The Map Of Honour

The Map Of Honour

Max Carmichael

Published by Tablo

Front cover
Taken from a photograph of stretcher bearers carrying white flag while returning
from battle with wounded soldier in Pozieres, France during World War I 1916.
Picture: Australian War Memorial Source: News Limited

Chapter 1

It was uncomfortably cold in the guard room of the First Australian Imperial Force School of Musketry near Lark Hill on the Salisbury Plains of England. Most of the off-duty sentries were huddled around the room's pot-bellied heater in an effort to keep warm. However, one of the guards, Private Ellis, sat apart from the group at the single table in the room. He was concentrating all of his attention on a small pile of erotic post cards that he had arranged before him on the table, and trying to decide which of the semi clad young women depicted on the cards he liked best.

The corporal in charge of the off-duty sentries entered the room and pushed his way to the front of the group surrounding the heater. He glared across the heads of those around the heater. 'Private Ellis! I thought you said July was summertime in this bloody country,' he grumbled.

Private Ellis did not respond.

'Yeah well, I suppose weather forecasting and tits weren't part of your university studies, was they, young fellow?' continued the corporal.

A couple of the off-duty sentries sniggered. The nineteen-year-old Ellis had abandoned the first year of a university degree to join the army, and many of his less educated comrades looked to him for guidance on issues they saw as requiring "educated" knowledge. He could rattle off historical facts about the various places of interest around the Salisbury Plains, and the towns and cities the Australians might visit when they had leave. However, his knowledge regarding the English climate had been brought into serious doubt. This particular reinforcement draft of Australians had arrived in May 1916, and Ellis had confidently predicted barmy summer days would be theirs to enjoy. Instead, the first three months of their stay at Lark Hill had proven to be cold and wet. In addition to this failing, his comrades were delighted to discover his knowledge regarding the female form was so slight as to be almost non-existent. In an effort to address this particular lack of knowledge, several of his older comrades had determined to see to this aspect of his education. The first stage of that process was the provision of the post cards that now held young Ellis's attention. Indeed, he had just decided that a petite blonde lady, who stared provocatively out at him while displaying her naked breasts, was his favourite when the guard room telephone clanged into life.

The Sergeant of the Guard answered the phone. 'Guard Room…yes…yes…I'll get on to it straight away…cheers.' He hung up the receiver and walked to the table where Ellis was continuing his study of the blonde lady's ample assets.

'Private Ellis!'

'Yes, Sergeant.'

The Sergeant glanced over Ellis's shoulder at the post cards. 'You like the blonde, I bet,' he commented.

Ellis grinned. 'She's seems very nice,' he replied bashfully.

'See too much of that sort of thing at your age young fellow and it will stunt your growth,' the Sergeant advised loftily. 'Fortunately, I can save you from yourself, my boy…I've a job for you. The phone to the Sergeant's Mess is out of order…nip across there and see Sergeant Green. Tell him he's wanted at Battalion Headquarters right away. He's to report to the 2ic as soon as he gets there…got it?'

'Got it, Sergeant.'

'Don't take a short cut across the parade ground, will you.'

'No, Sergeant.' The parade ground was considered a sacred site, only to be visited when one was actually on parade.

'You know to knock at the Mess door?' The Sergeants' Mess, the exclusive domain of the School's Warrant Officers and Senior Non-Commissioned Officers, the majority of whom were sergeants, was situated across the other side of the parade ground, directly opposite the Guard Room. Ellis as a private soldier would have to knock at the door and wait for one of the members to answer him.

'Yes, Sergeant, I knock and wait. What do I do if he's not there? Do you want me to go and look for him?'

'No, if he isn't there, come straight back here and tell me. Now get going. The 2ic is not a man to be kept waiting.'

Ellis was a little disappointed to be required even temporarily to forego his lascivious studies. Carefully, he placed post cards back in a grubby envelope and placed it on the table top. He knew very well that the moment he left the room one of the other sentries would purloin the cards and it would be some time before he got another look at them. However, his disappointment was tempered to a degree by the thought of meeting Sergeant Green.

Sergeant Green was one of the many Musketry School instructors, responsible for coaching soldiers as they practised shooting on the School's many rifle ranges. Like many of the other instructors at the School, Green was a veteran of the recent Gallipoli campaign, and Ellis's and his comrades were in awe of such men. However, particular revere was reserved for Sergeant Green as rumour had it that during that campaign, he had earned a deadly reputation as a sniper, and gained the nickname of "Killer Green." Strangely back in Australia, the fame he earned at ANZAC Cove was barely acknowledged. The war correspondents deployed to ANZAC Cove made no mention of Green choosing instead to extol the feats of other AIF snipers, such as Billy Sing who was known as "The Assassin." Yet so far as Ellis was concerned, there was a much more interesting aspect to Sergeant Green than his status as a marksman, for Green was an Aboriginal, and Ellis, a second-generation white Australian, had never met an Aboriginal.

Quickly, Ellis adjusted his uniform, pulled his slouch hat to the desired angle, and marched purposefully from the Guard Room. Minutes later, he reached the Sergeants' Mess and ran lightly up the three wooden steps to its front door, knocked loudly, and waited.

Moments later, the door opened and a Warrant Officer peered out. 'Yes mate,' the Warrant Officer inquired, 'who do you want?'

'Sergeant Green, sir,' replied Ellis.

'Right, hang on a moment.' The Warrant Officer turned back toward the interior of the Mess. 'Sergeant Green!' he called. 'There's a bloke here to see you.'

Sergeant Robert Green was at that moment buried in the embrace of a large leather covered armchair where he was quietly dozing. For the last two days, he had been coaching soldiers on the range, teaching them not to pull the trigger of their rifle, but to squeeze it. He was tired of telling them not to hold their breath, and a little deaf from the constant rifle fire of his students. The call to the door was an unwanted intrusion to his afternoon off. He opened one eye and focused it toward the main door where the Warrant Officer stood. 'Bugger,' he muttered. He sat up and eyed the disturber of his sleep warily. 'Thanks,' he said, 'I'll be right there.' He stood up and stretched, then with a weary yawn made his way to the Mess door.

Private Ellis had spent his time waiting at the Mess door deep in thought. He was one of many who had joined the AIF in a moment of patriotic fervour heavily spiced with a yearning for adventure. He believed the recruitment propaganda that the king needed his service and as he was proud to have honoured that need. He had yet to experience combat, but he thought it would be very like an exciting game of football, with the protagonists generally being jolly fine chaps who treated each other with respect. It was this thought that started him thinking about the morality of a man who chose to become a sniper. A sniper killed from cover, his victims having little chance to protect themselves, a situation that so far as Ellis was concerned was hardly sportsman like. This thought gave rise to another. Why was it, he theorised to himself, that some of the most famous snipers in the AIF were non-European? Did the fact that Billy Sing was Chinese, and Green an Aboriginal, have anything to do with the two men's ability to kill in cold blood? He had just about convinced himself that this must be the case when a polite cough returned his concentration to the task at hand.

Sergeant Green blinking in the sunlight stood at the top of the steps. 'G'Day,' Green said, 'what's up?'

For a moment, Ellis found he could not speak and that he was staring stupidly at the Sergeant. The famed 'Killer' was a short, rather ordinary looking fellow, who was at a guess only a few years older than himself. Green had an open, friendly face and the palest blue eyes Ellis had ever seen. The only feature that distinguished Green from anyone else who Ellis knew was his dark complexion.

'You want to see me, Dig?' Green prompted

Ellis pulled himself together. 'Sorry, Sarg,' he said hastily.

'You're wanted by the 2ic up at the School Headquarters. Right away, they said.'

Green frowned. Any attention from Major Allan Cook, the School 2ic, did not bode well for a happy conclusion for one Robert Green. He made no comment regarding this augur to Ellis, but simply nodded his assent...then he asked, 'Why didn't they phone the Mess?'

'The Mess phone seems to be out of order,' Ellis replied. 'The Sergeant of the Guard sent me to let you know.'

Green grunted disinterestedly. 'Okay, thanks.'

For a moment, Ellis waited, hoping to prolong the meeting, but Green turned back into the Mess and quietly closed the door.

Chapter 2

The Chief Clerk of the Musketry School glanced fearfully out of the Headquarters door for a sign of Sergeant Green's approach. The road from the Sergeants' Mess was empty and the Chief Clerk returned to his desk, fearful in the knowledge that he would be the victim of the choleric Major Cook's evil temper if Green was late.

In fact, even the kindest of Major Allan Cook's associates, believed he was mentally unwell. There was no medical diagnosis to support this theory, and in spite of concerns raised in hushed tones in the Officer's Mess, the Major's behaviour was a general concern that had never been appropriately addressed. Certainly, he was an angry and disillusioned man, and aspects of his behaviour could best be described as "odd." However, the majority of those who were unfortunate enough to come under Major Cook's influence were not prepared to accept this benevolent explanation of Cook's behaviour and simply considered him to be a right bastard.

Before the war, Cook had been a country lawyer and on enlistment he had used his professional qualifications as a means to gain an immediate appointment as a captain. In those early days of the AIF, his officiousness was mistaken for efficiency and he was soon promoted to the rank of major and appointed as a company commander. It was then that things started to go badly awry. Instead of further promotion as he was sure he deserved, others were selected to command battalions or to important staff positions. However, rather than addressing his own shortcomings, Cook blamed his men for this oversight and he began a ruthless program of discipline to ensure they did not disgrace him again. He awarded harsh punishments for minor infringements of military law, and while his commanding officer managed to head off some of his more excessive punishments, by the time the unit left Australia, Cook's men were united in a common hatred of their commander.

Cook was unmoved by their hatred; indeed, he thrived on it wrongly believing that while his men his men may not have liked him, that they respected him. However, about a week into the Gallipoli campaign when he and his men had been sent to a forward area at Pope's Hill above ANZAC Cove, Cook received a bitter lesson in the truth. Coincidently, this was the first time Cook had come across Robert Green and it was not a happy meeting.

At that time, Green was a corporal carrying out a special assignment for Brigadier John Monash, a task that had taken him into Cook's area of responsibility. When Cook challenged Green regarding this assignment, Green had informed him that knowledge regarding the purpose of his mission was on a "need to know" basis, and that so far as Green had been concerned, Cook did not need to know.

Cook found Green's attitude to be insubordinate and had him placed under close arrest. That had been a mistake. Somehow Monash came to hear of the arrest, and he had personally visited Cook's headquarters to order Green's release. During that visit, Monash had made it abundantly clear that Green was to be afforded Cook's complete cooperation.

Cook's reaction to Green's enforced presence was to increase the tyranny he inflicted on his own troops. In spite of the filthy conditions associated with trench warfare, he insisted his men spit and polish their boots and polish their brass. There would be, he had announced, a parade next morning when he would personally inspect each man.

No one believed Cook would call a parade, but they were all wrong. The next morning on the very edge of No-Man's Land, he ordered his men to form up in three ranks.

The result was entirely predictable. The no doubt astounded Turkish soldiers machine gunned the formation and several of Cook's men were killed and others wounded. He was sorry about that, but he firmly believed his decision to hold the parade was entirely justifiable. Indeed, he announced another parade would be conducted next morning to show the Turks that his men were not afraid.

The next morning as he stepped out of his dugout and blew his whistle for the parade to assemble, he was struck down from behind, by an unseen assailant who was armed with a tin of canned peaches.

The injury Cook suffered during the assault was not insignificant; he had a fractured skull and as a result he had been evacuated to hospital in Egypt for treatment. However, during his recuperation, reports of Cook's battlefield parades reached the ears of senior staff within the AIF and a court of inquiry conducted into the incident. Cook, however, was certain the inquiry had been called to identify and punish his assailant, and he eagerly offered his version of events to the board.

'This native fellow, Corporal Green and two of my men were close by when I was preparing for company parade. The men call him "Darkie," which is entirely appropriate as the fellow has more than a touch of the tar brush about him.'

The president of the board was a Brigadier, a man of little

patience. 'Yes, yes, Major Cook, but we are not interested in the racial profiles of your men. Please stick to the point. Do you know who, or what, struck you?'

Cook was flabbergasted by this rebuff. 'I assure you I do, sir,' he blustered. 'However, I hasten to establish Corporal Green is not one of my men! No indeed!'

'Oh, for heaven's sake!' the Brigadier snapped. 'Answer the blasted question!'

Cook smiled to himself. He felt confident his years as a civilian lawyer were standing him in good stead and that he was in complete control of the board's proceedings. He allowed himself to grasp the lapels of his uniform tunic with his hands, and armed with this pose of self-assurance, he continued his account. 'As I said previously, I was preparing for my morning parade. I blew my whistle to assemble the men and as I left my dugout, I heard one of my men say, "What do we do Darkie?" There may have been some profanity intertwined with the question, but that is the gist of it.'

'Do you know the identity of the soldier who asked that question?'

'No sir, I do not. Had I known I would have taken steps to discipline the fellow, for I can't abide profanity!'

'And what do you recall happened next?' the Brigadier asked wearily.

'I heard Green, the native Corporal, say, "I'll fix it."'

'That's all?'

'Yes sir, the next thing was I was struck down from behind, with a can of peaches, I believe.'

Several members of the board smiled wryly.

'Peaches,' the Brigadier inquired, 'how do you know it was a can of peaches? Might it not have been a tin of bully beef, perhaps? Besides, I understand the blow rendered you unconscious, so I am at a loss to see how you can be so certain of this.'

Cook was indeed certain a can of peaches was involved for he had a fondness for the fruit and had been deliberately withholding all rations marked "PEACHES CANNED" for his own enjoyment. However, the morning of the assault just prior to leaving his dugout for the parade, he noticed that one of the boxes containing his prized supply had been broken into. The obvious culprit was Green, for he was certain none of his men would dare do such a thing. This was, however, information Cook thought the Board need not be made aware of. 'Nevertheless, sir,' Cook replied, 'I have cause to believe that is the weapon that was used against me.'

'Hmm,' the Brigadier pondered doubtfully. 'I fail to see any such proof here as evidence. In any event aside from doubt as to the nature of the weapon used to assault you, our inquiries can find no witnesses to the assault, and I understand you did not see your assailant.'

'I assure you sir…' Cook began, but a warning hand from the Brigadier cut him off.

'Shall I tell you what the Board believes, Major Cook?' the Brigadier said in a gentler tone.

'Please, sir.'

'It is our opinion that the real assailant in this case was the enemy. We believe it is likely that the enemy threw a bomb at you which failed to explode, but hit you on the head injuring you and necessitating you're evacuation.' The Brigadier sighed and gestured toward the other members of the Board. 'Now Major, we want you to forget all this nonsense about Corporal Green. Concentrate on your recovery, man. We will contact you in the next day or so with our final decision. Good day to you.'

When the indignant Cook left the room, the Brigadier gave a sigh of exasperation. 'An arrogant fool,' he said flatly to his fellow Board members. 'I know what I will be recommending!'

One Board member, a colonel, seemed to harbour some doubt. 'What about this native fellow the chap kept prattling on about. Should we not at least investigate him?'

'I don't think so,' the Brigadier replied carelessly. 'I've received a letter from Brigadier Monash which I believe is relevant.' He shuffled through a file of papers on the table. 'Ah yes, here it is…I'll not read the whole thing, but the important part is as follows…

"I have no doubt Major Cook will endeavour to implicate a member of my headquarters, Corporal Green, in an alleged assault on his person. Corporal Green denies the assault. I do not trust Major Cook and have reason to doubt his suitability for command. On the other hand, I have absolute trust in Corporal Green a skilful and intelligent soldier."

'The letter is signed John Monash,' concluded the Brigadier as he set the letter aside. 'Monash may not be everyone's cup of tea,' he acknowledged, 'but he is a skilful soldier and a first-class judge of men. I remind you gentleman the purpose of this Board is to establish Major Cook's culpability in an incident that cost the lives of several of his men, not this Corporal Green fellow.'

A low rumble of accent greeted these words and another member of the Board loudly proclaimed, 'Sounds to me this Green fellow is just the sort of soldier we need, whereas Major Cook…'

The Brigadier smiled. 'Then I think we have reached our decision, gentlemen…'

It was no surprise to anyone except Major Cook when the Board found him to be negligent and unfit for further command. It was recommended he be quietly repatriated to Australia and then discharged from the Army.

Cook, however, was not so easily defeated. He had powerful political friends and after some earnest lobbying at the very highest levels, the recommendation of the Board was set aside. However, when he had recovered fully from his injury, he was not returned to his battalion and was instead moved to England and established in his current appointment.

Of course, Major Cook should have been thankful to his highly placed patrons, but he was not. He believed their influence should have been used to secure him a posting as the Commanding Officer, a CO, of a battalion. The position of Second in Command, or 2ic as the position was referred to in Army circles, was just that…second to someone else, and the refusal of his benefactors to push for such an appointment puzzled and embittered him to the point of madness.

In the months that followed, Cook introduced a similar administration to the School to that he had employed as a company commander. His singular pleasure became inflicting frustration on all those of lesser rank than he. As Second in Command of the School, this made just about everyone other than the CO, his target. A few others, such as the RSM, were also immune from his malevolence, but as for the rest… they became Cook's playthings, to be manipulated and taunted at his whim. He would cancel leave, insist on surprise inspection of the lines, and inflict harsh punishments for those who failed to meet his standards. On one occasion, he delayed signing the contracts with civilian suppliers for the School's rations, resulting in a shortage of food for the men.

Then one day soon after the main evacuation from Gallipoli, as Cook reviewed a list of those to be posted to the School, he noticed a familiar name: "Sergeant R. Green."

Surely, Cook thought, *it could not be the same man, but some discreet inquiries confirmed that it was indeed his nemesis.*

At first, Cook was full of righteous indignation that a black fellow should be posted to such a prestigious unit as the Musketry School, an opinion he expressed publicly. Privately, however, he was fearful that Green's presence at the School would revive the whole Gallipoli incident fiasco and render his position at the School untenable. He determined not to go quietly.

'Surely,' he complained to his CO, 'the history between this man and myself is known. Green assaulted me! He may well do so again! And beside any personal concerns I have, the fellow is a bloody native and should never have been allowed to join the AIF. I realise there is now nothing that can be done about his enlistment, but I must point out he is totally unsuited to any work here!'

The CO was fully aware of how Cook had come to be removed from command and placed in the posting he currently held. He had also heard rumours as to how Cook had been injured, and that Green may have had something to do with it. However, the CO was a practical man and he saw no reason to challenge the findings of a properly convened court of inquiry. His response to his 2ic was hardly supportive: 'I don't agree with you,' he responded. 'An expert marksman is exactly what we need here. I'm afraid you will just have to get used to Sergeant Green being here, Major.' Privately, the CO felt that if he had to make a choice between either Cook, or Green, he would far rather see the back of his 2ic.

Cook was incensed with the CO's attitude, but a few days later he was astonished to learn that Green was almost as unhappy as he was with his posting. Green had written a formal letter requesting an immediate transfer to a battalion in

France and in the normal course of administrative events, this letter landed on Cook's desk. 'I'm amazed the fellow can write!' he had joked to the Chief Clerk.

'Want me to bin it then, sir?' the Chief Clerk asked, gesturing toward a wastepaper bin.

'Good Lord, no!' Cook had exclaimed in horror, 'leave it with me.'

Cook lost no time in forwarding the letter, along with his own letter of recommendation supporting the request, to the AIF's newly formed 3rd Division's Headquarters. A few days later, both letters were returned and Cook was dismayed to see stamped across the pages "NO FURTHER ACTION TO BE TAKEN."

Cook made some discreet inquiries and found that someone at the Headquarters had vetoed Green's transfer.

In the weeks that followed, Green with Cook's active support made repeated requests for transfer, each one meeting the same fate, and eventually a despondent Green gave up. Strangely, Cook did not take advantage of the situation to inflict his malice on Green, preferring instead to leave well enough alone in case his Gallipoli folly would become more widely known. Nevertheless, he watched Green closely, hoping against hope that the sergeant would make some kind of error that would allow him to pounce.

Then the very morning that the Sergeants' Mess phone was out of order, and Private Ellis and his mates were rostered on for guard duty, a signal marked "URGENT" was delivered to Cook's desk. On reading the document's brief content, Cook was suddenly elated.

A knock on Cook's office door interrupted his reverie: 'Come,' he called sharply.

A relieved Chief Clerk peered around the half-opened door.

'You sent for Sergeant Green, sir?'

'Yes.'

'He's here, sir.'

'He is?' Cook's face positively beamed with anticipation. 'Excellent. Thank you, Chief, show him in please.'

Green marched into Cook's office, halted in front of the desk and saluted.

Cook ignored Green's salute and waved him toward a chair. Military courtesy demanded that an officer should either return the salute of a soldier, or if he was seated, or hatless, that he should at the very least assume a position of attention, or brace. Cook had no intention of being courteous to Green.

Green sat in the offered chair and waited for Cook to speak.

Cook made a show of tossing something into a wastepaper basket, before turning his attention to Green. He smiled happily. 'Well, Green,' he said, 'I have some very good news.'

Green already on his guard regarded Cook with even greater suspicion. 'You have, sir?'

'Yes, indeed,' Cook continued smugly, 'it seems we are going to lose you.'

Green felt a surge of joy, but he kept his face expressionless and replied, 'That *is* good news, sir.'

'Yes, but not,' Cook continued smugly, 'I suspect, so good for you, Green.'

'It's not, sir?' Green felt a pang of alarm.

'No. You have been unsuccessful in all of your preferred posting requests, but it seems someone at Headquarters 3 Division wants you. The posting order doesn't provide any details, so it could be anything. I don't suppose you cook, do you?' Cook chuckled at his own joke.

Green was horrified. 'No sir, I don't cook.'

'Didn't think you did. Still, I doubt they will have any

positions in your preferred line of work. Not many snipers at a Divisional HQ, eh?'

'No sir, I don't suppose there are,' Green muttered in reply.

'But plenty of tins of peaches, I imagine,' Cook said dangerously.

Green had never admitted his part in the Gallipoli assault on Cook to anyone. The few who were close enough to have possibly witnessed the assault were either dead, or were as determined as Green to bury the event so that no others were aware of the facts.

'Peaches, sir...why would tins of peaches interest me? I have no idea what you are talking about, sir,' Green replied evenly.

Cook smiled. 'Of course, you don't...well, that's all, Green. They seem to be in a hurry to gain your services for you are to report no later than nine tomorrow morning. The orderly room clerk will have some papers for you to sign. Shut the door when you go out.'

Cook immediately turned his attention to another of the papers on his desk. The interview had clearly ended.

Green got to his feet, saluted, was ignored again, and marched from the room. He was shattered. What indeed was he going to do at Divisional Headquarters? At least at the School he was outside and working with soldiers.

A clerk waiting in the outer office beckoned Green forward. 'Here you go, Sergeant,' the clerk said happily, 'important stuff first.' The clerk indicated a small pile of documents. 'These papers change your pay station...these others send your Q records...'

It took some minutes to process the paperwork during that time the clerk prattled away about the importance of the various forms, few of which made any sense to Green, but nevertheless, he signed wherever the clerk indicated. 'Only one to go now, Sarg. It's your receipt of the posting order. Oh, and you take this with you of course. There is this memo attached. You are to meet with Lieutenant Colonel Law tomorrow at 1000 hours, at his office in the headquarters.' The clerk paused for a moment and rummaged through a folder. 'Ah yes, here it is…most unusual for an NCO. You aren't to travel by train; a car will pick you up at eight in the morning.'

Green raised his eyebrows in surprise. Car travel was indeed unusual. He had expected to use the light rail system that linked the cities of huts and suburbs of tents that punctuated the military presence on Salisbury Plains.

'Well, good luck with your new posting, sergeant,' the clerk said as handed Green the posting order. 'Maybe they will give you an important job like being a clerk!'

Green frowned as he took the offered order. 'Very funny,' he growled, then with a curt nod to the clerk, he left the office and walked back to his hut to pack his gear.

Chapter 3

That night in the Sergeants' Mess, the RSM bought Green a beer. 'I hear you're leaving us, Killer,' he said as they took their first sips.

Green nodded. 'Yes, but not to a battalion,' he said bitterly. 'What the bloody hell could Divisional Headquarters want with me, sir?'

The RSM grinned and tapped the side of his nose with a forefinger. 'Things are afoot, my son. I wouldn't worry if I were you. I can't say too much, but you can rest assured Monash won't want to waste a man of your talents.'

The RSM was in fact referring to a rumour that General Monash's 3rd Division would shortly be bound for France. Since it's raising in February 1916, the Division had spent a considerable time in England training, leading to other Australian formations claiming the Division was only thinking about going to France, a claim that had coined the Division's nickname of "The Deep Thinkers." 'Don't you worry, mate,' the RSM concluded, 'we'll give 'em bloody deep thinkers. You mark my words, Killer, Monash is behind your posting.'

Green was not convinced. 'Then the General hasn't got enough to do if he's starting to worry about the postings for individual Sergeants!' he retorted hotly.

The RSM laughed then drained his glass in one gulp. 'Another?' he asked.

Green nodded. 'My buy,' he said.

'Not tonight,' said the RSM. 'Tonight, you keep your

money in your pocket.'

Green mumbled an embarrassed thanks.

'Mate, I don't think you appreciate the impact you made at Gallipoli,' the RSM began. 'I for one would not be here if you hadn't been around.' The RSM's face clouded momentarily as he remembered those early days at ANZAC Cove. He was a sergeant then, in Major Cook's company, and he had been present when the infamous tinned peaches attack took place. 'I remember that morning like it was yesterday,' he murmured. 'Cook was going to line us up again to call the role and the Turks would have shot the shit out of us again.'

'I don't know what you're talking about, RSM,' a straight-faced Green responded.

'Bullshit! After that first *parade* and knowing there was going to be another, I was so bloody frightened I didn't know what to do. You were the only bloke I could talk to and you told me not to worry, that you would fix it. You did, too. The pity of it was you didn't hit him hard enough.'

'I still don't know what you're referring to.'

'We needed your help and you came through for us.'

'I'm glad someone came to your aid, but I don't think I was in your sector at the time.'

The RSM grinned. 'You're a hard little bastard,' he said. 'I don't think I've ever heard you admit to doing that bastard.'

Green shrugged. 'Let's have a drink,' he said. 'All this make-believe has made me thirsty.'

News of Green's posting quickly spread and a party among the veteran sergeants and warrant officers developed. Someone produced a bottle of whisky, which prompted another to find a flask of green ginger wine. Beer, even though it was a local English brew, flowed freely and the party became a rather noisy affair. Songs were sung, each refrain bawdier than the last, and more and more drink was taken. None of the participants gave a thought to the fact that back in Australia, Green as an Aboriginal would not be allowed inside a bar, and that it would be illegal for him to drink alcohol. However, here in England, Green was one of them, a mate. This was not to say that the general attitude of the members of the Mess toward other people of colour had changed, but Green had endured the crucible of battle alongside them, a shared experience that had erased all the nonsensical, racially perceived differences they had grown up with.

On the other hand, Green could never allow himself to forget those same "differences" that existed back in Australia and elsewhere. He could not afford the luxury of basking in the reflected glory of acceptance by the men he had fought beside. There was always some young Digger newly arrived from home, who would object to taking orders from a black man, always another officer with similar attitudes as Major Cook's. Still, he revelled in the friendships the war had provided him, and he knew he would be sad to leave this particular loud and boisterous group of men who he was proud to call his mates.

The party became a little rough and a game of "Mess Rugby" began. In the general mayhem that ensued, the walls of the building seemed to bulge under the impact of the opposing scrums. Numerous bloodied noses, some loosened teeth, and a broken table spoke volumes of the success of the game. At one stage, the Duty Officer arrived and pleaded with the RSM to quieten them down, but after a few well-chosen words from the RSM, the Duty Officer went away, and the party continued unabated. Green joined in all of these activities with almost exaggerated zeal, but in the end, the amount of beer he had consumed claimed him and he fell asleep at a table. With shouts of triumph, his mates carried him to his room and unceremoniously dumped him upon his bed. He woke briefly and attempted to make a speech to thank them, but the words were slurred and crazy and so he gave up. They cheered him heartily and then he fell asleep again. The party was over.

Morning found Green tired and irritable, and in the throes of a massive hangover. He was too ill to eat any breakfast; the very smell of the fried bacon wafting from the kitchen was enough to make him retch. He smiled ruefully, grateful he would at least avoid a day of range practice with the associated constant brain piercing noise of rifle fire.

The promised car arrived, and he threw his few possessions on to its rear seat and climbed into the vehicle beside the driver. 'You know where to go?' he asked the driver.

'Yep.'

'Okay, then let's go.'

As the car passed the Guard House, the Old Guard, which consisted of Private Ellis and his mates, were about to go off duty and the next platoon rostered for guard duty were ready to take over. Military tradition demanded due ceremony accompany such an occasion, and the two formations, the Old Guard and the New Guard, were paraded on a cleared space in front of the Guard House to handover duties. The RSM was inspecting the New Guard, and as Green's car passed by, he paused in his inspection and waved.

Overcome with a feeling of great loss, Green waved back.

Chapter 4

The car journey to Headquarters 3rd Division was slower than anticipated. There was an unscheduled stop when the car's right rear tyre was punctured, necessitating the driver to replace it with the spare. Then a little further on, the journey was again temporarily halted for Green to be violently sick onto the road verge. However, in spite of these intermissions, Green was still able to present himself on time at the Headquarters' main reception area, where he was received by an overly officious sergeant of military police.

The military policeman looked Green up and down, and was clearly unimpressed by what he saw. 'Name?' he asked curtly.

Green pushed the posting order across the desk.

The policeman glanced at the order. 'Oh, so you're Sergeant Green,' he smirked, as if Green's somewhat dishevelled appearance was now explained. 'You're expected. You're the special one, you are.'

'I've no idea what you are talking about,' replied Green haughtily.

'Then I imagine you'll find out soon enough, sergeant,' returned the policeman equally as haughtily. He stamped a card which he pushed back across the desk to Green. 'Keep this with you at all times. If anyone challenges you while you are in the headquarters, show them this card. Got it?'

'Got it,' agreed Green, placing the card in the breast pocket of his tunic.

'Lieutenant Colonel Law's office is down that passage. You are a bit early, so you'll find a brew room about halfway down on your right. Help yourself. Someone will come and get you in about five or ten minutes.'

'Thanks,' Green said and hefted his echelon bag and pack on to his shoulders.

The policeman relaxed a little and held up a restraining hand. 'Ah, shit. No, mate! Don't take that lot down there! Pile your stuff over there in the corner. I'll keep an eye on it for you.'

In the wake of this friendlier atmosphere, Green smiled and put his baggage where the policeman indicated. 'Thanks again, mate.'

'All part of the service cobber.'

The brew room was a busy place with people of various ranks visiting, filling a cup or a mug with tea, then hurrying away to some hidden destination within the building. Green helped himself to a spare cup and leaned against a wall, quietly sipping the scalding liquid. His hangover was beginning to pass, and he able to give more serious thought as to why he had been sent to the Headquarters. It occurred to him that the most likely job he might be destined for was Headquarters Defence Platoon, probably as the platoon sergeant. 'Playing bum boy to some young prick of a lieutenant who had never heard a shot fired in anger,' he muttered despondently. He glared angrily into his teacup. Platoon sergeant under such circumstances would be bad enough, but he determined if they tried to make him a clerk, or a cook, he'd bloody well desert.

A tall Lieutenant Colonel entered the brew room. 'Sergeant Green?' he inquired politely.

Green set his brew aside and stepped away from the wall. 'Yes, sir. Lieutenant Colonel Law?'

'That's correct. Leave your brew. I've tea and cakes in my office. Please, follow me.'

Law led the way along a passage to arrive at a door which bore his name. He stood aside and ushered Green inside. 'In here, and take a seat...now, tea?' A tray holding a china tea pot, three cups and saucers, and a plate of cupcakes was positioned at one end of a large desk.

'Thank you, sir. Black, no sugar,' Green replied as he settled into one of the chairs.

Law poured the tea and passed Green a cup. 'Help yourself to a cake when you're ready,' he said.

'Thanks.' Green sipped his tea. Then, impatient to learn his fate, he added, 'Look here sir, I'm a bit puzzled. What's all this about?'

Law smiled. 'Can't tell you just yet; let's just say this is an initial job interview.'

Green reached for a cake. His hangover induced fasting had gone and he found he was ravenously hungry. 'So long as it's not for a cook, or a clerk's job,' he said meaningfully as he bit into the cake.

Law chuckled. 'No,' he said, 'it's not that kind of job, but you will just have to wait a few more minutes yet.'

Law seated himself behind the desk and glanced briefly at a file detailing Green's particulars before pushing it aside. He was used to interviewing interesting characters, but Green was particularly thought-provoking. In his pre-interview research, Law had discovered that Green was the youngest son of a white man, a South Australian pastoralist and entrepreneur who lived and worked in the South East of that state near the township of Penola. Green senior had shocked and horrified polite society by marrying an Aboriginal woman. Inter-racial marriage was common enough among the working classes, and while on occasion, an upper-class gentleman might indulge in a little bit of black velvet, they never married one of them! However, in spite of the gossip and snide innuendo, the Greens' marriage was indeed a love match and the two had no compunction in turning their backs on both the white and black societies in order to be together. Unusually, the children resulting from this union had remained with their parents. Government policy was to remove half-caste children from their parents and to make the children wards of the state and to place them in institutions, there to be trained as domestic servants. However, this had not happened with any of the Greens' offspring. Law guessed that Green senior had used his power and money to isolate his children from the practise. Law had also been intrigued to find that in stark contrast to the majority of Aboriginal children, all of the Green offspring were well educated—in Sergeant Green's case, up to Year 11 level, a commendable standard even for a white person. There was no doubt that Green and his siblings had lived a life of privilege denied the vast majority of their countrymen both black and white. However, he wondered if Green senior's wealth and influence had been enough to shield his children from the bigotry that infected white Australian society.

Law turned his attention to Green's military record. There was a report in the file suggesting Green senior had made every attempt to prevent his youngest son from enlisting in the AIF. That effort should have been easily achieved, for at the time, Aboriginals were actively excluded from the ranks. Law recalled the guidance for enlisting officers at recruiting depots promulgated earlier in the war: *"Aboriginals, half-castes, or men with Asiatic blood are not to be enlisted—This applies to all coloured men."* Apparently, Green senior had learned of his son's intention, and had ensured the local recruiters were aware of

THE MAP OF HONOUR

his son's heritage. There could be little doubt that furnished with this information, the local recruiting officer would have turned Green junior away. However, the lad was a resourceful fellow and overcame his father's interference by simply travelling in secret to a recruiting station in Victoria where he reapplied for enlistment and was accepted.

Law glanced at Green over the top of his teacup, the sergeant's complexion was certainly dark, and he wondered how he had overcome that particular hurdle at enlistment. However, Law noted grimly that whatever subterfuge Green had used his true racial background was eventually discovered, but by that time he was in Egypt about to deploy to Gallipoli, and no action was taken against him. Other than this infringement of the law, so far as Law could tell, Green's service record was impressive and almost unblemished. There was a small incident during his initial training, something about an affair with a married white woman, and another unproven accusation of assault during the Gallipoli campaign.

The rest of the report detailed Green's deeds in glowing terms, with several particular commendations provided by General Monash, leaving Law puzzled as to why the recommendations had not resulted in any award for bravery. However, when he considered the existing antagonism within the AIF's senior leadership toward Monash, the lack of awards for Green became clearer. Perhaps, he mused, Monash had an enemy in the higher echelons where the award of medals was considered. It would be easy enough to quash a recommendation at that level.

He glanced at the space on the page that listed Green's promotions, first to Corporal and later to Sergeant. It was hardly a meteoric rise; however, the issue of Green's aboriginality was probably the reason for the man's career had peaked at senior non-commissioned level. Social snobbery and racist beliefs, Law thought sadly, were so bloody stupid and wasteful, for he was sure Green's aboriginality provided the reason why the Australian press had studiously avoided any reports of Green's deeds on the battlefield to the Australian public. The worst of it was, if they had reported on Green, rather than much deserved adulation, there would have been a public outcry as to why a black fellow was in the AIF.

Aside from these background notes, the report stated that Green was of slight physique, a description that prior to their meeting had given Law to wonder if Green would be strong enough to undertake the rigors of a battlefield. That part of the report Law now dismissed, for while Green was certainly no muscle-bound hulk, he was clearly an extremely fit and powerful man.

As he watched Green sipping his tea, Law recalled another aspect of the report that he found to be almost alarmingly understated. The report simply stated Green's eye colour as "pale blue." While this was certainly correct, Law found that as he looked into Green's eyes, he was reminded of a bird of prey. Law had no doubt whatsoever that under certain circumstances, Sergeant Green would be a very dangerous man.

'So you're Killer Green,' Law said quietly.

Green blushed. 'That's what they've called me, sir,' he replied. 'I'm not into nicknames myself, although I've certainly had a few in my time: "darkie," "boong," even "nigger." They were bad enough, but I find "Killer" to be a bit,' he searched for a word, 'ostentatious,' he concluded.

Law smiled. 'Well perhaps the nickname is the price of fame,' he said. 'I've heard all about you, of course. You and Billy Sing were quite the celebrities of the campaign, were you

THE MAP OF HONOUR

not?'

'Billy might have been a celebrity,' Green replied, 'not me though. I just did my job. Besides, I'm sure others made a damn sight more positive contribution to the campaign than either of Billy or me.'

'Hmm, perhaps they did,' Law mused thoughtfully. He took a pipe out his breast pocket and began to fill it with tobacco. 'But that does not detract from your contribution,' he concluded. He smoothed the contents of the pipe bowl into the desired shape and struck a match. The flame flared briefly on the tobacco as he sucked the pipe stem, to be rewarded by the rich fruity flavour of the smoke.

Green shrugged depreciatingly.

Law was enthralled by Green's demeanour. In spite of having studied the man's background report, Law had expected to meet a rather basic human being, one who would be unable to resist boasting of his prowess.

However, the more he talked with Green, the more he realised how wrong this preconception had been. Green was articulate and confident, and Law had the impression the famed "Killer" Green would be at home in most social situations. He puffed briefly at his pipe and once again regarded Green through the cloud of tobacco smoke. There was no doubt in his mind that Green was indeed ideal for the mission he was soon to be offered. He set the pipe aside and began to nibble at a cake. 'Well, all that's behind us now,' he continued. 'France is very different, much tougher. Compared to France, the Gallipoli adventure was just a side show. The Germans are real soldiers, professionals.'

Green frowned. He had heard belittling comments regarding the Turks' skill at arms before, but it was an opinion generally expressed by men who had not fought at Gallipoli.

'Well, I can't comment on that, sir,' he replied evenly. 'I've not been to France.' He decided to change the subject. 'Where do you fit in to all of this, sir? he asked.

Law shrugged. 'I can't tell you much about myself,' he said. 'While I'm part of General Monash's staff, I also work for another organisation as well.'

A crisp knock on the office door interrupted further discourse on the subject, and without Law's leave, the door opened, and General John Monash entered the room.

Chapter 5

Monash smiled briefly as he placed his peaked cap on the hat rack. 'Sorry I'm a bit late, Law,' he said gruffly. 'A couple of minor issues took me away.' He glanced briefly at Green. 'Good to see you again, Robert.' His eye fell on Green's colour patch, which still reflected the sergeant's old unit. 'You'll have that colour patch changed to the blue circle on white, won't you Robert.' It was not a question, but a clear direction. Monash was determined to promote pride in the 3rd Division in every soldier under his command, and Green was not going to be an exception to that policy.

Green did not respond but stood stiffly to attention, his mind racing. The School RSM was right, after all, and Monash was behind his move from the School. The morning had just gotten a lot more interesting.

Monash seated himself in the spare armchair and waved Green back to his seat. 'Sit down, Sergeant, and relax for heaven's sake. You never used to stand on ceremony.' He turned his attention to Law. 'Is that tea?' Monash inquired.

'Yes sir…the usual?'

'Please…how far have you got with Sergeant Green?'

'I've reviewed Sergeant Green's background, and I agree with you. He would be ideal for our task.' Law handed Monash a cup of tea. 'You are aware of the relevant details concerning the sergeant, sir?'

Monash nodded and waved a hand dismissively. "All too aware,' he replied with a wry smile.

Law passed the plate of cakes to the General.

'Ah, my favourite. Thanks, Law.' Monash glanced at Green and then returned his attention to Law.

'You've not mentioned the mission yet?'

'No, sir.'

'Well, perhaps I should broach that subject with Sergeant Green now?'

'Certainly, sir.' Law sat down behind his desk and began again to watch Green intently.

Monash adjusted his seat so that he was looking directly at Green. 'You have no doubt guessed that I have another task for you, Robert,' he said quietly. 'It's similar to some of the jobs I gave you during our last campaign, but different too, and it's in France.'

Green nodded. He regarded Monash carefully. Past experience with the General had taught him to expect the unexpected.

'However, before I give you any more details,' Monash continued, 'you have the choice to accept, or reject the task. If you accept it, this briefing will continue in detail. If you reject it, the briefing will end and you will be posted to a battalion of your choice.' Monash smiled grimly, 'You won't be returned to the School of Musketry. Anyhow, before I ask you for a decision, I have to tell you this task is dangerous and there is every chance you won't return.' He raised a hand and gestured vaguely. 'Yes, I know, it's not much of a choice, a bit like playing Russian roulette with a fully loaded pistol, what?'

Green smiled politely at Monash's attempted humour.

'I'm sorry I had you sent you to the school,' Monash said contritely.

Green was shocked and tried to mask his surprise. Why would Monash do such a thing? It made no sense.

Monash noticed his expression. 'You must have underestimated the power of senior officers, Robert. It would have been inappropriate for me to advise you of my action, but I wanted to have you where I could get to you when I needed to. I never thought that our next scheme together would be anything like this one though.'

Green shrugged. 'The School wasn't such a bad life, you know,' he said defensively.

Monash frowned and wondered if perhaps he had misjudged his man after all, and that Green was about to refuse him.

'But if I'm honest,' Green continued, 'I'd have to say I was bored silly there. Tell me about the job, sir.'

Monash smiled. 'Thank you, Robert,' he said warmly, 'I hoped you'd agree. Things are a bit complicated, as you will now find out. Some people would say that I have no business getting involved, that at this stage, whatever is happening in France is none of my business. My position is, as it has always been, I just want to defeat the enemy, and if that means at times I adopt unusual methods, well, so be it. You will have to take a care Robert, for not all of those who will oppose your mission will be wearing German uniforms.'

Green smiled grimly. 'Nothing much has changed then, sir,' he said. Monash's struggles in pursuing many of his policies and to gain the promotion he needed to see his thoughts turn to deeds were well known. He was, Green mused, one of those men you either loved, or hated. He had to admit that at times he had been squarely in the haters' camp, but never for long.

Monash finished his tea in a gulp and turned to Law. 'Ah, that was bloody good, thanks,' he said with obvious satisfaction. 'Now, Law, it's over to you for the detail.'

Law stood up. 'Thank you, sir,' he said, and then he turned

to Green. 'You asked earlier where I fitted into all of this and I
think I will begin with a small explanation of my role. Aside
from my duties with General Monash, from time to time, I am
required to carry out other intelligence work for people further
up the chain of command.'

Green frowned. 'You mean you're a spy,' he said.

'Not really,' Law replied, 'but my work often brings me in
contact with people who are. And that is what has happened
on this occasion. I'll tell you a little more of that later. First, I
want you to look at this map.'

Green and Monash joined Law at his desk and pored over a
map which Law had spread across the desk top. 'This is a
section of the Somme in northern France,' Law explained for
Green's benefit. 'In particular, I want you to note the town of
Pozieres.' Law placed a fore finger on the map where the town
was depicted. 'These lines show current British and German
front lines,' he continued. 'Note that the Germans control the
town and the ridgeline above it.'

'How current is this information?' Monash asked.

'Correct as of 6:00 p.m. yesterday, sir,' Law replied.

Green was impressed. Law certainly seemed to be well
informed.

'Now I want you to look at this area,' Law indicated the
area directly north of the German front line. This is the
Courcelette area,' his hands moved broadly over the map, 'and
this is the town of the same name, all German controlled of
course. So far, the fields thereabouts have been pretty much
untouched by the war, whereas on the Pozieres side of the
ridge, just about everything has been churned up by shell fire.'

Green studied the map. The area Law indicated was
crisscrossed with tracks and hedgerows. He assumed the land
in between was farmland.

Law produced a rather grainy photograph and laid it on top of the map. Green glanced at the photo; it was a portrait of a German officer.

'Meet Colonel Walter Nicolai of the Imperial German Army. He's a rather important chap, for if he isn't the head of the German secret service otherwise known as the *Abteilung IIIb*, he's bloody close to it. In addition to this, the Colonel is a particularly powerful figure in German domestic politics.' Law paused and looked intently at Green. 'My masters,' he inclined his head toward Monash, 'my *other* masters, would very much like to permanently remove Colonel Nicolai from both of his fields of influence. They believe such an action would greatly inconvenience the enemy, and possibly even shorten the war.'

Green stepped away from the desk. 'So you want me to kill this bloke?' he asked.

'Yes,' Law replied flatly.

'Hmm,' Green continued carefully, 'I don't understand why you need me. Surely there are hundreds of men in France who could do the job.'

'That's true,' Law admitted. 'The problem is that British command takes a dim view of what they see as political assassinations. Bit rich really, when one considers the thousands of casualties they are responsible for, but apparently selecting one particular highly placed chap for death just isn't on. In short, so far as the British Army is concerned, they will not co-operate with this mission in any way.'

'Remember what I said, Robert,' Monash added, 'that not all the enemy wears a German uniform.'

'But don't worry too much at this stage,' Law interjected. 'We have a plan that should avoid any unpleasantness from that particular area.'

Green frowned. 'And I hope a plan to find the German

colonel, too. Talk about looking for a needle in a haystack!'

Law sipped the remains of his tea. 'Yes, we have thought of that. We have people very close to Nicolai and they are watching his every move. It seems that in the next few weeks, the good Colonel has business in Courcelette.'

'The town inside German controlled area?' Green asked.

'That's right,' Law replied. 'Our people will let us know exactly where and when we can expect him. That, however, is a bridge we can cross later, when you are on the ground at Pozieres.'

'We have arranged for you to be attached to the 3rd Brigade,' Monash explained. 'They're somewhere close to Pozieres now. The Brigade is commanded by Brigadier Sinclair-Maclagan. He's British, seconded to the AIF. You may have come across him last year?'

Green shook his head.

'No? Pity, but in any case, he will be expecting you at his headquarters. He's a good man, looks after his brigade well. However, the Brigadier is not privy to our plans. So far as he is concerned, you have been sent to the front to observe their techniques and procedures, particularly regarding the employment of snipers, and that you will compile a "lessons learned" paper on your return here. And Robert, under no circumstance may you tell Brigadier Sinclair-Maclagan what you are really up to. It would put him in an impossible position. He would feel duty bound to report the situation to his superiors, and that, of course, would jeopardise the whole scheme.'

'Your attachment will be for eight, maybe ten weeks,' Law continued. 'By the end of that time, if we've heard nothing more from our people behind the lines regarding the Colonel, you will come back here. However, during the next eight weeks, we expect the British Reserve Army Commander, General Gough, to launch a major offensive at Pozieres. That attack is almost certainly going to attract the attention of Colonel Nicolai. We don't expect that he will be too near the front line, but with luck, he will visit an area where you can deal with him. The attack will also provide you with the opportunity to infiltrate the German front line. You will be contacted once we hear any meaningful information.'

Green smiled. 'Sounds like a plan that I can work within,' he said. 'When do I leave?'

'Tomorrow,' Law replied. 'The Sergeant at the desk where you reported in has all you travel documents and so forth.'

Green chuckled. 'You must have been pretty sure I'd take the job.'

Monash did not share his mirth. 'Robert, believe me, I am sorry to have involved you in this, but when they asked for my help, you were the first person I thought of. Good luck, make sure you return in one piece. I will always have work for a man with your talents.' He shook Green's hand and moved to the door. 'Keep me informed, Law.'

'Of course, sir.'

Monash left the room, closing the door behind him.

Green set his cup on the desk top. 'I'd better get going too, sir,' he said to Law. 'I'll go and see the MP Sergeant and get my administration stuff sorted.'

Law shook Green's hand. 'Good luck, Sergeant. Get to 3rd Brigade as quickly as you can and then be prepared to move quickly. I'll be in touch.'

Green left the room, and Law was left alone with his thoughts. Things had gone rather well, he thought. Monash seemed pleased and Green very suitable for the task. All that remained now was for fortune to favour them with just an ounce of luck and Colonel Walter Nicolai would be no more. However, whether that death would shorten the war, Law very much doubted. In his opinion, the German war machine was too strong, and he was sure Nicolai's loss would be simply absorbed. During the initial planning for the operation, Law had given voice to these concerns, but he had been ignored. Now there was nothing more he could do but progress his part in the mission toward a successful outcome. He hoped Green was every bit as good as he believed him to be.

Chapter 6

As soon as Green left Law's office, he began to have second thoughts about the mission, and he realised he had allowed his own vanity to colour his decision. Ruefully, he acknowledged that his association with Monash made him feel important, that he was making a difference. 'You would think,' he said angrily to himself, 'that you would fucking learn, you idiot!'

A senior officer overheard the remark and balked away in alarm. He turned toward Green to reprimand him, but Green had already disappeared around a corner of the corridor. For a moment, the officer thought of pursuing the strange sergeant, but with a shrug he thought better of it. Besides, he was already late for his next meeting.

As Green approached the MP Sergeant's workstation, he took a deep breath and exhaled with a calming sigh. He realised there was now nothing he could do about the situation he found himself; he would just have to make the best of it. For a brief moment, he wondered what would happen if he went back to Law and told him he had changed his mind, but instantly decided at the very least such a decision would at the very least land him in some military prison. No, it would be better to die in France than be locked up in some bloody hell hole.

The MP Sergeant regarded him unhappily. 'Next stop France, eh?' he said as he pushed a bulging envelope across his desk toward Green.

For a moment, Green stiffened in alarm. Was his mission

already compromised? But then he remembered his cover story and relaxed. 'Looks like it, and all of a rush too. Bugger of a job, but someone has to do it.' He picked up the envelope. 'What's in this?' he asked.

'Travel warrants, money, and some 3rd Division colour patches. You're booked in at the local pub for tonight...give the old girl behind the bar a couple of bob and she'll sew them on for you.'

Green laughed. 'Bloody colour patches! I'm not sure if the damn things aren't the General's prime objective!'

The MP Sergeant smiled. 'Could be,' he agreed, 'but all the same, if I were you, I'd get 'em stitched on. The same car as brought you here is waiting outside; tell the driver to take you to the pub. You'll have to make your own arrangements to get to the railway station tomorrow.'

Green pocketed the envelope and gathered up his baggage and weapons. 'I'd best be off,' he said. 'Thanks for your help.' The car and its driver were waiting where Green had left them.

'You were quick, Sarg,' the driver commented as he saw Green. 'They told me to wait for you, but I thought you'd be a while.'

Green threw his gear onto the back seat of the vehicle. 'I don't suppose they told you where to take me?'

'The boss said I was to take you wherever you said.'

It made sense, Green thought. Had he turned Monash down, they would have provided him with a posting order to a battalion and an address to where the driver could take him. As things had turned out, the driver would now take him to the local pub. He wondered briefly who the boss was that the driver referred to and decided it would be either Monash, or Law. Given the sensitivity surrounding this mission, they would not have involved anyone else with any kind of information regarding Green or his choices of employment. He climbed into the front seat. 'The pub,' he directed flatly.

'Sure,' the Driver responded. He did not ask which pub. Clearly, he knew where to deliver Green and he did so quickly and without further conversation.

Green's stay at the pub was entirely uneventful. He was shown to a sparsely furnished room and given directions to the bar and the dining room. As soon as he had settled in, he approached the elderly land lady regarding the 3rd Division colour patches. Grudgingly, she accepted two shillings and took his tunics and his hat puggaree away to sew the new patches in place. Clearly, she thought the task was worth more, and Green agreed, handing over another two shillings when she returned the garments. The extra money was evidently well received, for when Green repaired to the hotel dining room, the old woman served him herself and provided him with beer 'on the house.'

The next day, Green began his short, yet complicated move to France. The first leg of the journey was to be accomplished by train to Dover, where he would board a ferry for Calais. From Calais his means of travel was less certain, but he had first to reach a place called Albert and from there, Pozieres. He leaned back against a wall of the extremely crowded railway station and contemplated the next few hours with distaste. He disliked train travel. He was of course impressed by the speed and the capability of a train, but after a while, cooped up in a carriage with so many others, he found it boring and stifling in the extreme. The station was crammed full of khaki dressed soldiers bound for the Front, and their families who had come to wave one last farewell. A melodramatic feature was imposed to an already poignant scene when somewhere along the platform, a woman could be heard tying to sing the popular tune "Tipperary" accompanied by an inexpertly played piano accordion. If the lonely vocalist had hoped to have the crowd join her in some kind of patriotic mass choral episode, she was to be disappointed. Men in uniform were slowly pushing their way toward the train. Women and children were either attempting to walk with particular soldiers for one last goodbye, or were standing like tiny islands in a khaki sea staring bewildered and tearful after someone who had already been swallowed up in the crowd.

It's a long, long, way to Tipperary,
But my heart, lies there!

The song concluded. There was no applause.

Green shouldered his kitbag and slung his rifle. It might well be a long way to Tipperary, he mused, but it was a bloody long way to Penola. He figured there was probably treble the small South Australian town's population right here on the railway station platform.

Hello, hello, who's your lady fair,
Whose' the little girlie by your side?

The unseen woman and her accordion accomplice had started another music hall melody and received similar attention to her last effort.

Green worked his way through the crowd toward the train. He had no concerns that the train was the right one for him. The uniformed tide through which he waded was only going to one place—France.

A station attendant using a megaphone was trying to marshal the uniformed passengers into carriages. 'All aboard for Dover! The train will be leaving in ten minutes! All aboard please!'

Green opened a carriage door and stepped aboard.

A friendly West Midlands accent greeted him. 'Here you

go, Sarg. Give us your rifle and kitbag and I'll put them up on the rack.'

'Thanks.' Green passed over his kitbag, but retained his rifle.

The carriage compartment was crowded with soldiers of the Warwickshire Regiment. Green recognised their distinctive antelope-like hat badge. His kitbag had been thrown into the luggage rack and below it was an empty seat, so he sat down there. His unknown assistant, a very young British Private soldier, offered him a cigarette.

'No thanks, mate. I don't smoke.'

'Coo well this is it eh, the great adventure! For king and country, hurrah!'

The soldier seemed to Green to be hardly old enough to have enlisted, and he found the lad's enthusiasm annoying. Yet he knew there had been a time when he had been just as keen. He had raced to the nearest recruiting station keen to "do his bit," only to be turned away on the basis that he was "**not substantially of European origin.**" He hadn't let that rejection stop him and he'd walked over sixty miles to the next town and enlisted there, claiming his dark skin was due to his mother being of Spanish extract. He had felt deeply ashamed at that subterfuge, not because he had lied to the army, but because he had been forced to deny his mother's culture.

His enlistment had infuriated his father. Green senior was not a man to be crossed, and his errant son knew full well that in disobeying his pater, he would be disowned and all family communication with his would be banned. In spite of this, he had received one letter from his mother, giving her blessing and telling him she loved him. After that letter, there were no more. He knew his father would have forbidden her to write and almost certainly would destroy any letter of his that arrived at the homestead. Even so, for a time he had written many letters home, but faced with the total lack of response, slowly and with deep regret, he gave up. He wondered if this Warwickshire youngster would face a similar situation with his family, or if anyone had told the young fellow that it was all a lot of crap, that there was no glory, and so far as Green could tell, the king and his country didn't care what happened to their soldiers, so long as somebody else did the fighting. With this souring thought, he pulled his slouch hat over his eyes, and pretended to sleep.

The youngster was not to be so easily put off and continued to fire questions at the disinterested Green. 'You're an Aussie, aren't you? I've never met an Aussie before; are all of you black? I bet you were you at the Dardanelles? What was it like? Smashing, I'll bet.'

Finally, an older soldier from the same regiment intervened. 'Come on, Smitty, leave the man alone. He wants to sleep.'

'I only wanted to know...'

'Well, you'll find out soon enough; now put a sock in it. There's a good chap.'

'Young Smitty's learned a whole lot already, ain't you, Smitty?' laughed another soldier in the compartment. 'Ask him about that little bint he rattled last night, go on!'

'Shut your mouth, Ormrod!' cried Smitty angrily. 'It ain't none of your business!'

'Might be her daddy's thought if he finds you've put a bun in her oven!'

There was general hilarity at this exchange, but the older soldier who had first tried to quieten Green's young admirer was not amused. 'Jesus Christ, boy! I promised your ma I'd look after you, and you've got into strife before we've even left

Blighty!'

The Guard's whistle and a tumult of tearful farewells from the platform saved Smitty from any further rebuke. With the exception of Green, the occupants of the compartment crowded to the carriage window to wave goodbye.

As the train gathered speed, most of its passengers sat in contemplative silence. Odds were that not many of them would make the return journey and perhaps with the exception of young Smitty and a few like him, they knew it.

Green surprised himself, for in spite of young Smitty's chatter and the uncomfortable conditions, he actually slept, waking only when the train began to slow at the end of the journey. He sat up and rubbed his eyes. The carriage was a hive of activity with the Warwicks hastily retrieving their gear and adjusting their uniforms.

'Nearly there, Sergeant,' said Smitty's older keeper. Smitty was leaning out of the carriage window and cheering at people they passed.

'How old is the lad?' asked Green, nodding toward the enthusiastic Smitty.

'Ah now, Sergeant,' replied the older man, 'that would be telling.'

'Hmm, don't you think he'd be better off out of it?'

'Course I do! Listen mate, I've been doing this shit since 1914. His dad was my mucker; he got it at Mons, and I've been dodging bullets and whizbangs ever since. Course I've tried to talk him out of it, but it's no go. He's tried to join up three times before and each time we found him and brought him back to his ma. This time…well, let's just say his ma gave up. So now he's here.'

Green shrugged. 'It's got nothing to do with me,' he said. 'I hope you both make it.'

The train slowed to a halt.

'Warwick Shire Regiment, fall in at the engine end of the platform!' An unseen voice of authority called Green's travelling companions away.

'Good luck, Sarg,' said young Smitty. 'Might see you over there, eh?'

'You never know,' replied Green. He shook the lad's hand and nodded to his minder. 'Keep your heads down.'

Then they were gone. Green picked up his equipment, slung his rifle, and stepped down from the train; the next part of his journey to the Somme would be by sea. He showed his movement order to a much harried Transport Officer and was pointed toward an already crowded ferry. Several hours later having endured a relatively smooth crossing of the Channel, the ferry berthed at the Calais dock.

Green waited on the crowded boat deck while the crew positioned the gang plank.

'Going all the way, Sergeant?' a voice at his side asked.

Green turned to find a British lieutenant standing beside him. 'Just about,' Green replied. 'Where's the train start from?'

'Good Lord, you want to avoid that if you can,' the lieutenant retorted. 'If the bloody thing went any slower, it would go backwards! Besides, it damnably uncomfortable, cattle trucks don't you know. My advice is to find a nice comfy supply column and hitch a ride. Only don't get caught; they tend to take a dim view of people striking out on their own. Do your orders mention the train?'

Green shook his head. 'No, I just have to get to a place somewhere near Albert.'

'There you are then; you've every right to look elsewhere for a mode of transport!'

The gang plank was secured into position and soldiers

began to file down on to the dock below. The lieutenant shouldered his pack. 'Well, must away, don't forget now, find a nice supply column, and avoid that bloody train!'

Green looked down from the boat deck at the turmoil of the dock and despaired of finding the train let alone a supply wagon. But the lieutenant's advice appealed to his 'old soldier' instinct to see to his personal comfort whenever possible, and he determined to at least attempt to follow it. He shouldered his pack and weapon, pushed his way into the disembarking troops, and began to make his way down the steeply inclined gang plank. Then just as he reached the dock, a rather insignificant sign on the façade of a long building situated on the far side of the dock caught his attention. The sign read simply: 'AAOC.'

'Blanket counters!' he mused using the somewhat derogatory term combat troops sometimes unfairly used to refer to the Australian Army Ordnance Corps. He felt certain if there was any chance at all of avoiding the train journey to the Front, the men who worked beneath that sign represented his best hope. He began to make his way toward the sign, through a throng of uniformed humanity. The trick, he knew, would be to avoid officious pommy bastards, particularly young officers thrusting for promotion. Either of those personalities would see him promptly directed back to the train.

It took some minutes to elbow and push his way through the crowd to the building that bore the AAOC sign. He peered in through a wide doorway. A mountain of stores laid out across the floor confirmed that he had arrived at a major warehouse. A number of soldiers in their shirt sleeves were working loading stores on to wagons and a corporal armed with a notebook appeared to be recording the product of their labour.

'No joy with that lot,' muttered Green. He needed someone with slightly more authority.

An office in the corner of the building caught his attention and he walked boldly toward it, but before he reached this destination, the office door opened, and an older man stepped out. The man wore a medal bar on his left breast indicating that he had seen service in the Boer War, and for a moment, Green and the man regarded each other in silence. Then the man grinned and extended a hand: 'Bloody hell, it's young Green!' he said.

Chapter 7

Green smiled broadly and grasped the man's hand, 'Warrant Officer Bennett,' he said.

'Well son,' said Bennet, stepping back and regarding Green with interest, 'you look all right, and a sergeant too, I see. Let's see, the first time I saw you was on the beach at ANZAC Cove. I didn't know whether to hand you over to the MPs, or turn the other way while you flogged me stores!'

'Instead, you helped me to whatever I wanted,' laughed Green.

'Shh! Not so loud, I don't want these young buggers to think I'm a crook!' Bennett nodded toward the working soldiers. 'Could you handle a brew?'

'Love one,' replied Green and followed Bennet back into his office.

'Take a seat.' Bennet indicated a dusty wooden stool. 'It's good to see you again,' he said. 'How did you find me?'

'Well truth is,' admitted Green, 'I didn't. It's a complete fluke. I am on my own and I saw your sign from the ferry.'

'Milk?'

'No thanks. Listen mate, I'm after a favour.'

Bennet laughed. 'So nothing's changed!' He pushed a steaming cup of tea across the table that served as his desk. 'Here you go,' he said. 'Now tell me, what's going on? Are you posted across here as reinforcement?'

'Nothing as easy as that,' replied Green grimly. 'Monash's division will come across here soon and he's sent me over to see how things are being done.' He was now totally committed to Monash's mission and the cover story came easily to his lips; even so, he felt some discomfort to be lying to a friend.

'Sounds like a sensible thing to do,' Bennett remarked, 'and it's no surprise he picked you. It was clear at ANZAC that he had a lot of time for you.'

'Yeah well, you know what the Toff's used to call me…Monash's pet nigger!'

'I know, I know. But that was then, and the blokes you were with, well, surely it's different now?'

Green shrugged. 'Yeah, most of them are all right. Some of the new ones still find it hard to take orders from a black fellow sergeant, but they get over it.'

'So, where do you have to get to?'

'3 Brigade.'

'Shit! It could take you a week by train!'

'So I'm told; that's why I came in here. I was hoping to hitch a ride on a supply convoy.'

Bennett snorted. 'That's no problem at all, but it could take even longer. The roads down round the Somme are pretty bad at the best of times, and the Hun likes to bomb and shell supply trains whenever he can.'

Greed was despondent. 'So maybe the train is the best way after all.'

'Not a bit of it!' Bennett retorted. 'How'd you like to get there tomorrow morning?'

Green laughed. 'What, you're into magic now?'

'Well, as good as, son. I've just received a stores request for urgent medical supplies from a Field Hospital at Amiens; 3 Brigade's near there. Nothing big, but apparently the medicos need it. In fact, I was just going out to organise it when you arrived. What we've done a couple of times recently for this

kind of thing has been to stick the package on an aeroplane and
fly it there. I send one of my blokes to sit in the back seat of the
thing and carry the stuff. I could send you to do the job.'

'Sounds good,' replied Green, 'but I've never flown before.
Are you sure it's all right?'

'Look, I won't lie to you, son. It's a dangerous trip. I reckon
just flying is bad enough. Personally, I wouldn't be seen dead
in one of the bloody things. But aside from that, the Hun tries
to shoot our aircraft down every time they see one and there
are about one hundred and fifty miles of dangerous space
between here and the Somme. The only plus for the whole
idea is, if you survive, you get there in a about an hour and a
half as compared to days in a bloody train.'

Green took a long sip at his tea and thought hard. There
was an embarrassing flaw in Bennett's plan; Green was
terrified of heights. For a moment, he was about to thank
Bennett and make his way to the railway station. Then he
remembered another Boer War veteran's advice to him as he
embarked on the ship bound for Egypt: 'take advantage of
every experience that is offered you...' The memory was
enough.

'Let's do it,' he said

Bennett smiled. 'Right,' he said. 'You had best stay here
until I square it all up. If you walk around outside, someone
will spot you and order you on to the train. You can kip in
here. Shitters are out the back, and we have enough extra
rations to feed a battalion, so you won't starve. I'll make a few
calls and then we should be ready to go sometime early
tomorrow morning.'

As events turned out, Green's flight was not quite as easy to
arrange as Bennett had hoped. While there was no problem
with his filling the observer's seat in the aircraft, the Major

commanding the Air Corps squadron was insistent that his pilot had an observer for the return flight too.

'He will need someone to man the old Lewis gun,' the Major complained. 'Bad enough when the Hun tries to jump one when the bloody thing is manned. No hope at all if we have an empty seat back there. Sorry old man, no observer for the way home it just won't do.'

Bennett was not to be defeated. A few more inquiries established that an able-bodied man at the Somme end, who was familiar with the workings of the Lewis gun, was going on leave in England. This man jumped at the opportunity to get to Calais in an hour and a bit, thus turning the two-day train journey into two days of additional time in the arms of his wife back in Britain. The man was happy, the pilot was happy, and Bennett was happy. Only Green remained as a less than enthusiastic party to the plot, particularly when the Major told him that he must be extremely vigilant during the whole flight and on no account could he close his eyes.

The next morning dawned damp and misty. Bennett had arrived at his warehouse office early and wakened Green. 'Bacon sandwich, mate? Best thing they tell me for your first flight.'

Green arose from the floor and stretched. 'Sounds good and smells even better,' he said as he took the offered food and ate it contentedly.

'Soon as you've finished, I've got a vehicle outside; we'll drive down to the airstrip. I'll just go and get the stuff for the medics.'

When Bennett returned, Green had his equipment on and his rifle and echelon bag safely stowed in the front of Bennett's vehicle, a light truck that bore a strange resemblance to a child's pram with an engine stuck on the front.

'Jump in,' said Bennett. 'It's about fifteen minutes down the track. I don't know how you'll go with this mist. The flyers don't seem to like it much. But the bloke who's flying you is a bit of a dare devil, so he'll probably have a go at taking off.'

Bennett's piece of casual advice in this regard did nothing for Green's confidence, and he was starting to regret his decision to take the flight.

As Bennett guided the vehicle toward the airfield, the mist began to lift, enabling him to drive a little faster. They passed columns of marching men, some of whom shouted angrily as Bennet's vehicle hit roadside puddles, showering the marching men with mud.

'Get on with you!' Bennett shouted back. 'Mud's good for you; it will make you grow!'

Green remained silent and concentrated on hanging on to his seat to avoid being thrown out onto the road. He constantly checked that his rifle was safe and that a leather cylindrical case attached to his big pack was not being damaged. The case held his spotting telescope; that and his rifle were the sniper's essential tools. He doubted that even Bennett's stores would be able to replace either item quickly should he lose or damage them.

In spite of Bennett's erratic driving, they arrived at the airstrip safely. Bennet brought the vehicle to a halt beside a neat sign which proclaimed the single word, "Dispersal." A Bell tent stood just beyond.

'What do they disperse?' asked Green as he gathered his gear.

'Fuck knows,' Bennet replied. 'Come on, the bloke we want should be inside the tent.'

Captain James Rosher AIF was cleaning his brown top boots, the kind that come up over a horseman's calves. On a chair next to him piled in neat order was a long leather coat, a thick woollen scarf, a pair of leather gloves, a flying helmet, and goggles. He looked up from his boot cleaning task as Bennett and Green entered the tent.

'Hello Bennett, two loads to deliver this time, eh?' Rosher returned to polishing his boot.

'G'day, sir. This is Sergeant Green; he's needed at 3 Brigade urgently, and these,' he showed Rosher two small packages, 'are wanted by the field hospital, also urgently.'

'Right oh, I'll just finish this boot and we shall be off! Ever flown before, Green?'

'No sir, I haven't.'

'Didn't think so; not many of you infantry types have. Can you handle a Lewis gun?'

'Yes, sir.'

'Good, good, hope we don't have to put that skill to the test, but one never knows.' Rosher finished polishing the boot, stood it beside its mate, and inspected his work. 'It will have to do,' he pronounced. 'Nobody up there is going to see them anyway!' He then proceeded to squeeze his feet into the boots, stamping each foot on the ground to make sure he had achieved a comfortable fit. Rosher was already wearing a thick naval style polo necked jumper beneath his uniform tunic, but now he wriggled into yet another pullover before struggling into the leather coat.

'It gets damn cold up there,' he explained to Green and Bennett. 'If you have any extra clothing in your kit bag, I recommend you wear it. Got a greatcoat?'

Green nodded.

'Put that on over the lot; that should reduce the size of your kit bag as well... we don't have a lot of space. Oh, by the way, if you need a leak or a shit, have it now. We don't run to flying toilets.'

'Where's your crapper?' asked Green. He felt very nervous, a little like he used to feel before the start of a game of football.

'Round the back of the tent. You'll see the hessian screen. Don't be too long.'

Green was quick. His bowels were particularly active, and he made a brief but noisy deposit in the yawning pit that served as the pre-flight toilet. He returned to the tent feeling a little foolish at his nervous state and began to pull a heavy jersey over his tunic, before struggling into his great coat.

'All finished? Wash your hands?' Rosher seemed to be enjoying the situation. 'Right oh Mister Bennett, you can shove off. Sergeant Green...let's go.'

Bennett shook Green by the hand. 'Good luck, mate. See you in about eight weeks.'

'Sure, sure,' replied Green. 'I'll let you know how I go, but I reckon I might come back by train.'

Bennett grinned. 'I'll watch you take off,' he said, 'should be good for a laugh.'

Green grimaced and followed Rosher out onto the airfield. Looming out of the mist, he saw the silhouette of the waiting aircraft. A mechanic was fussing over its engine, taking no notice of the approaching pilot and his passenger.

Rosher patted the side of the fuselage. 'This,' he said to Green, 'is the Sopwith 1½ Strutter, a two-seater biplane multi-role aircraft. That is to say we use can her for dropping bombs, or as a fighter against Hun aircraft. She is as good an aircraft as we have at the moment and can reach a speed of around two hundred miles an hour if she has to.'

Green nodded, but the thought of reaching one hundred miles per hour, let alone two hundred, was beyond his comprehension.

Rosher pointed toward the front of the aircraft. 'That's where I sit and drive her. You will note I have a fixed machine gun which fires through the propeller. Don't be alarmed; the weapon is synchronized and won't cut the prop off. You will sit in the rear pit,' Rosher pointed to the yawning observer bay situated immediately behind the pilot's cockpit, 'facing toward the tail. If we are attacked, you will operate that Lewis gun mounted there.' Rosher paused and smiled at his passenger. 'Don't worry, my aim is to get you there in one piece, so I have no intention of stooging about looking for trouble. I plan to stay low and go like hell to reach the Somme. If we run into trouble, we may have to climb into some clouds to hide for a while, or maybe this damn mist might help hide us. Now one more thing, as well as being bloody cold, it is very, very noisy. If you need to tell me anything, you are going to have to yell, or turn around and pass me a note.' He turned to the mechanic. 'Syd, help Sergeant Green get his stuff on board and then strap him in.'

'Come along now, Sergeant,' directed Syd. 'Careful where you put your feet now; we don't want to make a hole in her skin now, do we?'

Syd placed Green's kit bag and rifle in the body of the aircraft, making sure it was clear of the various control lines, and tied it in place securely. Then he strapped Green to his seat with a single leather belt, before handing him a flying helmet and some thick gloves.

'Put these on Sarg; it gets a tad cold up there.'

'So they tell me,' replied Green nervously.

After making sure Green could reach and operate the Lewis gun, Syd jumped down from the aircraft and moved to its front where he grasped the propeller. Rosher was already in his place. He turned and gave the thumbs up signal to Green, before returning his attention to the mechanic.

'Contact.'

The mechanic pulled down hard on the propeller and after several barking coughs, the Sopwith's engine bellowed to life. A few seconds later, the aircraft began to move slowly across the grass. When Rosher was satisfied that his controls and engine indicators were functioning correctly, he opened the throttle and the Sopwith bounded across the grass.

Green had never travelled so fast in his life. The noise of the engine alone was almost overpowering; the wind created by the aircrafts charge along the ground pressed the leather flying helmet into the contours of his head. He caught a brief view of Bennett standing by his vehicle; then he was gone. Below him, the grass rushed past in an emerald blur; the posts of the fence that bounded the airfield flashed by in a staccato of light and dark forms. Then with a leap that seemed to leave Green's stomach behind, they were airborne. He looked down in amazement at the rapidly receding airfield and then out toward the horizon. It was fantastic—he was actually flying! He glanced over his shoulder and saw they were heading toward a huge fluffy cloud, and then suddenly they were inside it, encased in a world of white. Moments later, the aircraft punched through the cloud mass, into brilliant sunshine.

Green gazed in wonder as an almost magical world of fluffy hills and valleys formed by the clouds below them was revealed to him. The sensation of speed that had so mesmerized him as they took off was gone and he felt he could step off the aircraft and walk around. Momentarily, he felt that he was an intruder, and he looked about half expecting to see some kind of guardian of the heavens, an angel, even God, watching him. But the feeling vanished in a throaty growl from the Sopwith's engine.

Rosher climbed to about one thousand feet, and then banked the aircraft away toward the southeast and the Somme. He looked back toward Green just as the Sergeant looked forward. Rosher smiled cheerily and waved. Green waved back.

After about five minutes flying time, Rosher put the Sopwith into a gentle dive, levelling off at about one hundred feet. He turned back to Green and shouted at him to attract his attention. Finally, Green heard and looked over his shoulder toward the pilot. Conversation was impossible, so Rosher began a brief pantomime, the point of which was to remind Green that he had to be on the lookout for enemy aircraft. Green immediately understood and turned back to his Lewis gun and began to scan the sky, swinging the muzzle of the gun in the same direction he was looking. Satisfied, Rosher turned back to his own task, bringing the aircraft lower and lower, until the Sopwith was around fifty feet off the ground, and then he opened the throttle a little to achieve a cruising speed of about one hundred miles an hour.

For Green, the sensation of speed returned as the aircraft rocketed across the countryside. Rosher dodged trees, leap frogged hedges, and just missed the roofs of farm houses. Every twist and weaving, every sudden brief climb and rapid decent, made Green's stomach heave. He had to force himself to concentrate on his allotted task and not to lean over the side and lose himself in a heaving vomit.

The glare of the sun came from their left front and it was in this quarter that Rosher was keeping his own watchful vigil, and after approximately half an hour into the journey, he was rewarded by a tiny flash of reflected light. Green, concentrating his watch to the rear, saw nothing, and the first warning of any alarm he received was a renewed bellow from the Sopwith's engine as Rosher opened the throttle to its full extent and began to climb toward a thick bank of cloud.

Green looked over his shoulder toward his pilot. Rosher pointed frantically upwards with his left arm. Green swung the Lewis gun in that direction, staring into the blinding sunlight. He could see nothing. He looked again and then through the eye stinging glare of the morning sun, he saw two dark shapes wheeling like eagles above the Sopwith, and in sudden fear, he realized the shapes were enemy aircraft. Even as he watched, one of the aircraft began diving to cut the Sopwith off, while the other was positioning itself to come at its rear. Green concentrated all his attention on the aircraft making toward their rear.

The aircraft Green was watching was much closer now, and as it banked to come directly behind the Sopwith, he saw a large black cross painted on its fuselage. He swung the Lewis gun toward the black cross, but his aim was spoiled as Rosher threw the Sopwith on its side and let loose with a prolonged burst of fire from his own machine gun. A split second later, the other enemy aircraft tore past, its own machine gun blazing.

Green had only just enough time to regain his composure when the second enemy aircraft began its attack. He could see the blaze of deadly light coming from its machine gun. Rosher was still desperately climbing for the cloud bank, twisting the Sopwith first one way and then another. A row of holes suddenly appeared in the aircraft's body inches from Green's front. Desperately, he swung the Lewis gun toward the attacking German and fired a quick burst. His shots must have been close, for the German pilot rolled his aircraft away and took a few seconds to compose himself before joining with his mate to renew the attack.

The cloud bank was now thirty seconds away, and Rosher was extracting every last ounce of power from the Sopwith's engine. The German pilots, sensing their quarry might yet escape them, redoubled their efforts. The first aircraft now attacked from above while the second came from the Sopwith's starboard side. Rosher was faced with the decision of continuing his flight, leaving his fixed machine gun out of the fight and Green with two enemies attacking from different directions, or he could turn and fight.

There was really never any choice. At thirty seconds' distance, the cloud bank might just as well have been a hundred miles away. Rosher knew he would have to fight. He threw the Sopwith into a diving corkscrew manoeuvre, spoiling the German's immediate attack, and then desperately pulled his machine around in an effort to gain the tail of one of his opponents. Green could only hang on, but then as Rosher desperately tried to steady the Sopwith for a shot at the first German aircraft, for a fraction of a second the other German was in the Lewis gun's sights and Green fired a prolonged burst. The German pilot shook as the stream of bullets struck him and tossed him into the corner of his cockpit; the nose of the German aircraft dropped and it began a long dive toward the ground. The other German pilot immediately broke off his attack and followed his stricken comrade. Rosher resumed his climb toward the safety of the cloud bank. The brief battle was over.

Chapter 8

It was just after half past eight on the morning of the 22nd of July when Rosher landed the Sopwith at an airfield just outside of the town of Amiens. He taxied the aircraft up to a sandbagged wall that protected a small hut, switched off the engine, climbed out of his cockpit, and walked back along the wing to where Green sat.

'Bloody well done, Sergeant!' he said, enthusiastically extending a congratulatory hand. 'I thought for a moment those bastards were going to have us for lunch!'

Green smiled and shook Rosher's hand. 'Complete fluke,' he replied, 'just a lucky shot.'

'Luck my arse,' retorted Rosher. 'As fine a bit of shooting as ever I've seen. You should transfer over to the Flying Corps my boy; we could use a man of your abilities.'

Green laughed. 'Thanks, but no thanks, if it's all the same to you, from now on I intend to keep my feet firmly on the ground. Fighting in the air is too bloody dangerous for me.'

Rosher helped Green unload his equipment and the two packages for the Field Hospital. 'I think we'll find someone in there to take the medical stuff,' he said pointing at the hut. 'But how you get to 3 Brigade will be up to you. At a guess they will be somewhere out on the plain between here and Albert. Did you see all the troops over that way as we came in?'

Green nodded. As they had emerged from the clouds, the plains between Amiens and Albert had appeared as a gigantic military camp spread out like one of the model battle fields

General Monash was so keen on making to familiarise the troops with new ground. Green had seen lines and lines of horses tethered in the morning sun, cities of tents, and where roads appeared, he had seen troops on the move.

'I'll be fine,' he said. 'There's bound to be someone going in the Brigades direction; I'll soon hitch a ride.'

'Well, good luck, Sergeant. I shall drop these inside this place and pick up my new observer. Hope he can shoot as well as you. If ever you change your mind about a transfer, give me a shout.'

Green had no luck finding a ride at the airfield and so shouldering his weapon and equipment, he walked into the town. It was market day in Amiens and townsfolk pushing or driving almost every kind of wheelbarrow or vehicle were adding their numbers to the road already crowded with military traffic. At the first crossroad Green reached, a single military policeman resplendent in red cap and white gloves stood point duty controlling the hectic human tide as though it were a crowd on the way to the Melbourne Cup. Green approached the lonely red cap and asked directions.

The policeman's directions were brief and to the point. 'There is an AIF Transport Office at the end of the third street on your left, Sergeant. Big sign out the front; you shouldn't miss it.'

Thanking the policeman, Green walked on. It was a surreal scene. Children walked alongside him, apparently on their way to school. Motorbikes were weaving their way through a horde of carts and wagons laden with market produce. Yet all the while, the sounds of battle seemed alarmingly close. The occasional staccato burst of machine gun fire that Green assumed was coming from aeroplanes that droned through the sky far above, the growl of a bombardment somewhere to the east, and the ever-present hurrying ambulances gave ample evidence that the war was very close. It was with some relief that he found the military policeman's directions were completely accurate.

The AIF Transport Office was a very modest affair; indeed, the office was only just large enough to contain a rather harassed young Lieutenant who was seated behind a very small table. Green opened the door and stepped inside. The young officer was on the telephone listening to someone of an obviously senior rank provide him with a vigorous and vitriolic assessment of the supply system.

'Yes sir...thank you sir....thank you sir...sir, this is a very small coordination office, we don't handle the actual supplies...no sir, I don't mean to suggest that you don't know what you are talking about...yes...yes...my OC is Major Headlamb...yes sir, I am sure he will be pleased to deal with your complaint...goodbye sir.' The Lieutenant replaced the telephone hand piece in its cradle and glanced toward Green. 'Yes,' he said, 'what do you want?'

'I need to hitch a ride out to 3 Brigade Headquarters, sir,' replied Green.

'Papers?'

Green produced his movement order. The Lieutenant glanced at them and handed them back. 'You got here bloody quickly,' he commented. 'What did you do, bloody fly?'

'As a matter of fact, I did, sir.'

The Lieutenant looked up at Green, decided he wasn't being insubordinate, and promptly lost interest in the issue. 'There's a car heading to 3 Brigade Headquarters in a few minutes. It's out in the yard. Tell the driver you've seen me.'

Green went to offer his thanks, but the telephone was ringing and with a sigh of deep exasperation the Lieutenant picked up the handset. He dismissed Green with a wave.

The yard the Lieutenant had referred to was a large cobble stoned area where several cars in various stages of repair were parked. The vehicles were lined up in front of what had until recently been a well-used horse stable. Most of the vehicles were up on blocks and a number of Australians were working at a forge and anvil making various kinds of spare parts for the disabled cars. One serviceable vehicle had just started to roll toward the gate, and using his best parade ground voice, Green shouted at the driver to halt.

'Sorry Dig,' he said to the startled driver. 'You have a passenger...me. I've seen the Lieutenant.'

The driver clearly objected to being delayed. 'I've a schedule to keep,' he grumbled as Green loaded his equipment into the back of the car. 'It makes no difference to you if the Corporal gives me extra duty for being late.'

Green ignored the man's complaints. 'How far to 3 Brigade?' he asked.

The driver threw the car into gear and guided it out of the gateway. 'It depends,' he replied, his voice oozing sarcasm, 'they might have moved again and then we shall have to find them. Then again, the Hun could be bombarding the road and we might have to go the long way round. The roads are chock-a-block full of troops at the moment and they won't get out of our way. Then again, these fucking cobble stones,' he indicated the road with a jerk of his head, 'might shake this poor old bitch to bits. How the fuck do I know how long it will take?'

Green shrugged. 'What's your name?' he asked.

'Private Blucher,'

'First name?'

'Karl.'

Other than this outburst and his few brief responses to

Green's attempts at conversation, Private Blucher proved to be a man of very few words, and they drove through the streets of Amiens in silence.

The first of Blucher's gloomy predictions proved to be accurate; 3 Brigade Headquarters had moved, for on arriving at its previous location, they were directed on to the town of Albert.

At Albert, they caught up with a rear party from one of the Brigade's battalions and were told the Brigade Headquarters was now at Rubempre. Blucher had become even more petulantly silent as the journey extended. Green made several more attempts at conversation, but receiving only grunts in reply, he gave up. Then the car overheated, and they had to wait by the side of the road for the engine to cool before they could continue. It was late afternoon when they finally arrived at the village of Rubempre.

There was no obvious sign of 3 Brigade Headquarters, but large numbers of Australian troops were hurrying down the street in the direction of the sound of the continuous bombardment. Ordering Blucher to stop the car, Green called out to a group of passing Australian machine gunners, their heavy weapons balanced precariously on their shoulders.

'3 Brigade Headquarters?'

The machine gunners did not pause in their march, but a sergeant at the rear of the group shouted out a reply. 'Down the street to the left; they're in the church.'

Green waved his thanks. 'Come on,' he said to Blucher, 'let's go.'

A few minutes later, Blucher parked the car outside the village church and Green got out.

'Wait here,' he told Blucher, 'and keep an eye on my stuff.' He slung his rifle and began to walk toward the church entrance.

'What about my schedule?' Blucher demanded angrily.

Green had had enough. He spun around and faced the petulant driver. 'Fuck your schedule!' he snapped. 'If you're not here when I get back, and if any of my stuff's missing, I'll find you and tear your bloody balls off! Do you understand?'

Blucher was aghast at the venom of Green's response and the mental image Green's threat conjured made it clear his passenger was not as mild mannered as he had first thought.

'Yes, Sergeant,' he replied hastily. 'I'll wait here. Your gear will be safe.'

Green regained his composure. 'Don't worry,' he said calmly, 'I'll see your Corporal and tell him why you are late.' He turned away from Blucher and trotted up the steps of the church.

A sentry at the head of the steps checked Green's papers and then directed him to a pew at the rear of the church, where he was assured "someone" would get to him.

About five minutes later, a Corporal came and took Green's particulars, told him again to wait, and then went away.

Green waited. He seemed to be the only visitor as nobody else came and sat in the pew with him. However, in the remainder of the church, an organized form of chaos prevailed. A constant stream of staff officers and soldiers scuttled back and forth, their movement implying urgency and tension. Something, Green decided, was definitely up.

After what seemed an age, a rather mature Captain approached the visitor's pew. 'Sergeant Green?' He sounded like a doctor asking for his next patient.

'Yes, sir.'

'I'm Captain Tollemache, the acting Brigade Major. We are expecting you, but you're about two days early. How did you manage that?' There was implied criticism in Tollemache's tone, as though he found Green's sudden appearance irregular.

'I hitched a ride in an aircraft, sir.'

'Ah well that explains it. Well done. Now I know your General has sent you here to study our employment of snipers in the field, but there is a problem.'

'A problem, sir?'

'Yes. Well as you can see, we are a bit busy. The Division is going up to the line to attack a place called Pozieres. This brigade is going to be on the right flank with 1 Brigade on our left. Tollemache paused and looked around as if worried he might be overheard. 'Well, the truth is, we are expecting a pretty hard time. The British regulars have had several attempts to take this place and have taken a rather nasty beating. So you see, we have been a bit preoccupied with planning and such and we haven't really organized anything for you.' Tollemache was genuinely apologetic. 'I've no doubt your General will be a bit put out.'

Green feigned disappointment at the situation. 'Possibly, sir' he agreed. In reality, he was not concerned. No doubt Monash and Law would not have expected him to arrive at 3 Brigade Headquarters so quickly, but he was confident they would be far from displeased with his progress. 'However,' he said, making an attempt to placate Tollemache's concern, 'I'm sure I can make myself useful.'

'Jolly decent of you, Sergeant,' Tollemache responded with some relief. 'It never does to upset Generals. What?'

Dutifully, Green chuckled at Tollemach's attempted humour.

'With your offer in mind Sergeant, I wonder if I could make a counter offer. Would you be prepared to carry out a task for us at rather short notice?'

Green was immediately on guard. 'What offer was that, sir?' he asked.

'To make yourself useful,' Tollemach replied. 'You see, your reputation has preceded you, and your turning up here now is quite fortuitous. The thing is, in my Brigadier's opinion, once we get into Pozieres, we are going to face a very confused situation, and until he can get an accurate idea of where our troops and the Hun actually are, he believes the Brigade will be vulnerable. Air photos won't help, the bloody place has been already heavily shelled by the British, and Division plans to give it another pasting before we go in, not to mention the hell fire the Hun will deliver as we attack. So I don't expect to be able to tell where the trench lines are. We need a number of people to move through the area immediately after the attack and mark where our people are on a map. I was rather hoping you might agree to assist.'

'I see, sir,' Green replied thoughtfully. Tollemache's request had taken him by surprise and his mind raced through the issues it presented. The plan had been for Green to wait for word from Law before he ventured into the front line, but Tollemache's request had introduced factors that were beyond the plan. To visit the Front now could place the whole scheme to kill the German colonel at risk. Green could become a casualty and be unable to respond to Law when his people advised that the target was going to be available. On the other hand, if he were to refuse to help 3 Brigade, there were bound to be questions asked as to what he was doing in France. Questions he was not in a position to answer, and any ensuing inquiries might well expose the true nature of his mission. Green had gained the impression from his pre-mission briefing that Monash was putting himself at risk by supporting this scheme. Green had no intention of doing anything that might solidify that risk. Therefore, he concluded the only thing he could do in this situation was to agree to carry out Tollemache's task. Indeed, as he rapidly gave further consideration to the issue, he could see some value additional value in doing so...an initial reconnaissance of the front would have some value, and placing Tollemach as the Brigade Major in a position where he owed Green a favour might well have some significance later in the mission. 'My orders from General Monash are indeed quite specific, sir,' Green continued. 'I am to study your methods of employing snipers, and I'm sure he could think of no better way to do that than by me visiting the forward troops.'

Tollemache was much relieved. 'Thank you, Sergeant,' he enthused, 'I'll send one of our Intelligence chaps with you as a guide. He's been up the line before to meet with the British, so he knows the way. You will have to leave at first light, and meet up with me in a place called "Sausage Valley" late tomorrow afternoon. We are in rather a hurry for the information, so I'll provide a vehicle to get you close. They tell me you got here by car, so you can take the same car and driver if you like.'

Green smiled grimly. He wasn't at all sure that Private Blucher would thank him for this new task, but he thought, *stuff him. It would do the moody prick a world of good.* 'You'd better show me the place on the map, sir.'

'Good. I'll send someone out to get your driver, and I'll introduce you to your guide. He can give you a map, your authorization to go forward, and so on. Wait here for a moment while I fetch him'.

A few minutes later, Tollemache returned in the company of a tall, thin, Lance Corporal. Tollemache beckoned to Green to join them by a wall on which a large map was displayed.

'Sergeant Green,' Tollemache began. 'This is Lance Corporal Elliot. I shall leave you two alone for a moment Elliot can give you a briefing on the map.'

Green extended his hand and was irritated to note that Elliot delayed accepting his greeting with almost studied insolence. 'Is there a problem, Lance Corporal?' he asked.

'Not at all, Sergeant,' Elliot replied evenly finally shaking Green's hand. 'It's just I am a little surprised we are employing someone for this job who has so recently arrived in France.'

Green smiled. Elliot was clearly an ambitious young man who thought he could do this particular task on his own. 'Well,' he said, 'that's just the way things go. Besides, I'm sure I can rely on your good advice during the visit. Now let's have a look at this map.'

Elliot gave a brief exposé of the general topography and concluded with his own assessment of the situation. 'About the only thing you can rely on so far as the bloody map is concerned,' he stated pompously, 'is the ridgeline. There's not much of the village left, and there used to be a windmill here,' he pointed to the map, 'but it's just a pile of bricks now. Mind you, the bloody Hun has managed to put at least one machine gun under the wreckage. Now tomorrow I'll want you to stick close to me and not to ask too many questions.'

Green raised an eyebrow inquiringly. Elliot was a little too cocky for his liking, but the Lance Corporal was saved from an immediate confrontation over the leadership of the coming patrol, when Blucher joined them at the map board. Green went to introduce the two men.

'I know Private Blucher,' snapped Elliot. 'In my opinion, we should get someone else to drive us. Blucher is a prick!'

'I've sat you on your backside once before, you jack bastard,' snarled Blucher. 'Looks like I'm going to have to do it again!'

Green stepped between the two men. 'Both of you shut up! Any more of this and I'll sit both of you on your backsides, understand!'

Elliot seemed to be shocked by Green's response, but he nodded. Blucher shrugged and looked up at the roof.

'Take a look at the map, Blucher,' Green said. 'Tomorrow morning, I need you to take Elliot and me up here.' He pointed to the map at a point close to the village named on the map as Contalmaison. 'You'll drop us off there, and then he and I are going to walk into Pozieres and then on to Sausage Valley. Once you drop us off, you can return to your unit. Got it?'

'Got it,' replied Blucher, and to his surprise, Green noticed a certain keenness in Blucher.

'Elliot, I want to take a couple of the air photos that best show the ridge and the windmill. And I'll need to take a map.'

'Yes, Sergeant.' Elliot replied unhappily. It was clear he was still angry that Blucher was to have anything to do with the task.

'Right, that's it.' Green said. 'Make sure you get a good feed tonight and as much rest as you can. Where is the cookhouse, Elliot?'

Elliot pointed. 'Out the back of the church,' he said sulkily.

'I'll see you both there at 4:00 a.m. tomorrow morning and we'll have a quick breakfast. I want to leave for Pozieres at first light,' concluded Green.

Blucher went back to the car park to prepare the vehicle for the coming day. Elliot walked off into the body of the hall, and as Green made a final study of the main battle map, he saw that the lance corporal was conducting a vigorous conversation with Captain Tollemach.

A few moments later, Tollemach called Green over. 'I've

just heard that the man I have detailed to drive you is Private Blucher,' Tollemache began. 'I'm very sorry about this, but he is completely unsuited for the task. Not sound, not sound at all.'

Green felt a surge of anger. It was time he established exactly who was going to lead tomorrow's mission. 'Well sir,' he retorted. 'I find myself at a bit of a disadvantage. I don't know Lance Corporal Elliot, but I do know Private Blucher, and while I am sure Blucher has his faults, I am quite happy with him as a driver.'

Tollemache glanced sharply at Green. 'This mission is vital, Sergeant.' he said, 'I cannot afford any weak links in the chain.'

'I understand that, sir, so perhaps after all it might be best to assign it to your own people rather than outsiders. Lance Corporal Elliot, perhaps?'

Tollemache raised his hands in surrender. 'No, no, Elliot would be entirely inappropriate,' he said. 'I need someone who can conduct interviews with Majors and Colonels, wrong kind of task for a Lance Corporal, hard enough for a sergeant. No, I need you to lead the mission. You feel that strongly about Blucher?'

'I do, sir.'

Tollemache shrugged. 'Well, he is only the driver, I suppose. All right,' he concluded, 'against my better judgment he can go.'

'Thank you, sir,' replied Green. Out of the corner of his eye Green saw Elliot shake his head in disgust, and then walk away. Blucher was in, and Green had established his authority as leader of the patrol. Yet in spite of this minor victory, Green felt a distinct unease about the team he was to lead. He had met many soldiers like Blucher. Generally, they hated taking orders from anyone, and often he found they were particularly averse to taking orders from an Aboriginal man. Elliot was another matter. The little bit of power provided by the single stripe worn by a lance corporal all too often led to trouble in the ranks. Lance corporals and their slightly more senior colleagues, corporals, were in the unenviable position of having to direct and discipline troops while still living among them. Sergeants and officers lived slightly apart from those they managed, a somewhat easier row to hoe. In Green's opinion, Elliot was one of those who had difficulty with his junior leadership role and responsibilities.

Green took a further twenty minutes to study the battle map taking particular care to note the various landmarks and troop locations. Then satisfied that he could learn no more from the available data, he left the church and went to look for the cookhouse.

The sun was low on the horizon as Green followed the aroma of stew. It was not, he decided, a particularly rich stew from the smell of it, but stew all the same. His last meal had been the bacon sandwich Warrant Officer Bennet had provided and now he was ravenous.

'Hey Sarg,' someone called him from the shadows of the church wall, 'Sergeant Green!'

'Who is it?'

'It's me, Blucher.'

Green was slightly annoyed at being delayed from satisfying his hunger, but believing Blucher was about to complain about tomorrow's task, he walked over to the driver. 'What's up?' he asked.

Blucher seemed embarrassed. 'They tell me you just stuck up for me in there,' he said.

Green was surprised. 'Do they? And who are they?'

'I've got some mates. Same mates that tell me you're

"Killer" Green the Abo sniper from Gallipoli.' Blucher felt an immediate pang of guilt at his reference to Green's race and sought to apologize. 'Sorry Sarg, I didn't mean no offence.'

'None taken,' replied Green. 'I'm black and proud. Look mate, can we make this quick? I'm bloody starving and the smell of that stew is driving me nuts.'

'Oh, yeah sure,' Blucher became flustered and he raced his explanation out in a torrent of words. 'Listen, I just wanted to say thanks. I haven't always been a driver; I was in a battalion once, but I kept on getting into strife. In the end, the CO got rid of me. That's why I'm stuck driving cars. I wanted to stay with me mates, but they kicked me out.'

'Yes, well I don't see how driving Elliot and me up to Contalmaison is going to get you back with them.'

'Yeah I know, but at least I can tell me self I got a bit closer to the front, if you see what I mean?'

Green wasn't at all sure he did. 'Look, just do a good job tomorrow; don't snot Elliot, and I'll put in a good word for you.'

'Thanks, Sarg.'

'Don't get your hopes up. I'm not sure a black fellow's word counts for too much.'

'Yeah, well thanks anyway. I'll see you in the morning.'

'Yes, in the morning.'

Green found the cook house and helped himself to two servings of the stew and several thick slices of bread. 'I don't know how I'm meant to cope with this,' grumbled the sergeant cook. 'You ain't rationed for here, and no, there isn't any butter.'

Green took no notice of the cook's complaints and after chasing his meal down with two cups of tea, he felt happily sated and left the kitchen area to find a place to sleep.

The Brigade staff continued to load the headquarters equipment onto trucks and wagons. There was a great deal of shouting, horns were blowing, and truck engines were being noisily revved. Green could see it would be hard to find a quiet place, but as it was a warm night, he reckoned he could find an out of the way spot and sleep under the stars. A French Army motorized ambulance trundled down the street toward him and pulled into the curb at the front of the church. The driver climbed out and walked off toward the church entrance; the second person in the vehicle, a nurse by her uniform, stayed near the vehicle.

Green nodded politely toward the woman as he walked past.

'Excuse me,' the nurse addressed him in heavily accented English.

Green turned back. Immediately, he noticed she had a pretty face, dark locks of hair peeping out from beneath her white nurse's veil. 'Good evening,' he said, 'can I help you?'

'*Oui*, yes, I hope so,' she replied hastily. 'Do you know if there is a ladies' toilet close by please? I'm afraid I really need to go quite urgently.'

Green shook his head. 'I'm new here myself,' he said. 'But I'll have a look. Hang on, oh I'm sorry, I mean wait here, I'll be back.'

He received a throaty laugh in response as he hurried away. At least, Green thought, she's not one of those uppity bitches he'd seen at the British hospitals back in England.

There was no designated toilet for females, but Green did find a toilet on the other side of the church, the door of which was adorned with a sign reading: "**For the use of Brigadier General Sinclair MacLagan Only.**" Checking that the facility was not occupied, Green returned to the ambulance.

The nurse was still waiting. 'Come on, love,' Green said, 'the nearest loo is just around the corner.'

Gratefully, the nurse followed him, but she recoiled in fear when she saw the sign on the toilet door. 'Oh no,' she said, 'I cannot.'

'Listen, love,' said Green, 'the Army has taught me many things, but the most important of all these lessons has been that shit and death have no respect for rank. I'll keep watch...you get in there; it will be all right.'

A spasm of discomfort crossed the nurse's face and she dashed inside the exclusive facility.

It had to happen. No sooner had the nurse had time to make herself comfortable within the confines of the privy, a tall and distinguished man left the church and walked toward the toilet. There was no mistaking Brigadier General Sinclair-Maclagan, or his purpose.

Green stepped out of the shadows. 'Good evening, sir,' he said quietly.

'Good evening,' Sinclair-Maclagan replied, not pausing in his advance.

'Sir,' continued Green, 'I wonder if you would mind waiting a few moments?'

'I beg your pardon,' replied Sinclair-Maclagan. He was unused to being questioned by a sergeant at any time, let alone while he was going to the toilet. 'I do mind, as it happens. Now get going before I become really angry.'

'I'm sorry, sir,' continued Green calmly, 'it just so happens that I allowed a lady, a French nurse, to make use of your toilet. I didn't think you'd mind.'

Sinclair-Maclagan turned and stared hard at Green. 'You what?' he exclaimed.

'I let a nurse use your privy; there didn't seem to be a

ladies' facility, sir.'

Sinclair-Maclagan was clearly lost for words, but finally he spluttered, 'I see, yes right thing to do, well done. How long do you think she will be?'

'Not long, sir.'

'Good, good,' added Sinclair-Maclagan as he studied Green's face more closely. 'Do I know you?' he asked.

'Sergeant Green, sir, I'm on attachment from General Monash's staff in England.'

'Ah yes, now I remember you. You were a sniper at Gallipoli. You worked for Monash there too, didn't you?'

'Yes, sir.'

The rustle of skirts behind the two men heralded the arrival of the nurse. 'I'm terribly sorry, General,' she said. 'It is not the Sergeant's fault. I am Madame Sainson, or more recently Nurse Sainson of the Croix-Rouge.'

Sinclair-Maclagan saluted and made a brief bow to the nurse. 'The fault is mine, Madame,' he replied. 'My staff should have established female facilities. I will see to it at our next location. Please accept my apologies and excuse me, for I too must answer nature's call and then return to my work.'

The nurse smiled and stepped aside. 'Of course, sir,' she said.

Sinclair-Maclagan made his exit and Green walked with the nurse back to her ambulance. 'Croix-Rouge' he said, 'that's the same as our Red Cross, isn't it?'

'That's right,' she replied, 'I work with Pierre the driver of my ambulance.'

Green smiled. 'Lucky man,' he said.

'Hah!' she laughed at Green's clumsy compliment, 'you are a cheeky Sergeant.'

Green was embarrassed. 'Look, I'm sorry, that was

impolite; please forgive me.'

'There is nothing to forgive.'

Pierre the ambulance driver was waiting at the vehicle. *'Nous devons partir1*,' he called to Madame Sainson.

She turned to Green. 'It seems we have to go,' she said. 'Thank you for helping me. Oh, I don't know your name—how rude of me.'

'It's Green, Madame, Sergeant Green.'

'Well, thank you again, Sergeant Green. Goodbye and good luck.'

Green waved as the ambulance disappeared down the road; then he resumed his search for a place to sleep. He chose a spot in the shelter of a derelict building's wall, where he rolled out his blanket, lay down, and was soon asleep.

A little after 1:00 a.m., he was woken by the distant sound of battle. Prolonged artillery fire lit the night sky with rippling flashes of light and the distant concussion of the exploding shells dislodged dust from the wall against which he had chosen to sleep. He got to his feet, slung his rifle, and walked back to the church. Most of the headquarters personnel were but gone, but a Rear Party, men left to bring on the less important stores, were out on the road watching the show.

Blucher appeared at Green's side. 'Struth,' he said, 'I suppose that's what the papers call an inferno.'

Green nodded. 'I reckon it's Pozieres,' he said. 'Be thankful you're not under that lot.'

'Is it German or ours?'

'Hard to tell from here; probably both, at a guess. Our gun's would have opened up first, and then the Hun artillery would have fired a counter barrage.'

There was a particularly impressive flash of light and a few seconds later the huge sound caused by the explosion.

'Jesus, what the fuck was that?'

'Maybe an ammo dump,' replied Green. 'Well, there's nothing we can do from here; I'm going back to sleep.' And without another word Green turned away and went back to his spot by the wall and slept.

Chapter 9

At first light, Green met Blucher and Elliot by the car. 'Have you had anything to eat?' he asked curtly and received a mumbled assent from both men. He looked at his watch. 'It's four o'clock; the sooner we get going,' he said, 'the sooner we get back.'

Blucher seized the vehicle's crank handle and after a single powerful twist, the engine spluttered into life; then jamming his rifle into the space between the two front seats, and throwing his pack into the rear seat, he climbed in behind the steering wheel. Elliot clambered into the rear seat and Green noticed a service revolver on the Lance Corporal's hip. 'Where's your rifle?' he asked.

Elliot smirked. 'Headquarters troops,' he said pompously patting the pistol holster. 'It's easier in the headquarters if you aren't cluttered up with a rifle.'

Green grunted. Where they were going was a long way from the Brigade headquarters, and a pistol was a notoriously inaccurate weapon even at the limit of its range of about 25 yards. Green firmly believed a rifle was a more appropriate weapon for an Infantryman, but he could not be bothered arguing with Elliot over the issue. So ignoring the lance corporal, he climbed in to the front passenger seat of the vehicle and made himself as comfortable as possible. Battle had taught Green the value of his rifle, and so he did not imitate Blucher's storage methods for his weapon, but carefully placed his rifle across his lap, the muzzle pointing out over the door.

Blucher piloted the car out onto the road, his neck reddening with anger as Elliot presumptuously directed him toward the road to Contalmaison. 'I've driven these roads a damn side more than you, Elliot!' he snapped.

Elliot ignored Blucher and leaned forward from the back seat to talk with Green. 'I was talking with the Intelligence Sergeant just before we left,' he said with an air of a man who had some superior information.

'Oh,' Green replied casually.

'Yes,' Elliot continued enthusiastically, 'he thinks the attack must have gone fairly well.'

Green's dislike of the Lance Corporal was intensifying, and he had no desire to engage in polite chit chat with the man. However, any news from the front might be important. 'What's he heard?' Green asked evenly.

Elliot smirked. 'Well, he hasn't heard anything as such; it's just a deduction that only an experienced man can make.'

'Is that a fact?'

Elliot did not detect the sarcasm in Green's response and pushed ahead with his condescending explanation. 'You need to understand how the attack was put together. They went in with 1 and 3 Brigades forward and the 2nd Brigade was in reserve. The battalions had a similar formation and the idea was the lead battalion would take the first objectives and then the reserves would leap frog them and take the next lot.'

'Very interesting,' Green replied evenly, 'but a good plan only lasts until the first shot is fired. How does he know it succeeded?'

Elliot smiled triumphantly. 'Ah, that's where battle experience counts,' he said. 'You see, the Hun has a standard tactic, and that is once an attack against them develops, they shell the living daylights out of the area immediately behind the attacking force. Cuts them off from reinforcements and supply; then after a while, they counterattack. Well, soon after our attack went in, the Hun heavily shelled the approaches to the village...therefore, our blokes must have taken the village.'

'Brilliant,' Green commented dryly.

'Yes, isn't it,' agreed Elliot, completely missing Green's sarcasm again. 'You learn a thing or two once you've been at the sharp end for a while.'

'Anything else you'd care to impart from your wealth of experience, Corporal?' Green asked.

Elliot sat back in his seat. 'Not really,' he said, clearly pleased with the way the conversation was progressing. 'As this is your first trip forward, you might like to know we are the first to take this road in daylight—should be quite an eye opener.'

Green immediately felt a pang of alarm. 'It might have been wise to have told me this before now,' he said. 'Let's hope the Hun is looking the other way.'

'Ah, he won't be interested in a single motorcar,' Elliot assured him. 'We're safe as houses here, so long as Blucher doesn't crash us into the ditch.

As the car continued its erratic progress along the road, Green's apprehension grew until about half a mile from Contalmaison they came upon a horrific scene. The road was littered with a variety of stores and equipment, and strewn within this mess were numerous human bodies and the carcasses of several horses, each bloated form issuing its own nauseating smell into the air.

Elliot watched with savage pleasure as Blucher began to dry retch. 'Welcome to the real world, Blucher,' Elliot sneered. 'Not so cushy out here, is it, eh? He turned his attention back to Green: 'It looks like a supply column caught it,' he said, indicating the carnage about them. 'Or maybe one of the headquarters wagons last night? Bit of a shock for someone like Blucher who's never been under fire. How about you, Sergeant? Have you been in the line before?'

'Once or twice,' Green muttered.

Elliot raised his eyebrows; it was apparent he did not believe Green's claim. 'Really, where was that? They don't usually let you darkies near the front, do they?'

Green frowned. It was unusual to hear the kind of rubbish Elliot had just avowed this close to the front line. Front line soldiers were rarely concerned by the colour of a man's skin, only by the worth of their work, but there were always a few bigoted idiots like Elliot. Most times he would ignore such comments, but he was keen to keep Elliot in his place. 'I'm sure that's why the Brigade Major sent you along,' he retorted sarcastically, 'to make sure I don't run away.'

Appreciating his comments had gone too far, Elliot blushed a deep crimson. 'I'm sorry, sergeant', he said contritely, 'I didn't mean you, just the other...' His voice trailed away as he realized he was on the point of making further offence.

Blucher tried and failed to conceal a snort of laughter.

'Shut your face, Blucher!' Elliot snapped furiously. 'I know you haven't been in the line, hardly heard a shot fired have you, let alone one fired in anger, eh?'

'Well, fuck you!' Blucher shouted in anger, and immediately slowed the vehicle. 'Let's see if you've learned to fight any better since I last belted you!'

'Shut up, both of you!' Green's angry command imposed an instantaneous if uneasy calm in the vehicle's cabin. 'Concentrate on this mission,' he continued coldly. 'Lance Corporal Elliot, if you can't offer any worthwhile comment...be quiet! Private Blucher, you keep concentrating on driving and keep your mouth shut!'

Blucher obeyed, returning the vehicle to its original speed. Elliot glowered sulkily, but he kept silent. Green ignored both of them. He was annoyed with himself for having allowed the situation to develop, but more particularly at his own part in the exchange with Elliot. Men were always tense and fearful as they approached a dangerous situation, and he knew he should have seen the problem and distracted his two companions earlier. He smiled wryly as he recognised his own anxieties were increasing with every cratered yard of the road they travelled.

Blucher noticed Green's smile and wondered what the sergeant was thinking about, but Green was unaware of the driver's curiosity, for he was lost in a moment of memory...

Gallipoli...Green was a Private soldier then. His unit had arrived at ANZAC Cove late in the afternoon of the 28th of April where they were allocated an area near 'Quinn's Post' and told to dig in. For the next three weeks they dug, wired, stood sentry duty, and listened to the sounds of the battle that raged all around, but the fighting never actually directly threatened them.

'They will hit us tonight for sure,' became the daily chant of the corporal in charge of Green's section. His words, undoubtedly intended to keep his men alert, served only to raise their stress levels, a situation made worse when the promised attacks failed to materialize.

Then one day after another night of tension, their Colonel called for volunteers to mount a raid on a Turkish trench system near Quinn's Post. One hundred men were required for the raid which was to take place shortly after midnight with the aim of destroying the enemy's trenches and to bring back prisoners. Young, keen, and still completely innocent to the reality of war, Green was one of the first to volunteer.

At eight o'clock that night, the raiding party assembled and were guided through a maze of trenches and gullies to the rear of Quinn's Post. There they waited for the appointed time to attack. Green could remember his excitement and a feeling of self-importance for having elected to take part in such a deliberately offensive operation. He also recalled the large slug of rum afforded each man, and the feeling of invincibility the strong liquor gave him. He rarely touched the stuff after that night, for it clouded his thinking, and with greater experience he found it best to remain in control of his actions.

At a signal, the raiding party had crawled forward and lay down out in front of the Australian wire that bounded Quinn's Post to wait for the signal to attack. Green remembered how quiet the night had become, and how a very white light sizzled into the air and illuminated the area as though it was daytime. He could hear the Turkish soldiers chatting in their trenches; they were about fifty yards from where he lay.

Suddenly, the leader of the raid blew his whistle and the one hundred raiders jumped to their feet and charged forward screaming and shouting.

It was a disaster. They were met with a murderous fire from the strongly entrenched Turks. Many of the raiders became entangled in new wire the enemy had erected across their front and were shot to pieces as they struggled to free themselves from this obstacle. Others were simply scythed down by rifle and machine gun fire. The twenty or so surviving raiders, Green among them, leapt into a steep gully but there was no safety there. Out of a series of tunnels in the gully walls poured a mass of Turkish soldiers. There was an initial exchange of rifle fire, but then there had been no time for shooting as the Turks fell upon the raiders in a fury.

There followed in the darkness of that gully a welter of slaughtering and savagery the like of which Green never imagined possible. Men stabbed, clubbed, and tore at one another in a frenzied orgy of death, but the Turks greatly outnumbered the surviving raiders and it was clear that unless they withdrew they would be wiped out.

Green had fought at the crouch, jabbing and slashing with his bayonet, choking the Turkish cries beseeching Allah for victory. But at the height of the fight, his bayonet became stuck in the ribs of an opponent and as he struggled to free the weapon, a rifle butt clubbed him to the ground, and he was left for dead.

When he regained his senses, there was no sign of any of his fellow raiders. He assumed the survivors had thought him dead and left him behind as they withdrew. Then through the gloom of the gully he heard several pistol shots, then silence, followed shortly later by another pistol shot. He realised the Turks were either killing the wounded raiders, or making sure the dead were indeed dead. It would be just a matter of time before he was discovered and dealt with in similar fashion, and he determined not to simply wait for such a fate to consume him.

It took Green an hour to crawl out of the gully, and by the time he felt safe from the Turkish executioner, the dawn was streaking the sky with blood red colour. This presented him with a new problem, for to try and negotiate the remaining distance back to Quinn's Post in daylight was nothing short of suicidal. The distance was negligible, a hundred paces at most and Green had found it so tempting to stand up and make a dash for it, but he restrained himself. Instead he endured a long hot day pretending to be one of the many dead that littered the field, and finally after dark made his slow and painful way back to Quinn's Post.

———————

The further they travelled along the road, the greater the evidence that it had been a recent artillery target. Blucher had to reduce speed to negotiate a way around numerous shell holes that littered the road surface, and on several occasions he was forced to bring the vehicle to a halt and perform difficult three point turns around yawning craters capable of swallowing the car whole, should he make the slightest error in his driving. He kept glancing across at Green, hoping the sergeant would realize the hopelessness of their journey and that he would order him to turn back.

Green was not watching Blucher. His attention was focused on a distant village he assumed was Contalmaison, which was being subjected to a severe German artillery bombardment. Dust and smoke shrouded the outline of ruined houses, swirling higher and higher with every new detonation. Green hated artillery bombardments; he had been shelled at Gallipoli, and had never got over the feeling of utter terror as he waited helplessly in whatever inadequate cover he had been able to find. But the experience had given him an extra sense that some old soldiers were able to develop, the ability to identify the projectile that among all those impacting in a bombardment was likely to land near or on him. However, as they bumped along this road, it seemed to Green that the noise of the vehicle's engine and its canvas covered roof was preventing him from fully exercising that particular skill, and to his annoyance he found that he was frightened. Every instinct was telling him that this road was a dangerous place.

Elliot, on the other hand, had recovered his confidence and had decided to demonstrate his knowledge of the area. 'When I was up here with the Pommies last week,' he announced pompously, 'I was able to impress their colonel with my knowledge of field sketching. I drew him a sketch so accurate he used it to register his supporting artillery on the Hun. I doubt even you, Sergeant Green, would have much of an understanding of the art. It takes real skill to draw an outline of exactly what one sees. I studied art at university, you know.'

Green was listening intently, but not to Elliot. He had detected a change in the concerto being played by the artillery. Suddenly, he flung the car door open. 'Get out!' he yelled: 'Get away from the car! Take cover!' Then he threw himself away from the vehicle and rolled into a small depression in the ground.

Blucher sat dumbfounded, staring at Green's vacant seat. He could see no reason for the Sergeant's sudden and strange behaviour, but above the cacophony of noise that surrounded them, he could hear a strange whirring sound that was becoming louder and louder.

With the car still moving forward, Elliot scrambled over the side of the vehicle, and fell heavily on to the road. Blucher looked around desperately. Where had they gone? Someone, Green perhaps, was screaming at him to get out of the car. The whirring sound was now almost overpowering. Then abruptly the sound dissolved into a blinding flash combined with noise so loud that Blucher could actually physically feel it strike his body like a hammer blow. The first artillery shell had impacted with astounding force into the field about fifteen yards to the left of the car. The concussion slammed into the vehicle and flung it onto its side. Miraculously, Blucher was thrown clear of the wreck. Dazed but otherwise unhurt, he crawled into the ditch on the side of the road and lay there shaking with fear. The bombardment had not finished. The next shell landed behind the vehicle, while a third and fourth shell impacted directly onto the car.

Suspended in the observation balloon's gondola, the German artillery observers checked the fire of the guns they had employed to destroy the car, and returned the destructive power at their command back to the larger target of Contalmaison.

Nothing that remained of Blucher's car bore any resemblance to it once having once been a motor vehicle. It had been utterly destroyed. Blucher got shakily to his feet, and stared at the smoking wreckage in dismay. Elliot lay unmoving on his back, a small trickle of blood running down the side of his face. Green ran to him. He knelt down and gently raised Elliot's steel helmet to check the man's wound; as he did, a large portion of Elliot's brain slid onto the ground. Quickly, Green removed Elliot's identity tag and stood up, waving to Blucher to join him.

'Is he all right?' Blucher asked as he approached.

'No,' Green replied quietly, 'he's gone west, I'm afraid.'

'What the fuck *was* that?'

Green shrugged. 'Artillery, 5.9's at a guess. Where's your rifle?'

Blucher pointed at the remains of the vehicle, the returned his attention to Elliot's body. 'What do we do with him?' he asked.

'Leave him here,' Green replied as he stood up wiping his hands on the back of his trousers.

Blucher was horrified. 'What? We can't do that! I mean, I didn't like the bastard, but I don't want to see him left on the side of the road like a dog!'

'Look around you, Blucher. I reckon there are about twenty dead men lying within fifty yards of us. The closer we get to the line, the more we'll find. At Gallipoli we used to use the bodies to rebuild our trenches, and I've no doubt they will be doing the same thing here. No one has the time to do anything for the dead at the moment. One day, after we've won perhaps, someone will come back and find them. Right now, we have enough to do, and the dead don't care anymore.'

'Well, it ain't right!' stated Blucher flatly.

'Tell you what then,' countered Green. 'You can carry his body back to Albert. I've no doubt you'll find a God-botherer who will be only too pleased to bury him for you. Or, you can come with me and start some proper soldiering. I'll give you five seconds to make up your mind.'

Green turned away from Blucher and began to check his weapon and equipment. He had retained his rifle and he had been wearing his basic equipment at the time of his undignified departure from the car. Now he adjusted his gear, and checked that the Lee Enfield had not suffered unduly in the impact of his landing. He remembered Elliot's revolver and bent down and removed both the weapon and its holster from the body and placed them on his own belt. Then he checked his watch. It was 4:45 a.m.

'What do I do for a rifle?' asked Blucher moodily.

'Well if you go back, you won't need one,' Green replied calmly. 'But if you come with me...' he paused and looked around. A few yards away the mangled corpse of an Australian soldier lay stretched out on the edge of a shell hole, the dead man's rifle still in his hands. 'You can borrow his. I don't think he'll mind.'

Blucher looked at the dead man holding the rifle and gagged. 'I'm coming with you,' he said with a determination

he did not feel, 'but I'm going to take that rifle over there.' He
pointed to a discarded Lee Enfield that lay a few feet away.

'Good,' said Green, 'see if you can find some ammo too.'

Steeling himself, Blucher went to rob the dead.

Green rifled through Elliot's pockets. He retrieved a map
and Elliot's papers authorising him to be in the forward area.
He opened the map and began relating it to the ground, trying
to establish their position. The road they had so recently
travelled continued to the north-east where it climbed a
ridgeline, a feature Green knew was German held territory.
The village of Pozieres lay directly to the north, or rather, it
used to lie to the north. Green could see that during the
previous evening, the combined might of British and German
artillery had reduced the village to little more than a few
ruined walls and mounds of broken bricks and timber beams.
The artillery fire had stilled now, but the occasional shell of
indeterminate origin still slammed into the ruins sending dust
and debris hurtling skyward. To the rear the ruins of
Contalmaison Villa were still being shelled by the Germans.
Satisfied that he had established roughly where they were,
Green folded the map and put it in his tunic pocket.

Blucher returned with his newly reclaimed rifle and
ammunition. The weapon's woodwork was smeared with
blood which Blucher was tentatively attempting to clean away.
'It stinks,' he complained, 'so does the ammo.'

'Sadly,' Green told him grimly, 'where we are going, you'll
get used to it. 'Thank heavens you still had your basic
equipment and water bottle on you when we got whizbanged;
otherwise, you'd really have something to complain about.' He
pointed to a nearby corpse whose belt and basic webbing was
straining to retain the swelling contents of the body. Blucher
imagined trying to retrieve the webbing and retched at the

thought.

Green moved to the lip of a shell hole and sat down. He beckoned Blucher to his side.

'What's a God-botherer?' Blucher asked as he squatted down beside Green.

'A Padre.'

'Oh, I hadn't heard that one before...it's good.'

Green smiled. 'Now you've decided to come,' he continued, 'I reckon it's time to fill you in on what your new job entails.'

Blucher nodded nervously, but somehow words would not form in his mouth.

'You've done bloody well,' Green continued. 'To be honest, I wasn't sure that you weren't going to turn back, but now you're here it looks to me like you intend to stay.'

Blucher indignantly found his voice. 'Hey, I said I'd come with you and that's what I'm going to do.'

Green smiled. 'Okay, keep your shirt on. You had better take these.' He handed Blucher the authorization papers Elliot had carried. 'You'll need these if the MPs challenge us on the way in, or as we come back. Keep them some place safe; I don't want to see you shot as a deserter.'

Silently, Blucher pocketed the papers.

'From now on you are going to be my "spotter",' Green said. In fact, he hadn't always used a spotter on Gallipoli, never in fact before Monash claimed him, and then only sparingly. However, once he got used to having the support of someone watching out and in effect coaching him on to a target, he realized a spotter's value. He had established a good relationship with an Irishman, Riley, but then just before the evacuation, the Turks shelled the knoll on which he and Riley were hidden and Riley had died. He was not entirely sure that

Blucher would prove to be of similar value, but he was all he had and he figured even if he was terrible as a spotter, he would probably prove to be more use than the unfortunate Elliot.

He detached a cylindrical leather sleeve from his web belt and handed it to Blucher. 'Inside this is my telescope. For Christ's sake, don't lose the bloody thing! Put it on your web belt and every fifty paces check it hasn't fallen off. When we get up there, we might have to do some shooting and I'll need you to spot for me, so that should I miss with a shot, you can bring me back on to the target. Got it? It's not hard; I'll teach you.

'Shit, do you think I can do it?'

'I wouldn't have asked you to do the job if I didn't think you could,' Green replied. 'The job that Elliot and I were going to do was to check the position of our blokes on the ground, mark it all up on a map, and get back to Brigade headquarters. I suppose they will use the info for planning our own artillery shoots and for the next lot of attacks, and that's the other reason why I need you... one of us at least has to get back with the information.'

Suddenly several hundred yards to their front the whole world seemed to erupt in dust, smoke, and horrendous sound of a major artillery bombardment. From within this storm of destruction brilliant light flared and died with flickering intensity. Then to their right front came another eruption, the gut-wrenching rattle of sustained machine gun fire. Green turned to watch but Blucher had slid down into the shelter of the deeper part of the shell hole.

'Must be a Hun counterattack,' Green shouted above the noise. 'Most of the small arms stuff is going away from us.'

'How can you tell?' Blucher shouted back from the bottom

of the hole.

'No crack thump.'

Somewhere in the back of Blucher's memory he recalled his pre-deployment training lesson where the he was told that a round fired toward him cracked as it went over head, and that moments later he might hear the thump of the report from the rifle that fired the shot.

'We'll wait a minute to see what happens,' Green called down to Blucher, 'and then we can probably keep going.'

Blucher scrambled up the side of the shell hole and joined Green, where he stared in horror at the bombardment. 'Into that?' he asked.

Green nodded. 'Still want to come?'

Blucher shrugged. 'Sure,' he said trying to sound more confident than he felt.

'Good man,' Green responded enthusiastically. 'We'll head north from here for about three hundred yards,' he gestured toward Pozieres. 'That should bring us to the first German trench our blokes attacked. If the attack went well, they would have passed over that trench and moved on to their final objective, which is the main road through the village. But by the sounds of that,' he inclined his head toward the sounds of battle, 'they haven't got that far and now the Hun is trying to drive them off.'

In truth, Green was feeling pleased with himself. He had worried that the battlefields of France would be so different from Gallipoli that his combat experience would stand for naught. However, the closer he got to the Front the more confident he became in his hard-won skills. Once again, he felt he could read the sights and sounds of battle.

The bombardment suddenly ceased, and the rifle and machine gun fire reached a new crescendo of sound before slowly dwindling away to the odd rifle shot. Faint screams and shouts could now be heard. Green looked toward the new sound. 'Well, there's no one rushing back in this direction. I take that as a good sign. Our chaps must have seen the counterattack off; we can get going again.'

Green's prediction as to the locality of the old German trench proved to be highly accurate, and within minutes of beginning their march forward, the parapet and other defences of what was known as the Pozieres Trench became clearly visible. They approached cautiously, mindful that the occupants of the trench might well be alarmed by their unexpected appearance and react violently. A few paces from the trench, they both took cover and Green called out, 'Hello the trench! Two Aussies, can we come in?'

A muffled voice responded. 'Be quick, there are Huns about.'

Green and Blucher slid down into the trench, to immediately recoil in alarm as they saw two German soldiers, seemingly on sentry duty on a nearby fire step and facing the direction from which they had just come. A low chuckle greeted their alarm. 'Don't you like our rear guard?' an Australian voice asked. The question provoked a new burst of laughter. Green smiled sheepishly and raised a hand in acknowledgment to a group of Australian soldiers lining the opposite side of the trench. A corporal from within the group stood up and strolled across to greet his two visitors. 'Where have you blokes sprung from?' he asked.

'We're from Brigade,' Green replied. 'What unit are you with?'

'Bits of this and that,' the Corporal replied grimly. 'But I suppose most of us here are from 9 Battalion, what's left of it anyway.'

Green looked at the resting men. They were indeed a disparate group. The colour patch worn on the soldiers' uniforms showed there were men present from every battalion in the Brigade. 'Shades of the first days at ANZAC,' Green muttered remembering accounts of how the forward assault battalions had lost much of their cohesion in the rush to reach the cliff tops at ANZAC Cove.

The Corporal nodded knowingly. Green turned away to take a closer look at the two dead Germans. There were no visible signs as to how they had died.

'Blast must have killed them,' the Corporal commented casually. 'This is the way we found them. They seemed to be doing a good job, so we left them to it. Of course, the joke will wear a bit thin soon, when they start to stink.'

Blucher was appalled, but when he turned away from the dead sentries he could see, just as Green had predicted, that the bodies of other German soldiers and those of several Australians had been used to build a parapet on the reverse side of the trench. 'Jesus,' he gasped. He walked away a few paces and vomited onto the trench floor.

The Corporal nodded toward the wall of human dead. 'The Hun had left the rear of the trench lower than the front, but of course their rear became our front. We had to build a wall.' He shrugged dismissively, as if to justify to himself the grizzly decision to use his fellow human beings as building material. 'Then of course the bombardment knocked it about a fair bit...' he mumbled.

Green nodded. 'I understand,' he said quietly. 'Don't worry about my mate; it's his first time. Now I'm in a bit of a hurry; can you show me where your Battalion headquarters is?'

The Corporal pointed to the right. 'About a hundred yards that way,' he said, 'they're in an old German dugout; you can't miss it, but for Christ sake, keep your heads down. The Hun has just counter attacked, but we saw the bastards off. Now they've a fuckin' sniper at work; I've just lost a couple of blokes. But if we work out where the bastard is, I'll give him fuckin' snipe. You can't miss the headquarters straight down that way.'

Green nodded his thanks and was about to leave, when the Corporal suddenly put out a hand and stopped him. 'Hang on a minute,' the Corporal said slowly. 'A man must be getting old. I know you, don't I? You're "Killer Green"!' He turned to his mates who up to now had taken no part in the conversation. 'Bloody hell, boys, we're in the company of a fucking celebrity up here!' He seized Green's right hand and began pumping it enthusiastically. 'Name of Judd,' he continued, 'you won't remember me, but we did our basic training together at Broadmeadows back in Aussie.'

Green smiled weakly. 'That was a while ago,' he said, 'but yes, I think I remember you.'

The other soldiers sat up and for the first time began to take an interest in their visitors. They crowded around Green and one by one shook his hand.

'This bloke,' Judd continued to the assembled group, 'is a fucking legend. Anyone here not know about "Killer Green"?'

A few of the soldiers raised their hands. 'Well, you've hardly been in long enough, I suppose,' Judd sneered, 'but some say he's a better shot than Billy Sing!'

One young fellow looked particularly puzzled. 'Who's Billy Sing?' he asked innocently.

Judd rolled his eyes and there was an audible groan from others in the group. 'Only the top sniper on Gallipoli,' Judd replied, 'that's all, and this bloke might have been better than him.'

Green blushed, and silently recalled how he had not been best pleased when he was first given that particular title.

———————————

It had all started after the abortive trench raid near Quinn's Post. Instead of being welcomed back to his unit, Green found he faced rejection. His CO had never been happy with having an Aboriginal in his battalion, and as soon as he saw Green, he accused him of having hidden while the rest of the raiding party fought. Angrily, the CO announced his intent to charge Green with having shown cowardice in the face of the enemy. Fortunately for Green, the only other survivor of the raid, a sergeant, had been witness to Green's actions during the fight and spoke up for him.

'You can say what you like about that black bastard,' the sergeant told the CO, 'but I tell you he's no coward. The little bastard fought like a bloody demon.'

Faced with this testimony, the CO was forced to abandon his plans to press charges against Green. However, Green's problems did not end there. A rumour circulated the unit that he was bad luck, and shortly afterwards many of the men refused to work with him. This situation provided the CO with another excuse to be rid of Green; after all he could not have one man causing such a disruption. Short of sending Green on some kind of suicidal mission, he decided to arrange for the fellow to be transferred to the supply depot down on the beach. The RSM advised Green of the transfer and Green dutifully reported to the supply depot, only to find they knew nothing of any transfer, and had no need of any additional men.

Alone and apparently unwanted, Green decided to return to the front and conduct his own private war against the Turkish Army. In this endeavour he found a willing ally in the elderly Warrant Officer named Bennet, the manager of a stores dump within the supply depot on the beach. *Bennet ensured Green was provided with various items he required, including a telescope in a leather carrying case.*

With his line of supply secure, Green would attach himself to any unit that was in heavy contact with the enemy, Australian, New Zealand, British—they were all the same to him. Then he would lend a hand. Some thought he was more than a little crazy, a little like Simpson and his donkey, but as Green proved to be a first-class marksmen, his assistance was almost always welcome.

It was during that time Green met Billy Sing and his spotter Tom Sheehan and another sniper Ion Idiress. Green stayed with them for about three weeks, learning many of the tricks of the sniper trade, such as the good sense of maintaining a policy of one shot per target. Should the marksman miss with the first shot, a second shot from the same position would almost certainly betray the sniper's position and allow the enemy to return fire. So Green had watched the experts, listened to their advice, and learned.

It was at that time that the matter of nicknames, or titles, arose. Sing had been nicknamed "The Assassin," Idriess as "Iron Jack," and soon Green had gained the title of "Killer." Green disliked his title but there nothing he could do about it. He killed the enemy because it was his job as a soldier, but he took no joy in the task. On the other hand, he formed the opinion that Sing and his companions were simply engaged in killing as many members of the Turkish Army as they could. While many of his fellow soldiers at Gallipoli thought this a laudable ambition, however, Green formed the opinion that a sniper's talents could be better employed.

He began to be extremely selective in his targets. Most snipers targeted Turkish officers and NCOs, but Green went further than this. He would superimpose himself onto ANZAC plans for an attack, targeting and attempting to nullify Turkish machine guns, and strong points. In addition to these activities, using skilful camouflage, he would move to a position from where he might observe the Turkish trenches. Then on returning to the Australian lines, he would report all he had seen.

His efforts were not always appreciated by those in command, and he was sometimes chased away from places where he could have been of great assistance. However, not all senior officers thought Green a nuisance. Brigadier John Monash had learned of Green's remarkable skills and recognised his potential, a potential Monash felt certain would be better employed within his Brigade.

Monash's meticulous planning of each of the operations his Brigade undertook, leant itself to employing Green to surgically remove perceived risks, or to obtain valuable information. After some thought on the matter, Monash decided to make a direct approach to Green, eventually finding him in a fighting bay at "The Neck."

'So you're the famed "Killer" Green,' Monash had begun without preamble.

Green turned toward the stranger who had interrupted his observation of the Turkish line. He noticed the red tabs and gold braid on Monash's uniform, was unimpressed, and turned back to his task. 'That'll be me,' he had grunted in reply.

Monash had smiled grimly, but was not deterred from his task. 'You're not a Light Horseman are you, Killer, and yet you seem to be hanging around with a mob of them. Billy Sing and Idriess both wear emu feathers in their hats. You should be with your brother Infantrymen.'

Green had laughed bitterly. 'I used to be, but the bastards cut me adrift,' he replied without turning back to face Monash.

Monash joined Green at the observation post. 'It must be tough, fighting on alone,' he commented as they stared out over no man's land.

Green grunted an acknowledgment. In fact, it was getting harder; even with Bennet's help he was often short of items he required.

'I tell you what,' Monash had continued, 'I'll make you a corporal *and transfer you to my headquarters. I'll advise you of targets I want eliminated, or of information I need, and then I'll leave you to get on with it.'*

Green was silent for a moment as he considered Monash's offer; it was just the kind of employment he had dreamed of. He stepped away from his observation post and held out his hand. 'Brigadier,' he said calmly, 'you have got yourself a deal.'

Now it all seemed so long ago, and he was stuck with his blasted nickname, and the notoriety that was associated with it.

Certainly, Corporal Judd was a happy man to be able to lay claim to knowing such a celebrity. 'Now you're a sergeant,' he enthused, 'and what's Billy Sing…still a baggy arsed private I hear.' Judd turned to his appreciative audience. 'Sergeant Green and I, we go way back,' and he gave Green a playful dig in the ribs with his elbow. 'I'll never forget the CSM calling the role that day on recruit course.'

'Neither will I,' Green muttered, gesturing to Blucher to start moving. But Blucher was enjoying his leader's discomfort. 'Hang on,' he said, 'I want to hear this. What did the CSM say?'

Judd began to laugh and before Green could further object, he continued his story. 'Well, you see, young Greenie was frightened the Army was going to toss him out on account of him being part Abo. So he was being extra careful to make a good impression. Anyway, we was on the parade ground learning how to fall out and report forward—you know the drill.'

Blucher and the rest of the group nodded happily. They had all experienced the same lesson as recruits. The NCO in charge would call the soldier's name and direct him to "Fall Out!" The soldier would come to attention take a step forward then march out of the ranks to halt before the NCO.

'Well the CSM calls out "Private Green." Greenie does his bit and marches out to the CSM.' Judd began to laugh again, and tears ran down his dirty cheeks; it took a moment before he could continue. 'The CSM says to Greenie, "Who are you? You ain't Green!" "Yes I am, CSM," young Greenie says.' Once again, Judd was almost unable to contain his mirth, but he managed to splutter on. 'Then the CSM says "No you ain't, you can't be Green...You're Black!"'

There was an explosion of laughter from the group, and in spite of his embarrassment, Green joined in. It was funny now, but on the day, he had thought his subterfuge to join the AIF had been discovered and he was about to be marched away to the guard room, to be unceremoniously thrown out into the street. Since then though he often wondered if that CSM had been having a joke at his expense, or if the CSM was actually letting Green know that he knew who Green was and he didn't care. One young soldier in the group, the lad who had asked about Billy Sing, had failed to see the funny side of Judd's story. 'I hated parades,' he stated flatly.

His companions laughed, but Green nodded his agreement with the soldier. The parade ground had always been a place of particular terror for him too. He was never confident that he could carry out the specific orders of the parade commander and that his errors would draw attention to himself. He had long convinced himself that anonymity was his friend, but under the eagle eye of Regimental Sergeant Major Robb, it had been a difficult state to achieve...

The RSM stood beneath the flagpole at the end of the parade ground, his great voice booming out words of command and striking terror into the heart of even the most artful recruit.

'Don't move! If you move, you horrible little man, I'll eat you, no pepper, no salt, dirty boots and all!'

Green actually imagined the RSM really would in fact eat any misbegotten recruit who offended him, and he determined to obey the RSM's every command and to remain perfectly still, but the harder he tried the greater an urge to fidget invaded his very soul.

A small black fly landed on the brim of his slouch hat. It paused there for a second then with a deft manoeuvre it transferred itself to Green's nose. Desperately he pursed his lips and tried to blow a jet of air at the insect to send it on its way.

The fly maintained its position, but Green's attempt to dislodge it from its landing point had not gone un-noticed. 'Leave that fly alone, you horrible little man! It won't eat much, but I will! I'll eat you, no pepper, no salt, dirty boots and all!'

For a moment Green thought the RSM was coming to get him, but a quick glance at the flagpole reassured him…the RSM was still there. Once Green had seen the RSM run across the parade ground to berate some poor unfortunate from point blank range… but not today.

And so Green's terror of the parade ground festered and grew. His preferred position in any drill formation was in the centre ranks, where he felt his surrounding comrades protected his identity. He even practised his rifle drill in front of the barracks room mirror to ensure his drill would be error free and never again draw that terrible curse:

'You, you horrible little man! I'll eat you, no pepper no salt dirty boots and all!'

'Do you know any other yarns, Corporal?' one of the other soldiers asked, interrupting Green's reverie.

Green held up a hand. 'I'm sure he does, but Blucher and I have to get to your headquarters.'

Judd picked up his rifle. 'Hold hard, Sergeant,' he said, 'I'll guide you, there's a couple of bits of trench where the Hun snipers are real bad. Don't want our celebrity getting knocked off now, do we? Come along then; I'm a busy man.'

Judd led the way along the trench. At various intervals, groups of soldiers had established strong points and were busily working at improving the trench defences. They took little notice of Judd or his two companions as they passed.

Chapter 10

Corporal Judd talked incessantly of the previous night's attack. 'We should have got a lot further on,' he told Green and Blucher as they followed him along the battered trench, 'but the bloody artillery blew us to hell and it wasn't all Hun artillery either.'

Blucher gaped at the Corporal in amazement. 'You mean our own side shelled you?' he asked incredulously.

'Too right,' Judd replied bitterly. 'I believe it was worse for the 11th and 12th Battalions, but we copped our share. Bastard gunners are too far away to see what they're shooting at. They don't give a shit so long as their bloody supper's hot for them when they've finished a shoot.'

Green grunted disapprovingly at Judd's disingenuous assessment of artillerymen. 'They would have been firing to a pre-arranged plan,' he said. 'You must have run into your own covering barrage.'

Judd sniffed indignantly. 'That's as maybe,' he said, 'all I know is our own artillery knocked the living shit out of the attack. But even that wasn't the worst of it. The right-hand companies had to attack along the face of the ridge, *between* the two lines of Hun defences; Christ alone knows why! Anyone with half a brain could tell they were going to take enfilade fire, and of course that's what happened; machine guns from the flank mowed dozens of the boys down. In a way, we were lucky on this end of the line, but those poor bastards on the right...' Judd's critique of the battle ceased and he held up a warning hand. 'Mind yourselves here,' he said, stooping to ensure he was well below the damaged parapet. 'There's a Hun sniper watching this gap; he's already knocked two or three of our blokes.'

Green and Blucher followed Judd's example and stooped below the remains of the parapet keeping low until they had passed the dangerous area and they were able to proceed in a more upright manner.

Judd resumed his running commentary. 'This is going to be a bugger of a place when the sun gets right up,' he commented. 'Don't look, whatever you do, but out there, over the top, it's carpeted with our blokes. Most are dead of course, but we still can't get to the wounded.'

Green could already detect the odour of death. Judd was right; soon the newly dead corpses would begin to swell and belch fetid gases into the air, a stench the living could not escape.

'Nearly there,' Judd said encouragingly. He pointed ahead. 'Do you see it there, that dugout on the point of the next corner?' That's where we have to go, but keep low, the parapet has been knocked about a bit...' a loud thump interrupted Judd's commentary. He sat down suddenly and slumped against the trench wall.

Believing Judd had merely tripped, Blucher made to step forward to help him to his feet, but a bellow from Green stopped him. 'Stay where you are! Sniper!'

Green crawled rapidly to Judd's side; he was dead. A small wound flecked with blood in the centre of the fallen man's chest spoke volumes of the German marksman's skill, and a flood of gore was forming where the dead man sat. Instinctively, Green knew the bullet must have punched a massive wound through Judd's back.

Blucher took an injudicious step forward and another bullet slammed into the trench wall, a hair's breadth from his face. 'Keep down, you bloody fool!' Green shouted.

Blucher was spared further of Green's remonstrations by the sound of incoming artillery shells. Green grabbed Blucher by the arm and pulled him forward. 'Come on,' he yelled above the ear-splitting detonations of the shells impacting along the parapet. 'If we don't get inside the headquarters, we're dead-uns!'

'What about Judd?' Blucher screamed as he ran after Green.

'Do you want to join him?' Green shouted as he ran toward the dugout the unfortunate Judd had identified.

Rubble caused by previous bombardments made the bottom of the trench treacherous, Green stumbled and fell, and for a terrible moment Blucher thought Green had been hit. He reached down and seized Green's equipment, hauling him to his feet.

'I'm all right!' Green gasped. 'Keep going!'

The trench behind them had dissolved into a cauldron of flame, smoke and dust, and in the growing shriek of another incoming shell they threw themselves toward the sanctuary offered by the dugout's entrance. The shell exploded with mind numbing power, and Green felt himself lifted into the air and then thrown violently forward; he landed painfully at the bottom of a steep flight of steps. For a moment, he thought Blucher had been caught in the blast, but a groan in the cloud of dust that blanketed the space he had fallen in told him Blucher was still with him.

Green sat up and massaged a sore knee. 'That was close,' he muttered.

Blucher was desperately fumbling around in the gloom on his hands and knees. 'Where's my rifle?' he said.

'Fuck your rifle. Have you still got my telescope?

'Put your weapons on the ground and get your hands up!' the order was barked from somewhere in the gloom of the dugout. A man stepped out of the shadows and pointed a pistol at Green. Green opened his mouth to speak, but the man cut him off. 'Quiet,' he said. Then he spoke to an unseen companion who was somewhere in the gloom beyond dugout entrance. 'I'll keep them covered while you search them.'

A second man came forward and quickly searched Green and the Blucher. He found Green's map and their written orders authorising their presence at the front. The searcher handed the documents to the man with the pistol. 'It's all right,' the man doing the searching said his voice tinged with relief. 'They're some of our chaps.'

The man with the pistol was not impressed. 'Well if they're not Huns,' he retorted tersely, 'they are probably fucking deserters.' He began to read Green's map. 'Who marked this map?' he demanded.

'Brigade Intelligence section,' Green replied evenly.

The man with the pistol turned his attention to the written orders and after a second or two he began to relax and signalled for Green and Blucher to lower their hands. 'You're from Brigade?' he asked.

'Yes,' Green replied. 'Sergeant Green and Private Blucher—we're looking for 9 Battalion Headquarters.'

'Well, today is your lucky day,' the man said. 'You've found us. This,' he said gesturing grandly into the dugout gloom, 'is the headquarters. The Huns make bloody good dugouts, don't you think? This one even had proper beds with mattresses. They would have been very happy in here, before we evicted them.'

In the spluttering glow of several wall-mounted candles,

Green could see a number of Australian soldiers, most of whom had paused in whatever activities they had been performing to watch the situation that had developed at the dugout entrance, then judging the brief drama posed no threat, they turned away. A few, Green noticed, seemed to be totally focused on the continuing bombardment, jumping at every detonation and casting anxious eyes toward the dugout roof above them. Everyone in the dugout was covered with a thick layer of chalk dust, making it impossible to see any individual's badges of rank. 'Are you the CO?' Green asked tentatively.

The man who had held the pistol laughed. 'Nah, I'm the RSM,' he pointed to a man who was stretched out on the floor, fully equipped and sound asleep, 'that's the CO. Lieutenant Colonel Robertson, the man who can sleep through anything.'

'I need to wake him up?' Green said.

'Sooner you than me, sport,' replied the RSM, 'good luck.'

Green knelt down and shook the sleeping CO. Lieutenant Colonel Robertson opened one eye and looked inquiringly at Green. 'Who the hell are you?' he demanded angrily. 'You're not part of my headquarters.'

'I'm Sergeant Green and that's my assistant Private Blucher,' Green replied, inclining his head toward Blucher.

Lieutenant Colonel Robertson sat up and rubbed some of the dust from his face. 'Of course you are,' he said, 'I recognise you; you're General Monash's sniper chap. But so far as I know, the "Deep Thinkers" are still in Blighty. What in God's name are you doing here?'

Green was amazed Robertson had recognised him, particularly as he had no recollection of ever having met Robertson. 'I'm on secondment, sir,' Green explained. 'Right now, Private Blucher and I are on a special task from Brigade.' He handed Robertson the letter of introduction Captain

Tollemache had provided. 'This should explain what we're up to, sir.'

Robertson read the letter and raised his eyebrows. 'Big job for a sergeant,' he commented. He looked toward Blucher. 'These orders say that one of you is a Lance Corporal.'

'Lance Corporal Elliot was killed getting here, sir. Private Blucher was my driver and he agreed to take Elliot's place. I'm afraid we lost one of your blokes on the way along the trench; Corporal Judd was guiding us here when he was sniped.'

Robertson shrugged. Men died here every second; one or two more hardly made any difference. 'So the Brigadier wants to know where we are?' he began. 'Well, there's not a lot of good news for him, I'm afraid, although it's not all bad either, by God.' Robertson got slowly to his feet. 'There was heavy fighting here last night, very heavy indeed. We were on the extreme right flank of the attack. Let me tell you, Sergeant, my men were bloody magnificent. Seven times they got smashed into the ground and each time they found a way forward. And not just my blokes—see that young fellow over there?' Robertson pointed to a slightly built lieutenant who seemed particularly tense, jumping at every detonation that impacted outside the dugout. 'That's Lieutenant Blackburn—he's from 10 Battalion, captured about two hundred yards of the Hun's trench, led bombing raids, and in his spare time provided me with all kinds of valuable intelligence. Between you and I, Sergeant, I'm going to recommend him for an award. And he won't be the only one. We ran into a Hun strong point and they pasted the hell out of us with machine guns and bombs. One of my lads, chap called Leake, took them on with the bayonet. I'm going to recommend him too.'

Green was silent. There was little he could say to affirm Robertson's obvious pride in his battalion's achievements.

'The bad news,' Robertson continued, 'is that this is as far we could go, so depending on how far 1 Brigade got in the village, our holdup here will have created a bloody great gap in our line. Whichever Hun is in charge over there knows his stuff. About half an hour ago, they counter attacked straight down where I reckon the gap is. But they made one mistake. Silly bastards tried to rush us in a tight formation; we shot them to bits. Mind you, it's a stalemate now; they can't get at us, but if we climb out of this trench... up on that ridge he's got more machine guns than he knows what to do with.'

Robertson was suddenly furious. 'The bloody staff,' he spat. 'What a pack of absolute bastards! They uselessly overcrowded the attack; the whole Division squeezed into a little over a 1,000-yard front, just one massive artillery target. But to send my battalion in between two lines of Hun trenches...' He paused momentarily before he continued in a cold fury. 'Too many men have been blown to bits and mown down like hay. Most of my officers have been killed, and all because of piss poor planning on their part! They have not even had the brains to consider the problem of communications and how the lack of ability in that regard is impacting on command and control. You know, I don't think we have learned a single bloody thing from Gallipoli, not a thing!'

Green was not surprised by the focus of Robertson's outburst. The staff had been notorious on Gallipoli for making ill informed decisions that had resulted in the unnecessary deaths of hundreds of men. Now many of the same men were responsible for the planning for this battle, and Green saw little reason to assume those men had changed their concept of war fighting. Nevertheless, he gave no indication of concurrence or dispute with the Colonel's opinion.

Robertson made a huge effort at self-control. 'You'll need a rough idea of my dispositions,' he said huskily. 'Do you have a map?' Green hastily produced his map and unfolded it to reveal the eastern side of Pozieres and Robertson regarded it with interest. He pointed a pencil at a symbol showing a junction point between the trench system known as "Pozieres Trench" and another substantial trench that followed a ridgeline bounding the eastern side of the battlefield. 'Munster Alley,' he said. 'It's full of Huns. We were supposed to reach the railway line, and for a short while some of our chaps got close, but the Huns bombed them out. So I hold this part of the old German line, plus a section of their line along the ridge.' He marked Green's map with a blue crayon.

'Do you have any idea where the rest of the Brigade got to, sir?' Green asked.

'Most of them are on my left,' Robertson replied, in this same bloody trench system. But it's all mixed up, more of a mob now than a Brigade. The 10th lost men too, but I think they have fared rather better than the rest of us; certainly if it wasn't for them there would be an even bigger hole in our line. I think the 11th got badly knocked about, don't know much about the 12th, but from what I hear, a lot of their men are now mixed in with what's left of the 11th.'

'What's the best way to get to them?' Green asked.

'Simple enough,' Robertson replied flatly. 'Go back the way you came and turn left, follow the trench line, and you can't help but run into them. We are expecting another counterattack at any moment and I'm currently working on achieving interlocking machine gun fire with the other units. It's the guns that will beat the bastards, but if we lose one or two of them, it will be down to bayonets to keep them out and I'm not sure we have enough of those to do the job.'

Green nodded. He understood the gravity of the situation

and in the same instant, the importance of the mission he and Blucher were undertaking was reinforced to him. 'We'd better keep going, sir,' he said. 'The quicker we can get this information back to Brigade, the better.'

'Of course,' Robertson agreed, but as he went to farewell his visitors, the German bombardment returned with a vengeance. All along the line shell after shell impacted with vitriolic intensity. Robertson glanced nervously at the roof of the dugout. 'This will test the skills of German engineering,' he quipped.

Green flinched as one shell exploded particularly close to the dugout entrance. 'I hope the bastards did a good job,' he replied anxiously. Gallipoli had left Green with an abiding fear of being shelled. It was a fear born of helplessness, at having to endure without any ability to hit back. However, he had learned that the damage the artillery of both sides could inflict was limited to the number of guns and ammunition they possessed, and all he had to do was endure and eventually the bombardment would cease.

A particularly heavy detonation seemed to impact directly on top of the dugout. The concussion from the blast snuffed out the candles lining the dugout walls and filled the dugout with dust and fumes. A long anxious moment followed where every man in the dugout waited fearfully for the roof to collapse, a catastrophe that would turn their subterranean shelter into a well-constructed mass grave.

The roof held.

Someone reignited the candles, but the feeble light provided in the dust filled space achieved little other than a slightly comforting glow.

Outside the barrage continued, and once again the attention of the occupants of the dugout focused on the roof.

A man in the corner of the dugout began to weep. Robertson rummaged around in a wooden box and produced a large stone flagon. 'RSM!' he called.

'Sir?' Out of the dugout's gloom the RSM appeared at his CO's side.

'Rum all round please, RSM,' Robertson continued shakily. He handed the flagon to the RSM.

'Certainly, sir.' Green watched as like some demented priest administering a hellish sacrament, the RSM moved about the cellar, pouring a generous tot of the fiery liquid into whatever receptacle the men had available.

The shelling suddenly ceased, to be replaced by a momentary stillness, which was almost as nerve shattering as the shelling.

The RSM was the first to react. The rum flagon was set aside. 'Right you lot outside!' his commanding voice shattering the silence and replacing the strange fear it had produced with a sense of urgency as men scrambled for the dugout entrance. 'Come on, you bastards; it's time to earn your pay!' the RSM roared encouragingly. 'Out! Out and into the trench! We don't want Mister Hun to catch us in here like rabbits in a burrow, do we now!'

The dugout quickly emptied of all except for a couple of signallers, the CO and Green and Blucher. 'Counterattack?' Blucher asked fearfully.

'Probably,' Green agreed. It made sense that the German artillery would cease fire to allow their infantry to close with the defending Australians.

Robertson beckoned to Green. 'Well Sergeant, as much as we have enjoyed your company, it seems now would be a good time for you to leave us,' he said. 'Don't waste too much time getting back to Brigade, will you.'

'We won't, sir,' Green replied. He picked up his rifle and equipment and made for the dugout steps.

Robertson took him by the elbow and again drew him back. 'The most important thing to get through to the Brigadier,' he said quietly, 'is our lack of supplies. We have no water, very little food, and our ammunition stocks are running low. I'm going to try and resupply my fellows tonight, but unless I get a major resupply, I won't be able to give them much. He has to get supplies forward.'

Green nodded and his thoughts returned to the eviscerated supply column he and Blucher had seen on the road in. 'I'm sure it's not through lack of effort...' he began.

Robertson held up a hand silencing him. 'I know, I know,' he began, 'the damned Hun artillery, but if Brigade doesn't get something to us soon, it will all have been for nothing.'

'I'll tell him,' Green promised, he beckoned to Blucher and together they climbed the steps of the dugout and out into the trench beyond.

Outside the dugout, in the ruined trench, the tension was palpable. All around, an amazing number of Diggers had survived the barrage to emerge from wherever they had taken cover and were now lining the battered trench, watching at the ready. However, among these living, lay the dead, some terrible in their mutilation, others seemingly untouched but just as dead, and here and there a splatter of blood mixed with particles of flesh and slivers of bone, all that remained of those who had been reduced to a state the soldiers referred to as "red mist." There was no discernible sign of the corporal who had died guiding them to the battalion headquarters.

A few yards away from the dugout entrance Green paused and drew Blucher down beside him. 'How are you doing?' he asked, 'Are you okay?'

Blucher frowned. 'Fine, I'm fine, let's get going.'

Green was surprised. Following all that had happened so far this day, he would not have been surprised if Blucher had had enough. At the very least, he had expected Blucher to question him with regards to a plan of action, but instead it seemed Blucher trusted him completely and was prepared to follow him unquestioningly. The very least he could do for Blucher in return, was to explain where they were going. 'Whoa,' Green cautioned calmly, 'no point in just rushing off; here's what we are going to do.' With the tip of his finger Green drew a rough map in the dirt of the trench floor. 'This is the trench, this is the village of Pozieres, and this,' he stabbed his finger into the dirt,' is Sausage Valley... got it?'

Blucher nodded.

'I figure we should follow the trench to the west toward Pozieres,' Green continued. 'If things are as bad as Colonel Robertson said, we should run into the other battalions along the way. We can plot their position on the map and then find this Sausage Valley place and deliver the information to the Brigade Major.'

'Sound's good to me,' Blucher replied.

'Any questions?'

Blucher had none.

Green smiled. 'You'll do,' he said as he got to his feet. 'Right, let's make a mile,' and with that he set off at a brisk walking pace along the trench in the direction of Pozieres.

His pace was not long maintained. The expected German attack had not materialised, and in the relative peace that had arisen, the living occupants of the trench began to transfer their attention from the possibility of fighting to repairing the damaged trench. Work parties crowded its narrow confines, the men toiling with a passion born of knowledge that as surely as death and taxes the Germans would shell the trench again, and when that happened their lives depended on the protection offered by the repaired trench. Adding to this congestion a stream of stretcher bearers carrying their bloodied burdens, accompanied by groups of walking wounded were making their painful way toward casualty clearing stations that had been established somewhere along the trench. As a result, Green and Blucher's progress was at first slowed, and then halted altogether.

'This is no good at all,' Green grumbled angrily. 'Come on, let's get up on top; it will be less crowded'.

The idea of leaving the shelter of the trench did not impress Blucher. 'What about snipers?' he asked nervously.

Green shrugged. 'It's a risk we are going to have to take. If we take fire, we can jump back into the trench.'

'Assuming the bastards don't hit us,' Blucher mumbled, but he followed Green to clamber out of the trench and walk along the shell pitted parapet.

New horrors greeted them. The newly dead, both whole and in mangled pieces, littered the trench top where the work parties had thrown them in their efforts to clear the trench. Then further out into what was now No Man's Land, a mixture of grey and khaki uniformed corpses lay quietly putrefying in the morning sunshine—a tragic record of the previous night's violent action. It was obvious that the grey clad German dead had been cut down as they tried to flee the Australian attack, while the khaki covered bodies were those of the attacking Australians who had been caught in the German artillery barrage or by enfilading machine gun fire from German positions on the ridge.

They were not alone with the dead on the trench top. Others had found the crowded trench impeded their progress and had reached a similar decision to Green. Some of these men moved hurriedly toward unknown destinations. Others searched among the dead, perhaps to find a loved one or a mate, or perhaps to remove useful items that the dead no longer needed. There were even a few intrepid souls who were taking advantage of the apparent cessation of hostilities to sunbathe in the brilliant sunshine. Green ignored all of these folk, and pausing only to urge Blucher to make haste, he led the way along the trench top. They had made considerable progress when a voice of authority from the depths of the trench hailed them.

Chapter 11

Green signalled to Blucher to halt then walked to the edge of the trench and peered down at the person who had called to them. A young captain had positioned himself in the middle of the trench from where he was endeavouring to reorganize the able-bodied men who approached his position into their particular units. Green thought he looked a little like a policeman on point duty.

'Come on, you bastards,' the Captain shouted to the troops around him, 'this is far from over! I want any 9 Battalion members to remain here. 10 Battalion men, your muster point is 100 yards back behind me! Any 11 and 12 Battalion men, wait over there!' he pointed to a wider area in the trench. 'You lot up on the parapet,' he glared up at Green, 'get down here and report to me!' He paused from his continuous directions as Green and Blucher slid down the trench wall to join him.

'Where are you from, Sergeant?' he demanded.

'Private Blucher and I,' Green replied, indicating Blucher, 'are on special duty from Brigade. We have important information for Brigade headquarters.'

The officer grunted, clearly unimpressed by anyone who came from an area further to the rear than his own company headquarters. 'Papers,' he demanded. Green and Blucher handed over their written orders. The Captain glanced at the proffered documents and grunted, apparently disappointed that these two men at least were on a legitimate task, but Green's papers took his attention. 'Green,' he said as he handed the papers back, 'you were with Monash at Gallipoli.'

Green nodded but made no other comment.

'Christ,' Blucher muttered, 'is there anyone in the AIF who doesn't know you?' He received an angry glare from Green.

The Captain grinned at the exchange. 'Blucher,' he said as he returned Blucher his papers. 'With a name like yours,' he quipped, 'are you sure you're in the right trench?'

Blucher shrugged. 'I've no doubt some of my cousins *are* on the other side, sir,' he replied wearily, 'but I think I'll stay here. I can't stand Sauerkraut.'

The Captain laughed and slapped Blucher on the back. 'Neither can I!' he said, 'can't even stand the smell of the stuff!' He wiped his nose on the back of his hand then turned back to Green. 'I don't suppose you have any water?' the Captain asked. 'My throat's as dry as the inside of a nun's crotch.'

Wordlessly, Green passed his water bottle. The Captain took one short mouthful, swilled it around his mouth, then slowly swallowed. He handed the bottle back. 'Thanks,' he said gratefully. 'Tell those boot lickers and nose pickers back there to get moving and get some water up here or we will all dry up and blow away.'

Green nodded grimly. 'We'll do our best,' he said. 'Can I trouble you to mark where you think the battalions are located now? We need that info back at Brigade urgently.'

The Captain took Green's map and after checking the notes Lieutenant Colonel Robertson had made, he made several notations of his own.

'That's it so far as I can tell,' he said as he handed the map back. 'I'm not sure where the 11th Battalion is. It should be somewhere further along the trench. Mind you, I've not been far past this point, so they might be just around the next bend. Or perhaps they got into the village. We lost a lot of formation in the attack, and now it's all very mixed up, a bit like the first day at ANZAC.'

Green nodded. The first day of the landing at Gallipoli, the Australian force had lost all order in the mad scramble to scale the cliffs to get at the Turks. He glanced at the revised map markings. 'Thanks for this,' he said, 'I don't suppose there's any of the Brigade forward of this trench?'

The Captain shook his head. 'Only dead ones I reckon,' he replied in a matter of fact tone.

'Any idea what's happened in the village?'

'Like I said, maybe the 11th got in there, but that's mainly 1 Brigade territory so if the 11th is there too, it's going to be crowded and pretty bloody awful.' The Captain paused and gestured toward the ruined village where desultory German artillery shells still slammed into random parts of it. 'I mean, look at that,' he continued, 'if they are in there, it must be tougher than it is out here.'

Green offered his water bottle again, but the Captain shook his head. 'Better not,' he said quietly, 'I might get addicted to the stuff.'

Green pocketed the map. 'We'd best be off,' he said.

The Captain nodded. 'Are you going back along the top?'

Green shook his head. 'No, he replied. 'I think we'll stick to the trench for a while; we don't want to push our luck, and it's important we get this information back.' Almost as he spoke, rifle fire broke out and the men who had been avoiding the trench rushed to return to its protection.

'Looks like I've got more business to attend to,' the Captain said. He turned his attention to the closest men who had slid down to relative safety. 'Right you lot, my job is to make sure you get back to your units. Any 10 Battalion men, your muster point is 100 yards back that way! Any 11 and 12 Battalion men, wait over there!'

Green and Blucher moved to resume their journey when the Captain called them back. 'Hang on, Sergeant Green, these two young bastards are from the 11th.' He pushed two bare chested youths toward Green. 'Drop them off when you find their battalion.'

Green waved his acknowledgement as the two errant 11th Battalion soldiers with their tunics in one hand and their rifles and webbing in the other, ever so casually joined Blucher.

'Put your tunics and webbing on!' he snapped at the two new arrivals. 'You should know that Private Blucher and I are in a hurry, so as of now, so are you. Do you know where your battalion is?'

'It's not far,' one of the newcomers replied sulkily as he dressed himself, 'down the trench about another hundred yards or so.'

'Right,' Green said, 'come with me. We need to get to your headquarters in a hurry. Blucher, bring up the rear and make sure these two don't skulk off somewhere.' Without a further word, Green began to trot along the trench.

One of the men fell in beside Green. 'Hey Sergeant,' the man said, puffing slightly with the effort of keeping up with Green, 'we aren't deserters, you know.'

'Never said you were,' Green growled, 'but as a matter of interest, what were you doing up there?'

'We were sunbathing,' the man replied indignantly.

'Bloody hell,' Green muttered, 'and what brought you back to the trench?'

'Snipers, they knocked a bloke just a few yards from us.'

'Well, maybe that will teach you to stay under cover,' Green said angrily, 'too late for the bloke who got knocked to learn anything, but you two, I hope you learned your lesson.'

'Hang on,' the other man interjected, 'I seen you two up there just before the snipers opened up!'

Blucher laughed. 'He got you there, Sarg!'

Before Green could answer, a tall figure of a man stepped out of dugout, barring Green's progress. 'Who the hell are you?' the tall man demanded.

'Oh shit,' muttered Green's new companion, 'it's the fuckin' RSM.'

The 11th Battalion's RSM ignored Green and Blucher and instead glared at the two 11th Battalion men. 'Well, well, well,' he chortled grimly, 'look who we have here, Privates Wise and Bennett. What hole did you two crawl out of? No, don't say anything; it doesn't matter. You're both on a fizzer, absent without leave for a start. I'll see what else I can hit you with to have you breaking rocks for the rest of your miserable lives!' The RSM paused in his tirade and turned mockingly to Green. 'Welcome to the 11th Battalion,' he began, then added menacingly: 'Now who the fuck are you?'

'That's for me to know and you to find out, you prick!' Green retorted hotly.

Blucher backed away in terror, certain that Green had gone mad.

The RSM bristled with anger. 'You bastard!' he retorted. 'Do you know who I am? I'm RSM…'

'Hardy,' Green interrupted.

'Eh?' RSM Hardy stepped closer to Green, 'Do I know you, Sergeant?' he asked cautiously.

'You should know me Dave; we've dodged enough whizbangs together.'

RSM Hardy's anger dissolved instantly and his face was creased by a happy smile. 'Well I'll stand fucking,' he declared. 'Robert bloody Green, it is you. I thought I recognised you when you turned up; then I thought it couldn't be.' Hardy noticed Green's colour patch. 'What's a Deep Thinker doing way out here at the front? Are you lost? The two men embraced like brothers, pummelling one another on the back. Hardy pushed Green out to arms-length and looked at him fondly. 'Christ, it's good to see you, Rob.'

'You too, Dave,' Green replied with feeling. 'It's been a while.'

'Oh my God,' Blucher muttered, 'here's another one that knows him!'

Hardy glanced inquiringly at Blucher. 'Who's your smart arse mate?' he asked threateningly.

Hastily, Green intervened. 'This is my new spotter, Private Karl Blucher. Mate, this is Dave Hardy, RSM of the 11th Battalion.'

Hardy shook Blucher's hand warmly. 'Pleased to meet you, mate,' he said genuinely.

'And you, sir,' Blucher replied somewhat fearfully.

Hardy turned his attention to the two 11th Battalion men. 'Piss off back to your platoon, you silly cunts. If either of you ever pull a stunt like this again, I will make you sorrier than you could believe.'

The two men pushed past Green and Hardy and disappeared down the trench.

'Silly young pricks,' Hardy muttered as he watched their departure; then he returned his attention to Green and Blucher. 'Now what brings you two reprobates to my part of this trench?' he demanded.

Green provided a brief explanation.

'Give us a look at your map,' Hardy said. He examined the now filthy document with sardonic humour. 'Do you know I've just had to send a young lieutenant out on a patrol without one of these,' he said indicating the map. 'Apparently, the staff believes maps aren't needed below battalion level! Lessons learned from Gallipoli... absolutely none!' He patted his pockets searchingly. 'Give us a pencil, will you? I must have lost mine.'

Green handed him a stump of a led pencil and Hardy drew a few quick symbols on the map each with a notation "11th AIF". He handed the map and pencil back to Green. 'Not much else I can tell you,' he said. 'I suppose we are like the rest of the Brigade, re-organizing after last night's stuff up.'

'Bad, was it?' Green asked.

'Bloody awful, actually,' Hardy replied sadly. 'Most of our officers, including all of the company commanders, were knocked in the shelling, and then the boys just went crazy. It was like the new blokes, our replacements like, were out to prove themselves to us originals and they just went for the Huns like fiends. Oh, we got to our major objective all right; nothing could stop them, and the Huns ran before us like rabbits. But the lads wouldn't listen to orders and they chased after them; some of them actually thought they were going to reach Berlin by morning. About two hundred of the blokes actually got to the bloody windmill on top of the ridge. That's way to the east of our part of the battalion's objective in the 9th Battalions area. From then on, it all turned to shit. The Hun artillery and some of our own gun fire knocked the lads for six, and then the Hun infantry came after them with bombs and chased them off. Only about ninety of the lads who reached the mill got back. Even then, it was hell's own job to get the survivors back here to consolidate. We lost an awful lot of men, Rob.' Hardy paused, remembering the attack and its consequences. He straightened his shoulders and shook his head as he dismissed images from his mind that would haunt him till his dying day. 'I suppose you'll want to see my CO?'

Green shook his head. 'No, the info you've given us will do.'

Suddenly in the distance, there came the familiar sound of artillery gun fire. Green and Hardy listened anxiously for the sounds of incoming shells; even Blucher was getting the idea and joined their expectant wait. Moments later, the crumping reverberations of a series of detonations shook the trench, but the shells had impacted some distance away. 'I think they hit the village,' Blucher muttered with relief.

'Bloody hell,' Hardy cried anxiously, 'that's where our patrol is, hunting snipers!' He ran to a fire step and stared apprehensively across No Man's Land. 'I hope that young bastard has enough sense to keep the boys out of the way.'

The German gunners increased the intensity of their bombardment. 'Jesus Christ, they must have a lot of guns and ammunition!' Hardy exclaimed as he watched as the ruined village once again convulsed and shuddered under the power of the German artillery. 'Look, the Huns seem to be concentrating their fire on the north east end of the village. They must figure that's the way our reinforcements and resupplies will come.'

Green and Blucher joined Hardy on the fire step and looked out over the devastated landscape. It was as Hardy had observed; the worst of the German artillery barrage was concentrated on one end of the village. Huge bursts of clay and bricks erupted from the ruined village where dust and smoke curtained the broken walls of destroyed buildings.

'Look!' Blucher cried excitedly. He pointed to a spot some six hundred yards away, where a dozen figures were running erratically back toward the trench. 'Is that your patrol? It looks like they're coming back.'

The three men watched as an uneven race between man and high explosive was contested before them. Each time the artillery projectiles screeched toward the patrol, the men of the patrol threw themselves to ground, and as soon as the detonations ceased, they were on their feet again running for dear life toward the trench. Green could not tell if the artillery fire was being directed toward the retreating patrol, or if it was mere coincidence that the shells appeared to be chasing it. This he knew was immaterial, for if the men of the patrol were to die by accident or by design, they would be just as dead.

The artillery fire suddenly ceased to stalk the patrol, and it continued its rapid withdrawal toward the trench unmolested. 'Thank Christ for that,' Hardy muttered with relief.

Green glanced at his watch. It was nearly 9:00 a.m. 'We have to go, Dave,' he said. 'One last bit of advice if you will, what's the best way to get to Sausage Valley?'

'Shit,' Hardy replied, 'I'm not sure. I've never been there from here.' He thought for a moment, still watching the patrols progress, and then he added, 'I reckon the simplest thing would be to stick to this trench and follow it in toward the village. I think there's a road junction where this trench cuts across two roads. At least there was; it might be hard to find now after all the shelling. Anyhow, if you find that road junction, take the road that heads more or less south. I'm pretty sure it will land you in the valley. But mate,' he paused and pointed toward the fury of the German bombardment, 'how the fuck are you going to get there through that?'

'Might be able to skirt it,' Green replied grimly. 'We'll have to try anyway.'

They parted company then, Green and Blucher making their way along the trench while behind them they could hear the great voice of RSM Hardy bellowing encouragement to the patrol. They walked on through the 11th Battalion's area. Green noted that this part of the line was thinly defended and he wondered if this was due to the number of casualties the Battalion had suffered during the night, or if it was because as at the 9th Battalion position, the CO of the 11th had made a deliberate decision to hold as many men back in reserve as he dared. He decided the answer lay in a combination of both.

The closer they came to the village, the shallower the trench became. The casualties from both sides lay here and there. Most were clearly dead, but a few cried out as Green and Blucher passed. 'We can't help them,' Green told Blucher. 'We have to leave them for the stretcher bearers.' Indeed, at various points, stretcher bearer teams were methodically searching the area for wounded from both sides.

'Over here!' Blucher shouted waving to one of the stretcher bearing parties. They waved back and began to slowly make their way to where Blucher had pointed.

'Don't do that again,' Green warned Blucher sternly. 'This is not the place to draw attention to yourself.'

They walked on following the trench line which by now was little more than a knee-deep drain. Green kept hoping that each corner in the trench would reveal the crossroads RSM Hardy had spoken of, but it was not to be. The artillery barrages of both sides had obliterated every landmark that had previously existed, leaving a confusion of broken buildings, and upheaved dirt. The occasional German shell still slammed into the area, maintaining a pall of dust and smoke that restricted visibility. They walked on, but Green was becoming increasingly concerned as to where they were going, for they seemed to be far closer to the ruined village than he believed they should be. Ruined walls of buildings loomed out of the smoke and dust, but instead of being to their right, the ruins seemed to be directly to their front. His concern was temporarily relieved when they found the remains of a road, which was bounded on each side by a deep storm water drain. He jumped into the drain and beckoned Blucher down to join him.

'What's up?' Blucher asked.

'I think we're off track a bit,' Green explained. 'We seem to be too close to the village, but this road,' he pointed at the formation above him, 'should help get us back on course.' He pulled out the map and lay it between the two of them. The roadway seemed to fit with the main road between Pozieres and the next village Bapaume. 'I think we are about here.' Green stabbed a dirty finger at the point on the map.

'Okay,' Blucher replied doubtfully, 'map reading isn't my strongest point, but that seems to make sense.' He got to his feet and looked left and right along the ruined road; then he sat down again. 'Jesus,' he intoned, 'what a fuckin' mess! There's fuck all left of the village.'

Before Green could answer, a sustained burst of machine gun fire swept the length of the road above them. Both men flattened themselves on the ground at the bottom of the ditch. The gunfire ceased.

Green recovered first. 'That was not aimed at us,' he announced carefully. 'If they had seen you, they would have got you when you stood up.'

'That's very comforting to know,' Blucher said from the bottom of the ditch.

'It came from somewhere up to the right,' Green mused. 'Question is... was it a German gun, or one of ours?' Carefully, he crawled to the top of the ditch to a position where he could observe the road. About fifty yards to the right of his position, he could see two khaki clad figures lying in the middle of the roadway. One of the figures was twitching feebly. 'A Hun gun,' he muttered, then smiled wanly at his choice of words. 'I'm a poet and don't know it,' he concluded.

Blucher joined him at the roadside. 'What's happening?' he asked nervously.

Green pointed at the two casualties. Both were still now. 'There seems to be a Hun machine gun somewhere up to the right. It got those two.' Sudden movement in the ditch near the two bodies attracted his attention, and he immediately swung his rifle toward it. 'Hello,' he continued, 'there's a mob of our blokes in our ditch, just below the two bodies. Do you see them?'

'Yes, I see them.'

'Come on,' Green said quietly, 'we might be able to help each other.'

Chapter 12

Moments later, Green and Blucher found they were sharing the ditch with four survivors of a work party engaged on carrying ammunition to the forward units. The party had been badly mauled. Besides the two bodies which Green knew lay on the road above them, there was another dead man on the very edge of the road and another lying at the bottom of the ditch, and alongside that body was an untidy stack of four large wooden boxes. The sides of the boxes were stencilled in white paint were the symbols "300 CART, .303 BALL, MK7 BDR, RL30-12-53" denoting the boxes contained small arms ammunition for the Lee Enfield rifle the standard issue personal weapon for British and Australian troops. Each box was about two-foot square and two-foot deep, with a rope handle at each end to facilitate the boxes carriage.

The four survivors were all private soldiers, one of whom had assumed the role of group leader. 'Name of Painter,' the leader said as he welcomed Green and Blucher to the group. He spotted Green's sergeant stripes and immediately began an overexcited explanation as to what had happened to the ammunition carriers. 'We got lost during the night,' Painter elucidated, 'and this morning we managed to creep along behind the Hun barrage until we reached this point in this bloody ditch. When we went to cross the road, we got hit. There's a bloody machine gun in a wrecked house just up there and it's got the whole road covered. They shot the shit out of us when we tried to cross. They got the Corporal and

two of the boys first up. We managed to get the ammo boxes
those blokes were carrying back, but lost another bloke doing
it. That's him in the drain over there.'

Green nodded. 'What are you going to do now?' he asked.

Painter seemed surprised that Green had not taken
command. 'The boys up in the village need this ammo,' he
replied grimly, 'one way or another we'll get it there.'

Green looked at the others in the group. They seemed to
exude the same determination. 'I'm Sergeant Green,' he said,
'and this is my mate Blucher. We are on a task from Brigade.
We got bushed trying to make it to Sausage Valley. Now I
think we can work out how to get back there now, but how
are you lot going to get across this road?'

'We might have a way,' Painter replied. 'Bill here found a
culvert pipe running under the road; he found it when he
dragged Syd's body back to the drain. He reckons a man might
be able to squeeze through, but it's not wide enough to take
the ammo boxes through.' He pointed at the four wooden
crates.

Bill seemed to have thought through the problem. 'If we
had some rope,' he said, 'we could send a couple of blokes
through the drain, tie one end of the rope to an ammo box,
heave the rope across, then the blokes on the other side could
pull the box over and heave the rope back.'

'It's a good idea but for one major point,' Painter concluded
morosely. 'No rope....'

Blucher fumbled in his small pack that hung down his left
side. 'How wide is the road?' he asked.

'About twenty feet,' Painter replied.

Blucher produced a coil of rope from the pack. 'I am, rather
I was a driver and it was always a good idea to have a bit of
rope in case you needed to tie something to the roof of the

car.'

They measured the rope. 'It might be a bit short,' Bill said enthusiastically, 'but how about if we take poor old Syd's webbing straps and tie them on to it. I reckon we'd have more than enough then.'

Painter was more pessimistic. 'And who's going to throw the rope across while the Huns riddle him with their bloody guns?' he asked sarcastically.

Green ignored Painters question and instead posed one of his own. 'Can we have a closer look at where this gun is?'

'Sure,' Painter replied, 'but we'll have to be careful. The bastards are ready and waiting for us.'

Green and Painter crawled to the edge of the road. 'Reference the nearest body,' Painter whispered, pointing with his chin at the body of his dead friend. 'Eleven o'clock at around about two hundred yards—there's a ruined wall; do you see it?'

'Seen,' Green whispered in reply.

'Now at the right-hand end of that wall there's a shadow down near the ground.'

'I see it.'

'They've dug some kind of a position there.'

Quickly Green surveyed the scene. 'Were you fired on from anywhere else?' he whispered.

Painter shook his head. 'I reckon they laid low last night when our attack went over them. They've been cut off from their mates and our clean up parties haven't found them yet.'

Green nodded in agreement. Painter's deduction was sound, for had there been a stronger German presence, they would most certainly have sent a patrol to kill or capture the surviving ammunition carriers. 'How many machine guns do you reckon they have?' he asked.

'One for sure,' came the whispered response, 'but there may be another. They put out enough fire for there to be two.'

Green made some mental calculations. If he assumed two machine guns, there would be a team of three men per gun, and there would probably be a protection party of another half a dozen. So there were too many for the ammunition carriers to successfully attack, even with his and Blucher's assistance. Clearly, the objective of this little problem had to be to help the ammunition carriers get their burden across the road, and then for he and Blucher to resume their own mission. That road though was a major obstacle. The German machine gunners could sweep it with fire; indeed, were he to raise his head from the cover he currently held, he was sure they could shoot him down. However, he noticed on his side of the road, around about one hundred and fifty yards away, the remains of a chimney standing like a headstone in memory of the obliterated building it had once served. Green felt certain that from behind that chimney he would be able to see into the German machine gun position.

'Come on,' Green whispered, 'I've seen enough.' Together they returned to the bottom of the ditch.

Green gestured to the group to gather round. 'I've an idea,' he began quietly, 'as to how you lot can throw your rope across the road without getting your heads blown off.'

The prospect of not having to face the machine gun fire on the road focused the ammunition carriers' attention on Green, and there were muttered sounds of relief from their ranks.

'Your plan of going through the culvert pipe is a good one,' he continued, 'but as Painter here pointed out, the poor sod to throw the rope over the road would be riddled like a sieve. What you need is covering fire to keep the Hun's heads down while the rope is thrown. Blucher and I will provide the covering fire; the rest of the plan will be like Bill outlined before. Two of you blokes go through the culvert and the other two can work the rope at this end.' Once you get all the boxes across the road, those of us on this side of the road will follow.'

Blucher looked startled. 'I thought you said we had to keep out of trouble,' he murmured to Green.

'Mate, this won't be any trouble at all,' soothed Green.

Painter looked doubtful. 'How are two riflemen going to keep one machine gun, perhaps two of the things, busy?' he asked.

'I don't think *he'll* have any trouble,' one of the ammunition carriers interjected. 'That's Killer Green. He was a sniper with Billy Sing on Gallipoli.'

Blucher rolled his eyes. Was there nowhere Green could go without being recognised?

'Never heard of him,' stated Painter flatly.

'Well, I have,' the man said,' and if anyone can get the attention of that machine gun crew, it's him.'

The other two ammunition carriers were obviously impressed; one actually asked for Green's autograph, but Green was not comfortable with the attention he was receiving and he pushed the autograph hunter's notebook away. 'Look,' he said tersely, 'if everyone agrees with the plan, let's get on with it.'

Painter and Blucher were the only two in the group who were unhappy with the plan. 'Well, the majority rules, I suppose,' said Painter reluctantly. 'It beats making another rush across that fucking road anyway.'

Blucher kept quiet. He had no doubts as to Green's abilities, but he had no confidence in his own.

'You all right, Blucher?' asked Green.

'Yes, yes,' Blucher replied hastily, 'let's do it.'

Green turned back to Painter. 'When I fire the first shot, there will probably be about a two second delay before they react. Make the best of it. Even if there is no delay, you should be safe enough to throw the rope as their fire will probably be angled away from you, looking for us. Got it?'

'Got it.'

The ammunition carriers organised themselves into the two groups and the two men nominated to crawl through the culvert departed. It was arranged they would fire two quick shots at the machine gunners once they were in position. Painter and the remaining man positioned the ammunition crates as close to the road as they could without raising the attention of the German machine gunners. They had removed the webbing belts and straps from the body of their dead comrade and tied the items to Blucher's rope. Painter had nominated himself to throw the extended rope over the road, and he crouched in the shelter of the boxes ready….

There was a tense wait; then they heard the two-shot signal indicating those who had crawled through the culvert were in position. The signal brought an immediate response from the German machine gunners in the form of an extended burst of fire, sending bullets pelting along the road.

Green glanced inquiringly toward Painter and received a thumbs up sign indicating all was in readiness.

Green turned to Blucher. 'Got the telescope?'

Blucher patted the instruments holster reassuringly.

Green smiled. 'This is where you get your first lesson in sniping, Blucher my boy, 'he said. 'There is nothing like on the job training, eh?'

Blucher gave a weak and sickly grin.

Green continued calmly and methodically with his

explanation. 'Right now, those Hun gunners are watching the spot where our two blokes fired from on the other side of the road. Do you see that broken chimney up there?' He pointed to the ruin. 'We are going up there and we will get down on the far side of it. Now nice and slow; do what I do...'

It was slow and exhausting work half crawling, half sliding toward the broken chimney. There was a bad moment when the machine gun fired a series of bursts along the road, but what had drawn this reaction was unclear. At length, they reached the side of the chimney furthest from the German position and paused for a moment to catch their breath. 'All right,' Green whispered when they had recovered. 'We'll both squeeze in here, hard up against the chimney base. I'll be on the outside, you closest to the chimney.'

Luckily, the artillery shell that had destroyed the house which the chimney had once served had blown most of the rubble away from base of the chimney and as a result they were able to achieve a comfortable fire position with a minimum of effort. Green's main concern was the condition of the chimney bricks, which appeared old and brittle. The bricks were fine to shield Blucher and himself from the Germans' view, but once the Germans discovered their position, the bricks would do little to protect them from a storm of machine gun bullets. Still, it was far better to be behind the chimney's doubtful cover than out in the open. Other than this minor drawback, Green was well pleased with their situation; they had reached their cover unseen from where they established the German post was about fifty, maybe sixty yards away. It was time for action.

'Now then, Blucher,' Green whispered, 'I want you to very carefully slide the telescope forward and look at the wall across the road. Let me know when you've done that.'

There were a few tense seconds as Blucher inched the telescope into position and focused the lens so he could see the broken wall across the road. 'I'm on it,' he whispered in reply.

'Good,' replied Green, 'now tell me what you see at this end of the wall.'

'Well, the top of the wall has collapsed down on this side, not much left of whatever the building was. Hang on,' he paused for a moment and when he continued his voice was tense with excitement. 'There's a bloody great machine gun and about half a dozen Huns. They're inside some kind of dugout—no, I reckon it's been a cellar; they've barricaded the entrance with wood and stuff and the muzzle of the gun is poking out through a hole.'

'Is there only one gun?'

There was a pause. The telescope brought the image of the German post alarmingly close, and Blucher felt he could reach out and touch the occupants, for he could clearly see their facial features, every detail of their uniforms, and the well-maintained condition of their weapons. He could even see the remains of a meal on some kind of ledge at the rear of their position. The machine gun, for there was only one, had been positioned behind a wall of sandbags, the gunner seated behind the weapon, alert and ready. 'Only one,' Blucher confirmed.

Green snuggled himself into the earth; taking a more comfortable firing position, he peered forward. 'Ah yes,' he whispered, 'I can see the gun and the bastard behind it. Now the important thing, Blucher, is when I fire, you must watch the other Huns. I want you to be able to tell me where they are in relation to the right-hand side of their firing bay. Use your knuckles to tell me. Like there's a man two knuckles in, I'll know what you mean then. Got it?'

'I've got it,' whispered Blucher.

The sudden report of Green's rifle made Blucher jump, but through the lens of the telescope, he saw the German soldier behind the machine gun thrown backwards and out of sight. The other Germans stared in horror, then disappeared from view.

Back on the edge of the embankment, the ammunition carriers began to work feverishly. Painter's first throw with the rope fell short, but the second allowed the team on the other side of the road to grasp their end and to pull the first of the ammunition crates across the road.

Blucher resumed his watch. 'Another one is behind the gun,' he whispered, 'and there's another three knuckles from the right looking out.'

Green was slowing his breathing. 'All right,' he whispered, 'they haven't spotted us yet. I'm going to knock the one that's looking out next. Keep watching...'

Again, the sudden bang of Green's rifle startled Blucher and the watching German seemed to jump with the impact of the bullet and then he fell forward, with the top half of his body hanging out of the firing bay.

The German soldier behind the machine gun let loose a wild burst of fire, traversing the weapon from left to right. There was another report from Green's rifle and the machine gun stopped abruptly.

'Shit... this is not good,' whispered Blucher. 'Two of them have come out from behind the wall. They seem to be heading this way.'

'Fuck!' said Green. 'I can't see them from here. You will have to watch them, and deal with them if they get too close.'

The machine gun burst back into life, this time its bullets searching the edge of the road to the left of the chimney.

Painter and his mate worked feverishly to position the next

two crates for dragging across the road. While the machine gun fired into the ruins, Painter made another successful throw with the rope.

Again, Green fired and again the machine gun fire ceased. Blucher wriggled out of his position and with his back against the chimney, he pushed the safety catch on his borrowed rifle forward. In growing panic, he realised he had never fired the weapon before, and wondered if it would work. Then he heard the two German soldiers sprint across the road and risked a quick peep around the side of the chimney. The Germans were thirty yards away, crouched down, probably working out their next move.

Blucher aimed his rifle at the larger of the two men and as he squeezed the trigger, he realised he had never killed anyone before. The borrowed rifle bellowed its challenge, the butt kicking wickedly into Blucher's shoulder. He glanced toward his target. One of the Germans lay on his back, his arms and legs jerking spasmodically. The downed German's companion gave a cry of despair and ran back across the road toward the wall. Blucher aimed hurriedly at the fleeing man, fired... and missed.

Within moments of the survivor's safe arrival back with his comrades, the German soldiers knew exactly where their hidden assassin lay. Concentrated machine gun fire hit the chimney like a jack hammer, sending broken bricks and dust flying. Blucher threw himself to the ground and wriggled away from the ruined house to regain the shelter of the ditch. Seconds later, Green slid down the slope backwards to join him. When they looked back toward the chimney, it was little more than a pile of loose stones and dust.

The last of the ammunition crates had been pulled safely across the road.

Bending double to ensure they did not present any kind of a target to the now furious Germans, Green and Blucher raced back to join the two men from the ammunition party.

Blucher was jubilant. 'He knocked four of them,' he told Painter and his mate, 'four!'

Green was quiet, sad even, but none of the others seemed to notice, and even if they had, they probably would not have understood. After all, who had heard of a sniper that hated killing?

Painter was keen to leave. "Come on,' he urged, 'if there are more Huns in that cellar you saw, this place is going to be bloody unhealthy in about five minutes.'

He led the way to a deeper section of the ditch where a clay culvert pipe about a little over two feet in diameter protruded from the embankment. Clearly when it rained, the culvert allowed water to flow beneath the road.

'You three go first,' said Painter. 'I'll bring up the rear.' He took up a firing position, watching for any inquisitive German that might have been sent to find them.

The other ammunition carrier removed his pack and basic webbing. He stuffed the webbing into the pack and then pushing it and his rifle before him, he crawled into the tunnel. Blucher followed this example and moments later he too vanished into the pipe.

'Better give them a few moments to move through a bit,' Green suggested as he prepared his own equipment.

Painter nodded. 'Not too long though—it won't be long before the Huns send a patrol down here.'

Green stuffed his basic pouches and web belt into his haversack, but his bayonet would not fit and remained outside of the pack where it flapped around annoyingly. He looked at the size of the culvert pipe and felt uncomfortable about pushing his pack through it, and opted instead to tie the pack to one of his ankles.

'Are you sure you don't want me to go last?' he asked Painter.

Painter shook his head and silently motioned Green to hurry.

Green shuffled over to the culvert entrance and crawled in. He was immediately alarmed, for while he was not a large man, his shoulders were wide and muscular and he found he could only just fit into the pipe. He tried to use his elbows to drag himself forward, but he found in that position his shoulders were being squeezed tightly against the pipe making it impossible to pull himself forward with his arms. After a few moments of experiment, he discovered his best means of progress was to push against the walls of the culvert with his feet, but it was a slow and painful process. Green began to become convinced that the pipe was narrowing in front of him and while he tried to control his fear, he found himself becoming more and more anxious. Blucher was still in the pipe in front of him and he heard Painter coming close behind him; their bodies seemed to be blocking the daylight and air from penetrating to where Green lay. The effort he was expending to move forward was leaving him breathless. He was perspiring heavily, the sweat running into his eyes stinging them painfully, but because of his cramped position he was unable to wipe his face.

Then quite suddenly something seized his foot and held it tightly. At first, he thought it was Painter, but then he realised it was his big pack that he had tied to his leg. He tugged with his leg, the bag held fast, something was caught, and then he remembered the bayonet flapping on the exterior of the pack. It must have become wedged in a crack, or perhaps a join in the pipe.

Daylight suddenly appeared before him. Blucher was clear of the pipe. Green sucked in great lungs full of air and tried to quell his rising terror. He tried again to free his leg. He jerked and pulled; pain shot up his leg; he remained held fast. Now he could feel Painter's head pushing against his feet and knew that he too must be suffering. Painter was a big man and Green was amazed that he had been able to travel along the pipe. Desperately, Green tried again to free himself, and again he failed.

Painter was in agony. He had had copied Green in tying his pack to his ankle and he found that the only way he could fit into the pipe was to extend his arms above his head, and then to worm his way forward along the pipe. In this position he had in fact made better progress than Green, but when Green had become stuck, the delay resulted in agonizing cramps in Painter's neck and shoulders. He was desperate to escape and in his effort to do so, his arms slipped past Green's legs and his head rammed up tight against Green's feet. Neither of them could make any forward motion.

For several agonizing minutes, Painter could not understand why Green had stopped. He tried to call out to him, but the Green's form wedged as it was in front of him, acted as a barrier to his shouts. At last he realised that Green was stuck, but he was now too exhausted to move backward to a point where he might use his hands to find the obstacle. He began to push at Green's feet and pack with his head. Green feeling this pressure tried to move forward again. Painter pushed, Green pulled and then inexplicably the bayonet fell free of the crack that had held it. They were free.

Chapter 13

Green slid clear of the culvert and fell exhausted into a shallow hollow at the entrance of the culvert. Blucher and one of the ammunition party dragged him clear and propped him up against the embankment. The experience had nearly done for Green. He had been buried once on Gallipoli when a Turkish shell collapsed a trench on to Billy Sing, Tom Sheehan, and himself. Sing and Sheehan had been lightly wounded but not completely covered by the fallen trench. Green had been entirely interred. The memory of the brim of his hat sliding down across his face keeping the earth out of his nose; the weight of the earth gradually forcing the hat further down on his head, taking the skin from his nose with it; the soft earth slowly compressing down on his chest and tightening around his body preventing his breathing. Iron Jack Idriess had desperately clawed at the earth with his hands and had managed to reach one of Green's legs and just in time had dug the rest of him out. That experience had left Green with a fear of confined spaces, and having been stuck momentarily in the culvert pipe, he was left in a delicate frame of mind.

Painter's arms and head appeared at the culvert opening and there he remained firmly wedged. Desperately, the others fell upon the culvert opening, digging with their bare hands and smashing the pipe with their rifle butts. After five minutes' work, Painter too was free his mates dragged him to the side of the embankment where he collapsed.

The German soldiers in their post seemed to realise that

their quarry had eluded them and in angry retaliation sent a sustained burst of machine gun fire whipping along the roadway. Green sat up and listened to the rounds cracking over his head; he was still recovering from his ordeal, but now he was concerned for the general security of the group. He saw the others were crowded around Painter. No one was on sentry. 'Blucher!' he croaked. 'Leave him, get over there and keep a look out for Huns,' he pointed at a likely observation position. 'You,' he picked out one of the ammunition carriers, 'go down the other way and watch.'

Satisfied they would now have some warning if the Germans came looking for them, Green slumped back on to the ground.

After about ten minutes, Painter got to his feet and he staggered over to where Green lay.

'It's nearly eleven o'clock,' he said. 'We are half a day late with this ammo. We have to go.'

Green nodded and sat up painfully. 'How far do you have to go?' he asked.

Painter shrugged. 'Last time I saw them they were up near the church; it's probably about a mile that way.' He pointed northward into the centre of the ruined village.

'Blucher and I will help carry it to the first Aussie position we come to,' Green announced, 'and then we'll have to leave you to it.'

'Fair enough,' Painter extended a hand and pulled Green to his feet. 'I'm not sure what the two of you did back there,' he said, 'but I know we would never have got this far without you. Thanks.'

'Not a problem,' replied Green evenly, 'but let's not waste time congratulating one another; we need to get away from here and fast.'

The four ammunition crates comprised a heavy and an awkward burden, requiring all six men to lift and carry the load. Painter organised the group into two carrying teams, the first team of two men carried a single ammunition box between them. Painter and Green were still suffering the effects of their ordeal in the culvert, so they comprised this team. The second team of four men carried the three remaining boxes, and the two men in the centre of this team took the weight of two boxes. Thus loaded, the group made its slow and difficult way along the ditch to the west, away from the German post. Then at a distance Green judged as safe, they climbed out of the ditch and headed north into the heart of the ruins of Pozieres.

They groped their way through the residual smoke and dust from the artillery fire and stumbled past crumpled walls that were once homes, now ruined wrecks with items of clothing and smashed ornaments of the former occupiers intermingled with broken masonry and other twisted building material. It saddened Green to think of the loss suffered by the families who had once lived there, and he was thankful that the Gallipoli campaign had been fought in a relatively deserted area. Blucher, however, was horrified. He had never seen destruction on such a scale, and he felt sure the village could never be rebuilt. 'Why would the Germans do all this?' he asked in dismay.

The ammunition carrier with whom Blucher shared his load snorted in amusement. 'Ain't all the Huns' fault,' he said. 'He's just finishing the place off. We shelled the crap out of it before our attack last night, and the Poms shelled it to perdition before all of their attacks the other week. Mind you, they never got into the place, so the Hun had no cause to shell it then.' He paused and looked about. 'They're certainly making up for it now, eh?'

On several occasions, the artillery barrage drifted toward them, forcing the group to find cover in shell holes, but by some miracle, they were spared further casualties. Curiously, they almost welcomed these interludes for while they crouched in abject terror in whatever cover they could find, they were at least relieved from the weight of the ammunition boxes. Then when the shelling moved away again, they clambered wearily to their feet and stumbled on.

Only Painter and the other ammunition carriers knew where they were going, and when Blucher inquired as to their destination, he received a muttered response: 'We're going to church,' or was it 'we're going to the church'? Neither alternative made any sense to Blucher.

Green, on the other hand, was addressing a more perplexing problem. It was now after 11:00 a.m. Should he and Blucher continue to assist in carrying the ammunition, or should they turn back to Sausage Valley and deliver the information they had gathered? If they were to leave the ammunition carriers, it was doubtful they could deliver their precious load to the front line and men would die. If they stayed and helped deliver the ammunition, the Brigade staff might make decisions based on ignorance of the real situation and men would die. He was still pondering this problem when a hoarse voice hailed the group.

'Hello the ammo party!'

The ammunition carriers came to an abrupt halt and stared into the smoke and dust to their front. A lone Australian soldier was carefully approaching them. 'It's Steve Baxter,' Painter announced quietly, 'the 2ic's runner. What the fuck is he up to?'

Baxter began to hurry toward them. 'Thank Christ I've

found you,' he said in obvious relief. 'The boss is planning all kinds of mischief and we might not have enough bullets to go around.' He paused and looked around the group of ammunition carriers. 'Where are the rest of the blokes?' he asked unnecessarily.

Painter shrugged. 'We've picked up a couple of helpers from 3 Brigade Headquarters,' he announced wearily, 'Sergeant Green and Private Blucher.'

Baxter nodded a welcome. '3 Brigade Headquarters, eh? What are you doing here?'

'Complete accident,' Green replied.

Baxter was not really interested in any explanation, and he returned his attention to Painter. 'I'll give you a hand with the boxes,' he said. 'Things have changed a bit since you left, so I'll guide you from here.' With that, he took an end of one of the boxes Painter was hefting and led the way through the ruins.

Baxter proved to be quite talkative and was soon pointing out objects of interest along the way. 'That big pile of bricks over there,' he said, 'was a Hun strong point. The Poms called it "Gibraltar," and they told us it was impregnable, but earlier today Captain Herrod and Lieutenant Waterhouse with about fifteen blokes from the 2nd Battalion captured it right enough. So we don't have to worry about the Hun machine guns as much, not from in there anyway. The big danger here is the Hun artillery. The bastards really set about poor old 4th battalion last night; the barrage dropped right on them.'

Green glanced at the ruins of the once vaunted German strong point. It was obvious a savage struggle had taken place for its control. He could see at least thirty dead Australians and a number of German soldiers lying on the roadway. He turned his attention to a wide-open space that stretched away from the fallen post. 'The main street?' he suggested to Baxter.

'That's right,' Baxter replied. 'We have to go along it for a while and then we break off to the left, up a hill to the church, or what's left of it. We'd better make a mile. Just keep an ear out for the Hun artillery.'

They made ready to move off, when Blucher called out and pointed. 'Hey look, there's someone over there with a white flag.'

Green placed his end of the ammunition box back on the ground and turned toward where Blucher was pointing. About 100 yards away at the very edge of a group of dead German and Australian soldiers, a single Australian was lying on his back, one arm raised toward the sky and in the hand of that arm something white fluttered. 'Telescope,' Green snapped.

Quickly Blucher handed him the instrument.

Baxter was impatient to keep moving. 'We can't waste time here,' he said dismissively as Green adjusted the lens of the telescope. 'It's just another dead-un.'

'I don't think so,' Green murmured as he viewed the soldier through the telescope. 'That's no flag! It's a despatch packet. Looks like the poor bastard was a runner, he got hit, knew he was done for, and held up the package to attract someone's attention.'

Blucher was shocked. 'You mean he died that way?'

'Looks like it,' replied Green. 'We'd better try and get the dispatch; it must have been important.'

Baxter shook his head. 'That's not a good idea,' he said. 'If someone goes out there and gets hit, that stuffs up the ammunition carrying teams.'

Green shrugged. 'We were managing all right before you came along,' he said. 'We could manage again. But I agree we need to maintain our ability to carry the boxes, so only one of us better go.'

A sudden scrambling sound interrupted Green and when he looked, he saw that Blucher was sprinting across to the roadway toward the dead man. Reaching the dead runner, he gently removed the precious package, then turned and sprinted back to where Green and the others waited.

Blucher handed Green the despatch. 'He was a 2nd Battalion bloke,' he said sadly, 'big strong fellow with blonde hair.'

'Did you get his identity tags?' Green asked as he took the package from Blucher.

'Oh shit, I didn't think... I'll go back!'

'No don't, it's too late; forget it.' Green tore open the despatch. 'You can do me a favour though,' he murmured as he scanned the document. 'Never do anything like that again'.

'I didn't know you cared,' Blucher quipped.

'I don't,' Green replied emphatically as he handed the telescope back, 'just remember our main job is to get info back to Brigade. I need you to stay in one piece in case I get knocked. One of us has to deliver the information.' He paused as he digested the importance of what he was reading then he turned to the ammunition carriers. 'This despatch is almost as important as the ammunition we're carrying,' he announced. 'Baxter, I want you to take it and deliver it personally to the CO of the 2nd Battalion. The rest of us will get the ammunition to the nearest 2nd Battalion post; then Blucher and I will leave you to it. We have our own mission to complete.' He handed the despatch to Baxter. 'Get going mate, and take care; that despatch holds vital information.'

Baxter was ashamed at his dismissal of the situation that Green had interpreted so accurately. He would not meet Green's eye, but he nodded, acknowledging that he would do as Green said. He readied himself, tightening his webbing and adjusted the sling of his rifle before issuing a direction of his own. 'Keep going up the hill,' he told Painter. 'The nearest post is on the edge of the cemetery.' Then he turned and ran up the hill toward the ruined church.

Twenty painful minutes later, the ammunition carriers were quietly ushered into an Australian strong point. 'Keep your heads down and don't make too much racket,' warned the Sergeant in charge of the post. 'The Hun is pretty close here.'

'How close?' Blucher asked nervously.

The Sergeant smiled. 'About ten yards,' he said grimly.

'That's close,' agreed Green, 'bomb throwing distance.'

'Only good thing about it,' the Sergeant continued, 'is that we are too close to one another for either side to blast the other with artillery.'

'You mean no bombardment?' Blucher exclaimed. 'Why, it'll be a pleasure to visit.'

'Don't speak too soon,' the Sergeant warned. 'It really don't matter what kills you—shell, bullet, bayonet, or bomb—you're just as dead.' He looked more closely at Green. 'Say, I know you, don't I?'

'You'll be the only bastard who doesn't,' muttered Blucher and received another warning glare from Green for his trouble.

'Rob Green,' the Sergeant continued, extending a hand toward Green, 'I thought it was you. But I see you're a Deep Thinker; how the hell did you get here?'

Green did not recognise the sergeant; nevertheless, he shook his hand warmly. 'It's too long a story,' he replied. 'Did that runner arrive here?'

The sergeant nodded and continued to shake Green's hand. 'Baxter? Yeah, he came through here like a bloody steam train and went straight on to Battalion Headquarters.'

'Good,' Green declared as he disengaged his hand from the Sergeant's grip and glanced at his watch. It was ten minutes to twelve; time was running out. 'Look, I'm sorry,' he said, 'but Private Blucher and I have to keep going. Painter will fill you in on what's happened. Can you tell us the best way to get to Sausage Valley?'

Green's haste to be gone seemed to annoy his fellow sergeant. 'Bloody hell,' the Sergeant responded heatedly, 'it was hardly worth your coming up here if you have to leave straight away! It's a pity to see you wasting your talent rushing about the place, when we could do with you here.'

'I'm sorry, Green said again, 'we have another job to do; it can't be helped.'

The Sergeant shrugged and turned away. Green was about to repeat his request for directions when Bill, the ammunition carrier who had conceived the idea of crossing the road through the culvert, intervened. 'Sausage Valley is easy enough to find,' he said. 'Look over there to the southeast; see that tower?' In the distance, through a haze of smoke and dust raised by the German barrage, the sun glistened on the walls of a tall structure. 'That's the church at Albert,' Bill continued. 'Use that as your marker and you can't go wrong. Don't try to find any other landmark; it's probably been blown to bits, or you'll lose it in the dust and smoke, so head for the church tower. There's the odd sniper about, but as you can see, the worst of the journey will be the Hun shelling.'

Green stared long and hard at the distant tower, trying to engrain its direction into his brain. His gaze returned to the ferocity of the German artillery barrage, and he wondered how the hell he and Blucher could survive a passage through that maelstrom of high explosive, flying steel and debris.

Blucher cleared his throat and spat. 'At least it's going to be a damn sight easier going back down this bloody hill without those bastard ammunition boxes,' he quipped.

Green glanced at Blucher and grinned. 'Yes,' he replied quietly, 'we should make good time.' Then with Blucher at his heels, he walked back down the hill.

Chapter 14

As Blucher predicted, the return journey down the hill was far easier. The German artillery continued to pound an area to the southwest of the village. Occasionally, some of this destructive energy was directed back onto the ruins, but not enough to hinder Green and Blucher. At the bottom of the hill, Green called a halt and in the shelter of a ruined wall, he spread the map on the ground. 'Can you see that blasted church tower?' he asked Blucher.

Blucher stood up and gazed toward where he thought Albert lay. There was a sharp crack and he spun around before collapsing to the ground and holding the side of his head.

Desperately, Green crawled to Blucher's side and dragged him back closer to the remains of the wall. 'You're all right, mate,' he told Blucher, trying to keep the fear from his voice. 'You're all right.'

Blucher, his teeth tightly clenched in pain, did not reply.

Satisfied that Blucher was under cover, Green wriggled to the end of the wall and looked about. There was no one to be seen. He wriggled back to Blucher. 'Must be a sniper somewhere,' he told Blucher quietly. 'I can't see him, but he's there all right.'

Blucher nodded but did not take his hands away from his head.

'Might need your help to smoke him out,' Green continued calmly. Gently he prised Blucher's hands away from his wound. Blood covered the whole of the left side of Blucher's head, but as Green probed for the site of the wound, he almost laughed with relief. The bullet had carved a gash across the top of Blucher's ear. 'You've been ear marked, mate,' he told Blucher. 'There's a lot of blood, but your ear is the only wound. Can you sit up?'

Blucher lay still. 'So me brains aren't going to fall out?' he asked tentatively.

'What brains?' Green replied scornfully.

Blucher sat up and lent his back against the wall. 'What do you want me to do?' he inquired.

'Good man,' Green said fervently. He removed his own helmet and passed it to Blucher. 'Get your bayonet out and when I give you the word, use it to push my helmet just above the wall. Make it look like someone is having a look over the top.'

Blood had got into Blucher's left eye and he angrily wiped it away. 'I get the idea,' he said. 'Where will you be?'

'At the other end of the wall,' Green replied as he began to crawl into position. 'If the bastard is there, he might have a go at the helmet. He would have seen the two of us stop here; he'll reckon he got you and he'll want me too.'

'Greedy bastard', Blucher quipped as he wiped more blood from his face.

A few moments later, Green gave a low whistle, and Blucher pushed the helmet so that the rim was just above the wall. Within seconds, a bullet slammed angrily into the wall immediately below the helmet, but in the same instant, the sound of that impact was drowned out as Green fired.

Green crawled back to Blucher. 'I think I got him. I saw his rifle flip backwards, he explained. 'He was in the remains of a roof.'

'Good,' Blucher replied curtly, 'I hope it bloody hurt the

bastard.'

Green produced his field dressing and wrapped it around Blucher's injured head. 'We had better get going,' he said as he finished tying the bandage. 'That sniper may have some mates.'

———————

Two hundred yards away, Jäger2 Bayerlein paused to rest and leaned back against the wall of the ruined house he had taken refuge in. He needed to consider his situation. He was a professional soldier, proud of his trade and skills as a scout and sniper, but he had made a fundamental mistake. He should never have allowed young Himmler to shoot at the Australians. Himmler was meant to accompany him, to watch and learn, and indeed he had been pleased with the way the lad performed. The Australians were amateur soldiers, easy meat for well-trained professionals and an excellent training aid for youngsters like Himmler to practice on. Bayerlein had personally killed six that morning, but then things had gone badly wrong. Himmler had pleaded with him to be allowed to shoot the two Australians who had wandered so carelessly down the hill. Bayerlein saw no harm in it... he had even given the lad his special rifle with its telescopic sight to take the shot. He should never have done that.

The lad had hit one Australian and then they had seen the other one peering out from the bottom of their wall. He had prevented Himmler from firing at him then, but he had not been quick enough to stop him shooting at the helmet when it had appeared at the top of the wall. He spat with disgust, the oldest trick in the book! Well, it had cost Himmler his life and ruined his favourite rifle. The Australian's bullet had hit the rifle on the breech, smashing its mechanism before driving onward to hit Himmler in the right eye.

Had Himmler lived, he would have given the lad a good beating. However, he was especially angry with himself, for he too had been fooled by the Australian. He had been concentrating on the place where they had first seen the second Australian looking out from the bottom of the wall. Instead, the Australian had shot and killed Himmler from the other end of that wall.

Bayerlein had not anticipated such cunning could have existed in an amateur Army like Australia's. Perhaps, he mused, it had been a lucky shot, but a feeling deep within his soul told him that this was not so. He knew he should not have treated his enemy with such contempt, and he hoped wherever Himmler's soul had gone that it forgave him for not being a better teacher.

He retrieved Himmler's rifle and carefully withdrew from the remains of the roof, and took refuge behind a ruined wall. There to further his anger and disappointment, he saw the two Australians leave their cover and cross the road. One of them had a heavily bandaged head, but the second who was obviously the marksman, was a dark-skinned man. He had watched them in amazement. Did the fools think they were safe? He shrugged for in fact they were safe enough. Even though he had Himmler's weapon, he was not confident it had been zeroed correctly and so he chose not to fire at them. But he would remember that dark-skinned man; maybe they would meet again.

He continued to watch the two Australians as they began to hurry toward the area where the artillery still pounded the ground to dust. He concentrated on the dark-skinned one, and gave him a mocking salute. 'I hope you make it,' he mused as he saw him disappear into the smoke and dust. 'You are too skillful a warrior to die at the hands of a blasted artillery man. I want to kill you myself.' Then he settled back in his hide to wait for nightfall when he would go back to his own lines.

———————

Incredibly, as horrendous as the German artillery barrage was, men still lived and worked beneath its fury. Reinforcements braved the man-made storm hurrying forward toward the thinly held Australian line. Work parties straining under the weight of their loads of ammunition, food, water and defence stores laboured onward in the knowledge that their loads were desperately required. Slowly, yet ever so steadily, the Australian front line was being reinforced and consolidated. This turn in the fortunes of battle was a fact not lost on the German commander. His bombardment of the approaches to Pozieres was designed to isolate the Australian front and enable him to counter-attack. However, now he recognised it as wasted effort. In one of the vagaries of war, just as Green and Blucher were about to enter the worst of the barrage, he ordered his artillery to pause in its destructive duty while he reassessed his options.

———————

For a short time, Green and Blucher hardly noticed the difference as they hurried onward. They ran from shell hole, to shell hole, neither of them believing they would survive. Blucher had largely recovered from the shock of his wounding, but it was he who first detected the pause in the incoming artillery fire. With renewed hope, they hurried forward. They were not alone. All around, groups of soldiers were emerging from whatever cover they had been sheltering in and began to hurry away in various directions.

'Which way?' Blucher asked Green, but before he could answer, a slight puff of breeze dissipated the dust and smoke and for a brief moment he saw the sun glinting on the distant church spire at Albert.

'Come on,' Green replied, 'not far now.'

They found a road which appeared to be heading in the right direction, and after a few minutes walking, they attracted the attention of a military policeman.

The policeman beckoned them toward him. 'Papers,' he demanded. It was clear he felt Green at least should be back in the line.

Wordlessly, Green produced the required documents. The policeman perused the papers before handing them back. 'Thanks, Sergeant, you'll find a Casualty Clearing Station around the next corner,' he said as he waved them on. 'They'll have a look at your mate. Good luck.'

The Casualty Clearing Station was where the MP had said it was, complete with a sign announcing it as "Casualty Corner."

The sign amused Blucher. 'That's good,' he laughed.

'What is?' asked Green.

'Well, it's a corner and all the casualties are making for it. "Casualty Corner," it's clever.'

'That bullet came too close to your brain,' Green growled, but then he stopped. 'Hang on, that's even better. Wait here!'

Without waiting for Blucher's response, Green ran forward toward a Model T Ford ambulance that was being loaded with wounded, and a familiar figure of a Croix-Rouge nurse.

'Madame Sainson!' he called. 'Madame Sainson!'

She turned and for a moment did not recognise him. 'Yes?'

she replied.

'It's Sergeant Green, Madame. We met the other night at 3 Brigade Headquarters.'

'Oh yes,' she seemed very weary, but nevertheless pleased to see him. 'Are you wounded?'

'No, no,' replied Green, 'but my mate is. He's had a bit of his ear shot off.'

'Well, he should see the orderlies,' she said. 'We are taking the more seriously injured back to the hospital.'

'Yes, I see that,' said Green hurriedly, 'that's why I've come to you. Will you be going close by to Sausage Valley? You see, my mate and I have been on a special patrol for the Brigadier General who you met the other night, and we have to get our information back to him urgently. If you could give us a lift, it would save us a lot of time.'

Madame Sainson blushed. 'Oh dear, yes, I remember the Brigadier; I hope you did not get into trouble on my behalf. I am sure we can arrange something.' She called to her driver and the two spoke together for a moment. The driver did not seem too enthusiastic about two extra passengers, but relented with a shrug.

'He will do it,' smiled Madame Sainson. 'Now where is your friend? I will look at his ear while the rest of the wounded are lifted into the back.'

Madame Sainson quickly cleaned Blucher's wound, ignoring his hisses of pain. 'Oo la la,' she breathed as she redressed the ear, 'you are lucky man.'

'Unlucky, you mean,' Blucher muttered, 'half an inch to the left and he would have missed me altogether!'

Madame Sainson ignored his levity. 'There,' she said briskly, 'your ear no longer bleeds. Keep the new dressing on for a few days if you can, but you are not too badly hurt. You have probably had worse cuts while shaving.'

Pierre the driver indicated to Green that he was ready to go. 'Will you travel in the back?' he asked in heavily accented English.

Green shook his head. 'We can stand on the running boards,' he replied, deliberately selecting the side of the vehicle closest to Madame Sainson, while Blucher, resplendent in his clean dressing, was left with the driver's side. The driver revved the motor and the ambulance jerked forward.

At first, it was a slow journey and the driver made every effort to avoid the worst of the holes in the road. Even so, every bump caused moans of agony to be heard from the casualties in the vehicle's rear. Madame Sainson was clearly concerned, and on several occasions ordered Pierre to halt to enable her to check her patients.

Then the German artillery began again impacting close behind them. The driver opened the vehicle's throttle, and began speeding along the road, twisting and turning through the major shell holes and bouncing over lesser obstacles. The cries from those in the rear of the ambulance were pitiful, and Green and Blucher clung to the side of the vehicle for dear life. No amount of pleading from Madame Sainson could make the driver slow down. '*Une coquille et nous sommes tous fini! Vous voulez que?*' he shouted back at her.

Fortunately for all on board, Sausage Valley was close by, and at that moment was not receiving the attention of the German gunners.

'Is this where we get off?' Green shouted above the noise of the ambulance engine.

Pale faced and desperately holding on to the door, Madame Sainson could only nod. The driver, however, was showing no sign of even slowing down.

Blucher reached across the panicked driver and reduced the throttle; then as the vehicle slowed, he took hold of the wheel and steered the vehicle on to a flat piece of ground. For a moment, the driver looked as if he would try to regain control of the vehicle, but then he took his feet from the gear pedals and turned off the engine.

Blucher patted the Frenchman on the back. 'It's all right, mate,' he said. 'You'll be away again soon enough.'

Madame Sainson climbed down and ran to the rear of the ambulance. Two of the wounded were dead; Green and Blucher helped her lift them to the ground.

'Was it my fault?' she whispered as they lay the last body on the ground.

Green looked at the dead men. One of them had lost both legs above the knee and an arm at the shoulder; it was a miracle he had lived to see the back of the ambulance. The other seemed to be a mass of bloody wounds, the worst of which had removed the side of the man's head. Death must have been a welcome release for both of them.

'No one's fault,' he said gently. He removed the identity discs from both bodies and handed them to her.

'I will check the others,' she said.

Blucher stared at the two bodies. 'Fuck, what a mess,' he said.

'Doesn't do to brood, mate,' Green warned. 'Come on, we'd better find Captain bloody Tollemache.'

He went to the rear of the ambulance and looked in. Madame Sainson was administering a morphine injection to one of the wounded. 'We have to go,' he said. 'Will you be all right?'

She finished pushing the syringe plunger home then climbed from the vehicle and stood beside him. '*Oui*, I will be fine, but them,' she gestured toward the rear of the ambulance and shrugged.

Green turned to go, but she caught his arm. 'Will I see you again?'

Green laughed. 'I bloody well hope so, Madame!'

'I hope so too,' she replied. 'I will look out for you.*Avoir de la chance.*'

Green looked puzzled.

It was Madame Sainson's turn to laugh. 'Oh, I am sorry. I forget you have little French. I said, "Be lucky."'

'You too,' said Green, and then he turned and with Blucher following went to find Captain Tollemache.

'So what was all that about?' asked Blucher.

'What do you mean?'

'All that with the nurse, is she sweet on you?'

'Don't be fucking stupid. I've only seen her twice.'

'Twice? When was the other time? You've been holding out on me, Sarg!'

Green turned and faced Blucher. 'Leave it!' he said angrily. 'I can't afford any of this crap! Just leave it!'

Blucher cringed away like a hurt puppy. 'All right, keep your shirt on,' he soothed. 'I was just pulling your leg.'

Green walked on. He was angry at himself for being angry with Blucher, but most of all, he was angry at a world he believed would never allow a woman like Madame Sainson and a man of colour to be together.

It was 3:00 p.m. when they found Captain Tollemache. He was drinking tea and seated on the running board of a Crossley 20/25 staff car.

'You made it,' he said as Green and Blucher approached. 'Where's Elliot?'

'Dead,' replied Green flatly.' we got shelled on the road as we went forward.'

Tollemach seemed unconcerned. 'Have some tea?' He indicated a steaming billy that was set on the edge of a small fire. 'I don't have any cups, I'm afraid.'

Green removed his big pack and took out two mess tins. He dipped one into the billy and handed it to Blucher, then filled the second for himself.

Tollemach leaned forward in a conspiratorial manner. 'Now tell me,' he said, 'how did you go?'

Blucher fumbled in his tunic pocket and produced Green's notes. 'Bit blood stained I'm afraid,' he said. He handed the paper to Tollemach, who took it reluctantly, holding it between a thumb and forefinger.

'Good Lord, what did you do with this, use it as a bandage?'

'Private Blucher's ear,' explained Green. 'Ears bleed a lot.'

'I see, and do you have a map?'

Green unfolded the map and placed it on the ground in front of Tollemach.

Tollemach studied Green's work and the notes. 'Excellent!' he said. Bloody well done the both of you. This is just what we need to plan the artillery barrage for the next attack.' He turned to Blucher. 'How is your ear?' he asked.

'Bit sore, sir.'

'Do you need a doctor? There's a doctor over there in that tent,' Tollemach pointed to a small tent with a large red cross painted on its roof.

'I should be right, sir,' Blucher replied; then borrowing Madame Sainson's words, he added, 'I've had worse cuts shaving.'

Tollemach raised an inquiring eyebrow. 'Well, if you're sure, you can come with the Sergeant and me back to Brigade. I expect you will be keen to get back to your unit.'

Blucher did not respond, and instead glanced toward Green appealingly.

Green saw Blucher's look. 'Excuse me, sir,' he said to Tollemach, 'I wonder if I might have a word in private?'

Tollemach frowned but nevertheless beckoned to Green to follow him as he walked a few yards away from the car. 'What's the problem?' he inquired.

'No problem, sir,' Green explained, 'it's just that Private Blucher has performed exceptionally well today. In my opinion, sir, he would certainly be an asset to any battalion in the line, but right now he would be of even more value to me.' He paused to allow Tollemach to digest his remarks. 'You see, sir, a sniper is normally deployed with a spotter. Now in theory for the job I have been sent here to do, I don't need a spotter, but today's experience has shown me that in fact I do need one. I wonder if you might consider allowing Blucher to remain with me for the remainder of my attachment.'

Tollemach could not hide his surprise. 'Good heavens!' he exclaimed. 'It's not that I doubt your words, Sergeant, but Blucher has in the past being nothing but a bloody pest!' He aimed a kick a small clod of earth at his feet. 'I'm amazed,' he continued. 'Still, if you think you can make use of him, I will make the necessary arrangements. I dare say the transport NCO will be jolly glad to see the back of the chap!'

Green smiled. 'Thank you, sir,' he said, 'if he survives, I'm sure you will find him useful after I've gone.'

Tollemach was impatient to be on his way. 'I shall leave it to you to break the news to Blucher,' he said briskly. 'He may not be so keen when he hears our next destination is Brigade Headquarters. It's back the way you have come, well, not exactly where you have come from, but it's near the eastern edge of the village. Pity there was no way to contact you before and I couldn't arrange to meet you there, as I wasn't certain where the headquarters would finish up. Nothing for it I'm afraid, we shall have to walk.' He turned to his driver. 'You can head back to Albert, Jim. We'll have to wait and see when you can come forward.'

The driver tipped the remains of the billy tea over campfire and packed the billy in the car. 'See you later then, boss', he said in farewell to Tollemach as he drove away.

It was early evening by the time Tollemach, Green, and Blucher had negotiated the maze of trench works and shell holes to arrive at 3 Brigade Headquarters. The headquarters was located in the remains of a large cellar to what must have been a fine house. The headquarters troops had undertaken considerable work to reclaim the underground structure and to strengthen its roof and frontage with pine logs and sandbags. A determined looking, but very young soldier stood guard at the entrance and on recognising the Brigade Major, he waved the trio forward.

Brigadier General Sinclair-Maclagan was clearly pleased to see the safe return of his principal staff officer. 'You're a tad late, Tollemach,' he observed as the exhausted trio entered the headquarters.

'Yes sir,' agreed Tollemach, 'but I think you'll find it worth the wait.' He handed Sinclair-Maclagan Green's map and Blucher's notes. 'These fellows have done a first-class job,' he concluded, gesturing toward Green and Blucher.

Sinclair-Maclagan turned toward them and immediately recognised Green. 'Good Lord,' he said, 'Sergeant Green, you do pop up in the most unexpected places! Have you prevented any other senior officers from visiting the lavatory?'

Green smiled. 'No, sir.'

'And you are?' Sinclair-Maclagan asked Blucher.

'Blucher, sir.'

Green offered some additional explanation. 'Sir, Private Blucher was the driver who delivered Lance Corporal Elliot and myself forward this morning. He volunteered to take part in my patrol when Lance Corporal Elliot was killed.'

Sinclair-Maclagan shook Blucher by the hand. 'Good, good, well done, Blucher. Now let's have a look at this map of yours, Green.'

He studied the map and glanced at the notes. 'Excellent,' he said and beckoned to a junior staff officer. 'Take this along to the guns,' he said. 'It shows our forward positions as of 10:00 a.m. today. Have them check the plan and make any necessary adjustments.' He turned back to Green and Blucher. 'Rum?'

Green declined, but Blucher readily accepted the invitation.

The junior staff officer returned. 'Excuse me, sir, an important message from the signallers.'

Sinclair-Maclagan took the offered note and read it. 'Damn,' he said. He turned to Tollemach, 'This will interest you, BM. It seems the new signal's telephone wire is not surviving the Hun bombardment.'

'I had heard this, sir,' Tollemach replied. 'Bloody stuff is brittle and just by bending the it; it tends to snap, so subjecting it to high explosives....' his explanation trailed away.

Sinclair-Maclagan turned back to the staff officer. 'Keep trying to fix the lines,' he said. 'In the meantime, we shall have to back every message up with a runner.'

'Yes sir,' replied the staff officer. 'We are getting short of runners though; too many of them are becoming casualties. Is it all right to get some volunteers from the reserve units to act as runners?'

'Of course.'

The staff officer hurried away, and Sinclair-Maclagan

turned to Green. 'Which brings us to you, Sergeant Green,' he continued. 'You have my sincere thanks, you too, Private Blucher. That was a job well done. BM, I shall leave it to you to ensure that Sergeant Green's liaison work can be carried out, and I assume Blucher can be returned to his normal duties.'

Tollemach glanced at Blucher. 'Sergeant Green has requested Private Blucher be assigned to him for the duration of his attachment here, sir. I see no reason why that can't happen.'

Sinclair-Maclagan nodded. 'Of course, of course,' but he was already giving his attention to a message that an exhausted runner had just delivered.

Tollemach turned to Green and Blucher. 'I think we can take it the Brigadier has given his approval. For better or worse, Blucher is all yours, Sergeant'.

Blucher could hardly contain his relief. 'Thank you, sir,' he said gleefully. 'I won't let you down.'

'It's not me that should be worried, but Sergeant Green,' Tollemach said stiffly. 'Besides, you may not thank me once you've followed Sergeant Green around for a few days. I do believe we are in for a rather nasty mauling. We're launching another attack tomorrow night just after midnight. The Brigadier wanted to wait until the situation was clearer, but the Divisional Commander has ordered us forward.' He turned to Green. 'As you are here to observe, Sergeant, you might get a good opportunity to carry out your orders then. However, I suggest you wait until the morning before moving any further forward.'

'What do we do now?' Blucher asked after Tollemach had gone back into the headquarters dugout.

'Nothing,' Green announced simply.

A few yards away, a disused trench offered the two men some degree of isolation from the headquarters and with much relief, they clambered into it and on lying down against the trench wall, they fell instantly asleep.

Chapter 15

Blucher poked Green gently in the ribs with his boot. 'Get this in you, mate.' He offered Green a steaming mug of tea. 'The cooks said we can grab some breakfast in a few minutes.'

Green sat up and rubbed his eyes. 'Thanks,' he said as he accepted the mug of tea. 'What time is it?'

Blucher shrugged, he did not own a watch, but another soldier passing by called out an answer. '7:00 a.m., Monday, 24 July.'

Green was about to thank his informant when the whirring sound of heavy artillery shells passing overhead sent everyone in the vicinity cowering for cover. Moments later, a series of massive explosions erupted and as the ground heaved from the resulting concussion; those close to 3 Brigade Headquarters sighed in collective relief. Someone else, albeit not far to their north, had been the German artillery target.

Numerous headquarters soldiers appeared out of trenches and dugouts to watch the bombardment. Brigadier Sinclair-Maclagan and Captain Tollemach had climbed on to the roof of the headquarters dugout, binoculars at their eyes, studying the artillery impact area. 'It's right on top of the 3rd Battalion, sir,' Tollemach confirmed anxiously. 'They seem to be firing from somewhere back behind us near Courcelette.'

'Get on to our guns,' Sinclair-Maclagan snapped. 'I want counter battery fire on Courcelette; our boys can't stand too much of this!'

Tollemach ran toward the signallers' telephone centre,

shouting as he ran. 'Get me our guns, lively now!'

'Well, I reckon that stuffs breakfast,' Blucher grumbled.

'Quiet,' Green snapped, 'I'm counting explosions.'

'Sorry,' Blucher muttered.

Green shook his head. 'No need,' he replied, 'this is bloody awful!' He shook his head, unable to believe the data he had just calculated. He shook his watch and satisfied it was still working, he began to count again only to confirm his original observation. 'One hundred forty-four,' he shouted above the increasing din. 'At least one hundred and forty-four shells a minute, I can actually see the bloody things as they pass over.'

'What's that you say?' a voice called from behind him.

Green turned and saw that Sinclair-Maclagan was standing beside him. 'One hundred forty-four shells a minute, sir,' he replied; then he added unnecessarily, 'That's a huge number of guns they've got, sir.'

Sinclair-Maclagan moved close to Green so they could speak without having to shout above the noise, but even then, communication was difficult. 'I've ordered counter battery fire,' he said. 'Hopefully our guns will put a stop to this.'

'Will the attack still go in?' Green asked.

'Eh? Hmm, yes, I expect so. I just hope this bloody shelling leaves us someone to attack with!'

The bombardment began to drift back toward the headquarters, and the ever attentive Tollemach appeared at Sinclair-Maclagan's side. 'Sir, we need you in the dugout.'

For a moment, the Brigadier seemed about to object, but he allowed Tollemach to lead him away.

Green watched fearfully as the barrage crept back toward him. He hated shell fire with a passion, but he had never seen anything on the scale of this bombardment, and he wondered how anyone could survive its ferocity. Spent shrapnel began to flutter down around him and he knew he should take cover, but he found he was unable to cease his vigil. It was as if the explosions held him in a hypnotic grip from which he could not escape.

Blucher seized him by the leg. 'Get down here, you crazy bastard!' Blucher screamed. He pulled Green roughly from the parapet to the trench floor.

The fall broke Green's trance and he was once more in charge of the situation. Four other men had joined them in the trench, and now Green calmly directed them toward the shallow scrapes in the trench wall known to the troops as "funk holes," before he joined Blucher in another.

Then the bombardment was upon them.

The noise was so intense that it assumed a physical shape that could be seen in the rush of dust and debris that accompanied each explosion, and felt as a corporeal body blow. Each man was lost in his own world of noise and terror, and isolated beyond the comfort of those who cowered in the earth alongside them. Green tried to tell himself that the German artillery would soon run out of ammunition and the shelling would cease, and as he began to realise this was vain hope, he felt the fear rising in him and he began to struggle to retain control.

For a time though, their particular section of the trench was spared a direct hit. Most trenches were constructed with a series of sharp corners at regular intervals, designed to deflect the blast of a shell exploding in the trench, away from the next section. Several times shells impacted in other sections of their trench, but the corners did their work, dissipating the effects of the blast and shielding them from the shrapnel. Then their luck finally ran out.

There was an overwhelming blinding flash as a shell landed

directly on their part of the trench. A power so terrible that it plucked Green and Blucher from their funk hole and threw them around like autumn leaves before a wind. Then there was darkness.

Blucher recovered first. At first, he believed he was entirely buried and in his panic to reach the surface, he was surprised when the earth fell from his body and he was able to get to his knees with little effort. Yet he found he was still tethered to the ground by something attached to his neck. Puzzled, he traced with one hand the object that held him, and to his relief found it was his rifle sling. The sling was still attached to the weapon, which remained buried beneath him. Quickly, he retrieved his rifle, then remembered Green's telescope; it was still attached to his belt. 'Anyone about?' he shouted, trying to keep the panic he felt from his voice. 'Anyone...?' A few feet away, a pair of booted and trousered legs protruded from the collapsed wall of the trench.

He reached out, grasped the legs, and pulled. To his horror, the legs and the bottom half of a body came free of the earth and fell bloodily against him. The trench beyond the severed legs and pelvis of the unknown dead man was completely destroyed, and instinctively Blucher knew the other four men who had been in that part of the trench were all dead. But where was Green? With fearful dread, he began to believe that the legs and pelvis he had pulled free of the rubble were the sergeant's.

Behind him someone was violently coughing and gasping for air. Still grasping one of the dead man's legs, Blucher looked toward the sound.

It was Green.

'Jesus,' Blucher wheezed, looking at the leg he was holding, 'I thought this was you!' He pushed the leg away and crawled to Green's side.

'Gut full of dirt,' Green spluttered an obvious explanation and promptly vomited over Blucher's hands. 'Sorry mate,' he muttered.

'It's okay, it's okay,' Blucher responded, not even bothering to wipe his hands. He put an arm around Green's shoulder and gently guided him into a deeper section of the collapsed trench.

'Where are the others?" Green asked unsteadily.

'Gone,' Blucher replied.

Green began to dry retch. 'I've been buried before,' he explained between heaves, 'at Gallipoli. It scared me shitless then; they had to dig to find me. This wasn't too bad...'

Blucher could do little other than to place a comforting arm about Green's shoulders.

Another shell exploded on the ground immediately beyond the parapet, and out of the very flame of the explosion, Tollemach appeared. Amazingly, he was unharmed, and he quickly jumped down into the trench beside them. He glanced at Green, who was still retching up the contents of his stomach. 'Concussion,' he pronounced flatly. 'Come on, Blucher, we have to get him out of this; you can do nothing more here.'

They assisted Green to clamber out of the remains of the trench and across the torn ground to the headquarters cellar. The determined young soldier who had greeted them earlier was still at his post, but he was now pale faced and shaken; even so, he helped get Green inside and to prop him up against a wall.

Someone thrust a clay flagon toward Green. 'Rum,' the holder of the flagon declared.

This time, Green did not decline the fiery liquid. He drank greedily and immediately vomited again.

'That's the stuff,' Tollemach declared as he stepped around Green's regurgitation and handed the flagon on to Blucher.

Another soldier emptied a bucket of earth over Green's deposit. 'I'm sorry,' Green offered, but the man had already walked away into the gloom of the headquarters interior.

A series of massive explosions, far closer than any of the other impacting shells, rocked the cellar, extinguishing most of the candles that lit the room. They were quickly relit and in the eerie glow that followed, Green noticed a group of runners sitting quietly in a line along one wall of the dugout. They were waiting to be sent outside into the teeth of the barrage with orders for the forward troops. A few paces away, a signaller sat at a small table on which a field telephone exchange had been established. At regular intervals, the signaller would push a plug into the exchange box and twirl the handle on his phone, but while Green watched, there was no answer to any of his calls. Deeper into the dugout, Green could see the figure of Brigadier Sinclair-Maclagan apparently deep in thought and standing before a large wall mounted map. Occasionally, the Brigadier would gesture at the map and speak to one of the men standing near him. He seemed oblivious to the bombardment that raged outside like some demented beast—Green tried to draw strength from his example.

'What now?' Blucher shouted above the din.

Green felt too ill to care. He shrugged and managed to shout in response, 'We'll just keep out of the way.'

Time inched by. Sometimes the barrage seemed to lessen; at other times it returned with renewed fury. The roof of the headquarters received a direct hit, fortunately from a smaller calibre artillery gun than others being fired by the German gunners. Some logs and sandbags dislodged, allowing a shaft of light to penetrate the space below, yet the main structure remained solid. However, the hit had a terrifying effect on Green. He edged toward the headquarters entrance and it took every bit of his failing courage to stop himself from running outside. Tollemach and another man were suddenly beside him. Wordlessly, Tollemach handed him a mug of tea that had been heavily laced with rum.

Tollemach's companion watched with disapproval as Green drank greedily. 'He shouldn't be having that!' the man shouted above the noise of the bombardment.

Tollemach ignored his companion's exclamation, and waited just long enough for Green to finish the tea. Then retrieving the cup, he walked away, deeper into the dugout. The other man followed.

Night fell and still the shelling continued. The line of runners Green had earlier observed was now dramatically diminished, and the signaller at the telephone was becoming more and more frustrated at the lack of response from those he endeavoured to contact. And still the German artillery tortured Pozieres and its immediate surrounds. Green wondered what had happened to the counter battery fire Sinclair-Maclagan had requested, for it was plain either the request had been refused, or the British artillery return of fire had been ineffectual.

It was an additional source of alarm for Green that he had no notion of what was happening beyond the relative safety of the headquarters cellar. However, late that night, he noticed the headquarters staff had achieved a new rate of frenetic activity and he deduced something had either happened, or was about to happen in the battle beyond the cellar. As if in response to this assumption, the shells falling in the immediate area of the headquarters diminished. The noise of the barrage continued, but its epicentre was now further away to the north.

Tollemach was suddenly at his side. 'Good morning, Sergeant Green,' he said cheerily. 'How are you feeling now?'

Green stood up, he still felt ill, but he was determined to show he could still make a contribution. 'Better sir,' he replied, 'the rum helped and now with the shelling gone...'

Tollemach was genuinely pleased. 'Good, good, you've had a rough trot.' He paused, apparently uncomfortable with a subject he was about to pursue. 'If you are willing,' he continued awkwardly, 'we might have another task for you.'

Green flexed his aching back and let his arms hang loosely at his side, and felt a little better. 'Certainly, sir,' he replied. Inwardly, he felt he would rather face the barrage outside than endure any further time in the cellar.

'You had better come down to the map,' Tollemach said without further preamble.

'Can I come too?' Blucher asked nervously. 'Only, I'd rather not be left behind.'

'Certainly,' Tollemach replied, as he led the way deeper into the cellar. 'I had rather assumed you would accompany Sergeant Green.'

A large sketch map titled "**POZIERES– Correct as of Midnight 24th July 1916**," adorned a portion of the cellar wall. Tollemach moved to the map and using a pencil as a pointer, he began to explain the situation. 'We are about here,' he began stabbing the pencil at a point to the south east of Pozieres. 'The attack went ahead as planned,' he made a sweeping motion with the pencil indicating the direction the attacking battalions had taken, 'and we have achieved a degree of success. The 5th Battalion has managed to secure a portion of the Old German trench here,' the pencil hovered over a portion of the bottom right hand corner of the map. 'But the

Hun is still in possession of positions either side and on the ridge above their positions. They are running out of ammunition and it is the Brigadier's intention to use the 7th and the 9th Battalions to reinforce the 5th and to carry more ammunition forward to them.' He paused and glanced questioningly at Green and Blucher, but they remained silent.

'The telephone lines are still out, but we have set runners off to the 7th and 9th Battalions with orders to implement the Brigadier's intent. The trouble is we can't be certain the runners reached their objectives, so we need you to do a similar task to the one you performed yesterday. Move forward and check that the 7th and the 9th are carrying out the task. If they are not, order them to do so. If they are, see if you can check that the reinforcements and ammunition is getting forward; then come back here and give us the good news.'

Green nodded. 'When do we leave?' he asked.

'Now,' Tollemach replied. 'Every minute is vital. If the reinforcements and resupply don't get through, it will all be for nothing.' He handed Green an envelope. 'If you need to convince either CO of your authority, the contents of this will do the trick.'

Green glanced at Blucher. 'Ready?' he asked.

Blucher gave a weak grin. 'What are we waiting for?' he replied uncertainly.

They collected their weapons and equipment and made their way to the dugout entrance. The earnest young soldier was still there, and he wished them luck as they left. 'He can't be more than fourteen,' Blucher muttered as they passed.

Green did not respond; for some reason, he found himself thinking of the young Warwickshire Regiment lad he had met on the train back in England and wondering if he still lived.

It was around 6:30 a.m. when Green and Blucher reached

the forward positions. Clearly Sinclair-Maclagan's runners had reached the 7th and the 9th Battalions, for both units were busily engaged in carrying out the Brigadier's orders. Up on Pozieres Heights, the sounds of a vicious fire fight could be heard. Toward that clamour, along a narrow corridor, parties of Diggers were carrying boxes of ammunition, water, and rations forward to the beleaguered 5th Battalion. Using the same slim passageway, groups of wounded were making their way back away from the fighting. Grimly, Green noted that once the wounded escaped the onslaught of bullets and grenades, they faced another trial before they reached aid, for the German artillery continued to rain fire on the ruined village and its surrounds, and through that hell, the wounded men would have to pass.

Blucher looked longingly over his shoulder back toward Sinclair-Maclagan's headquarters. 'What now?' he asked knowing the answer, but fearing to hear Green confirmation.

'Up to the ridge to see how the boys are travelling,' Green replied flatly.

'I thought you'd say that,' Blucher muttered, but he made no attempt to dissuade Green and dutifully followed him toward the fighting.

Green had recovered much of his good spirits now that he was free of the confines of the cellar. He still maintained a wary eye on the artillery barrage, but out in the open he felt if death found him, it would be quick and clean, not slow and suffocating buried under rubble and earth. 'We'll go close enough to see what's going on,' he told Blucher. 'Then we'll go back. We have to keep clear of strife to be able to take the news back to the Brigadier.'

They attached themselves to the rear of a group of Lewis gunners who were hurrying forward to add their firepower to that of the 5th Battalion. The gunners set a punishing pace, dodging from shell hole to shell hole and clambering in and out of abandoned German trenches. In a few minutes, the whole group slid into the main part of the Old German trench, much to the annoyance of a 5th Battalion soldier who happened to be underneath the descending mass of humanity. 'Mind how you go,' the man complained as he struggled from beneath one of the gunners. 'You bloody near broke me teeth!'

'Well, get out of the way or I'll make a better job of it,' growled the Lewis gunner.

Green stepped between the two protagonists. 'Ease up,' he snarled. 'Save your fighting for the Huns!'

The Lewis gunner turned away. 'That's gratitude for you,' he grumbled to one of his mates. 'We've only come to help!'

'Can you direct me to your CO?' Green asked the 5th Battalion man.

'Follow the trench to the left,' the man replied grumpily. 'The headquarters is in an old German dugout. You should see what the bastards had... grog, tucker, and real beds. We're in the wrong fuckin' army. Hang on, I'll take you there.' A few moments later, their new benefactor presented Green and Blucher to Lieutenant Colonel Frank Le Maistre.

The CO of the 5th Battalion shook Green's hand and grinned. 'You were a baggy arsed corporal the last time I saw you, Sergeant,' he said.

'And you were a bad-tempered Major, sir,' Green replied happily.

Blucher shook his head in exasperation but made no comment.

'Well, to business,' Le Maistre said abruptly. 'What brings you here? It can't be for the good of your health.'

'We need to check how the battle is going and then report

back to Brigadier Sinclair-Maclagan,' Green explained.

'The battle is bloody awful,' Le Maistre retorted. 'I've lost a lot of men—at this stage I don't know how many. My northern flank is exposed, and the boys are fighting it out with Mills bombs. The reinforcements have helped though, and we are holding a strip of trench between the road and the railway. Mind you, that's only about a quarter of what we were supposed to capture, bugger all I can do about that.' Le Maistre paused as a particularly heavy exchange of grenade explosions took place. 'Bloody hell,' he muttered, 'the bastards won't give up, will they? Look, the worst of this affair is going to be holding this bloody trench. I mean, we've lost so many good chaps grabbing it, but we'll lose more and more keeping it. Will it be worth it? I'm glad I'm not the one who must make that decision; that's what the bloody staff has to work out.'

The firing and grenade blasts increased to an alarming crescendo. 'I must go,' Le Maistre said quickly. 'Tell the Brigadier we are holding our own for now.' Then shouting for his RSM, Le Maistre ran down the trench in the direction of the firing.

Chapter 16

Tollemach was particularly pleased to see them, although they had already received similar information to that which Green and Blucher brought, via another runner. Nevertheless, he was gratified to have that information confirmed. 'Find us easily enough?' he asked as he ushered them into the headquarters cellar.

'Yes sir,' Green lied. In fact, finding the headquarters again had been a nightmare. Whereas the British artillery had reduced Pozieres to a ruin, the German barrage of the 24th and 25th July had turned the whole area to the status of a ploughed field. Little remained that could be called a landmark, and it had been a complete fluke that they had arrived in the correct place. Aside from that difficulty, the German artillery continued to bombard various sections of the Australian line, although Green formed the opinion that the German gunners were being more frugal with their ammunition, for there were gaps of up to half an hour in their fusillade of shells. It was during one of these interludes that Green and Blucher had stumbled on to the headquarters.

Like every other trench and dugout in the Allied line, 3 Brigade Headquarters was rather worse for wear. The entrance had received a direct hit, and a dark stain on the remaining rubble was all that remained of the earnest young Digger who had previously guarded the doorway. Inside, the roof showed evidence of further damage and as they followed Tollemach deeper into the cellar, Green began to feel his fear of being entombed alive return.

'I was particularly anxious that you returned today,' Tollemach continued conspiratorially. 'We are going to be relieved tonight. It's just as well, for I don't think any of us can stand much more of the shelling.'

For the first time, Green noticed the condition of the surviving staff. A combination of lack of sleep and the effects of the continuous shelling had reduced most of them to a zombie-like condition. They were managing to function, but only just. Even Tollemach and Brigadier Sinclair-Maclagan had developed robotic characteristics. It was time, indeed beyond time, for all of them to have a rest.

'Rum?' Tollemach offered. 'I'm afraid we don't run to tea—lack of water, don't you see.'

Green and Blucher both accepted a pannikin of the spirit and drank.

'You can't stay long,' Tollemach continued. 'We received another order this morning, just after you left, in fact... you are to return to Sausage Valley forthwith. A Lieutenant Colonel Law will meet you there at the main kitchen of all places. I've no idea what it's about, so I suppose you had better go.'

Green nodded, but Blucher was dismayed. 'So that's it,' he said sadly, 'I'm back to driving.'

'Oh for heaven's sake, man,' Tollemach snapped. 'I really don't care where you go! Go with Sergeant Green if it makes you happy. I have other things to worry about.'

'I'm sorry sir,' Blucher replied, trying hard to conceal his glee. 'I'll go with Sergeant Green.'

Green frowned but kept silent. He wondered how Lieutenant Colonel Law would take to the extra member of the team. He knew Blucher would be handy to have along, but Monash and Law's obsession with the security of the operation would be a significant hurdle to cross. In a moment of defiance, he thought, *Stuff them both—Blucher can come and I'll sort it all out later.*

It was dark when Green and Blucher left 3 Brigade Headquarters and made their weary way to the west and comparative safety. However, getting back to Sausage Valley was even more difficult than it had been leaving it. The maze of trenches they had followed on their outward journey had almost been obliterated by the previous two days' shelling, and keeping direction was a challenge. Curiously, the German artillery that caused this difficulty and still continued to pound what little was left of the village of Pozieres, now served as a navigational aid. By keeping the barrage to their right, they knew they were bound to arrive at their objective. Even so, the dawn was beginning to break as they approached Sausage Valley, and it was then the bombardment moved to the south, cutting off their line of advance.

'Keep going?' Blucher suggested as they watched the impacting shells.

Green had had enough. 'Bugger it,' he replied, 'I'm damned if I'm going through that.' He slumped into a shell hole and Blucher clambered in and sat down next to him.

'When are you going to tell me about this Colonel Law bloke?' Blucher asked, taking advantage of their halt.

'Nothing to tell yet,' Green replied. 'We will have to see what he wants. Listen, if you have any sense, you'll get a transfer to one of the battalions. I'll put in a good word for you and I'm pretty sure the Brigadier and Captain Tollemach would too. If you stay with me... well, I don't know how you will end up.' Green fell silent and stared moodily at the bottom of the shell hole.

'But it's up to me?' Blucher asked.

'Up to a point,' Green replied. 'Colonel Law will have to agree to you joining the team.'

'There you go again,' Blucher muttered. 'What team?'

For a long while, Green did not answer, for he wondered how much he should divulge to Blucher. It hardly seemed fair to allow Blucher to accompany him any further without giving him some idea of what he was getting himself into. On the other hand, he asked himself how well he really knew Blucher. Blucher had proved himself to be reliable in a fight, but how reliable would he be on a night's leave and a skin full of grog? Finally, he decided to compromise. 'Mate, I can't tell you much at this stage, but I'm actually in France on a special job.'

'Not observing snipers, I'll bet,' Blucher remarked sharply.

'I won't take your bet,' Green responded grimly. 'It's all very hush hush, and bloody dangerous. Now that's as much as I'm prepared to tell you at this stage. However, I will need an assistant and if you still want to come, I'll certainly recommend to Law that you are included.'

'I'll come,' Blucher said flatly.

An hour later, the shelling to their front ceased and half an hour after that, they stood at the entrance to Sausage Valley. 'I wonder what constitutes the "main kitchen"?' Green pondered, for in the early morning light he could see several locations where food was being cooked and distributed.

'It'll be the biggest one,' Blucher suggested. 'What about that one over there?'

It was a good guess. Lieutenant Colonel Law was standing by a wheeled field cooker sipping a steaming mug of tea. At first, he failed to recognise Green and when he did, he seemed irritated by Green's condition. 'Good God, man,' he spluttered, 'what the hell has happened to you? You look as if you've been dragged through a pig sty backwards!'

'That's not far from the truth, sir,' Green replied wearily.

'They tell me you have been to the front!' Law continued angrily. 'I don't think that was in your brief! What if I had needed you in a hurry?'

'I was living up to the cover story you gave me,' Green replied hotly. 'When 3 Brigade were sent forward, I could not very well refuse to go, could I?'

Law's shoulders sagged. 'No, I don't suppose you could,' he replied quietly. Then noticing Blucher for the first time, he raised an inquiring eyebrow. 'Who is this?' he asked.

'Private Blucher,' Green replied. 'He has been attached to me more or less permanently and has proved to be a valuable assistant.'

'What do you mean "assistant"?' Law bristled.

'I mean that when a sniper is in the field, he generally employs a spotter. The spotter guides the sniper on to the target.'

'Private Blucher,' Law addressed Blucher without looking at him. 'Why don't you join that queue over there and get yourself something to eat?'

Blucher hesitated, but Green confirmed Law's direction with a nod.

Once Blucher was out of ear shot, Law turned angrily on Green. 'How much have you told that man?' he demanded.

'About the operation... Nothing at all,' Green replied calmly. 'But you should know if the operation is to proceed, I will need a spotter, and you should also know that I have now worked with Blucher and I trust him.'

Law was not convinced. 'I am amazed you should even associate with such a man—I mean his name, he's clearly of German descent!'

'So is Monash,' Green retorted hotly, 'and I'm a black

fellow. Not everyone in the AIF is a white Briton.'

Law straightened as if he'd been struck; then he began to laugh. 'You've got me there, Sergeant,' he gasped as he controlled his mirth, 'but it's just as well Monash is on this side of the line, for with him we just might win this war. Let's hope your man Blucher is as good as you say.'

Green relaxed. 'Thank you, sir,' he said warmly, 'I assume Blucher is in then.'

Law held up a warning hand. 'Yes, you can use him,' he said, 'but I don't want him given any details just yet.'

'That's fine, sir. I was about to suggest much the same thing myself.'

'Good, good, now things are afoot, we need to be ready. I still can't give you a date when you will need to move, but I must now have you near at hand so that once I receive word, we can act quickly. To that end, you and friend Blucher can take a spot of leave. I want you to stay at a house in Amiens and while you are free to wander around the town, I don't want you leaving town. Once we get word of the target, speed will be critical. I can't afford to waste time looking around France for you.'

Green nodded. 'We need a rest,' he said. 'A few quiet days will be very welcome.'

'And a wash,' Law commented wryly. 'You both stink!'

'Thank you, sir,' Green replied wearily. 'Washing was not high on our list of priorities of late.'

'Quite, quite,' Law blustered. 'Right, I'll leave you to round up Blucher,' he was once again business-like and brisk, 'and get something to eat yourself. I shall go and organise my driver. I'll come and find you in say twenty minutes?'

A little after the twenty minutes he allowed, Law returned. He bundled Green and Blucher into his car and with a curt word to the driver, they drove away. After that, Green's memory of events was confused. He fell asleep almost as soon as the car began to move, and as a result, he had no idea how long the journey took. Nor had he any memory of passing through Albert, or the quick stop at Divisional Headquarters where Law had left them in the car while he attended to some matter.

Green finally awoke when Law loudly announced they were in the Saint-Leu quarter of Amiens. 'That house there,' he said, pointing to a two-story terrace house, 'is your billet for at least the next ten days.'

Green sat up and yawned. 'So long as it's got a big feather bed,' he declared.

Blucher got out of the car and stood hands on hips assessing the house. 'Looks all right to me,' he said. 'I think I'll stay.'

'I'm so glad our accommodation arrangements meet with your approval, Private Blucher,' Law said sarcastically. Then he handed Green two leave passes. 'Don't leave the house without these passes,' he warned. 'The Military Police are hunting deserters.' He produced two envelopes and handed one to Green and the other to Blucher. 'Your pay clerk won't be able to find you for a while.' Law explained, 'So I've arranged this advance. By the way, this amount will not appear in your pay books. Look on it as a bonus, but please don't spend it all at once.'

Green and Blucher mumbled their thanks.

While these military administration matters were being attended to, the front door of the house opened, and a woman of indeterminate age walked wearily down the steps and toward the car. Law noticed her approach and went to meet her. '*Bonjour, Madame Claire, tu vas bien j'ai confiance?*'

'*Assez bien merci,*' Madame replied dourly, '*tu es en retard.*'

Law shrugged. *'Je suis désolé madame le trafic que vous connaissez.'* He handed her an envelope. *'Le loyer Madame'*, he announced grandly.

Madame Claire eagerly opened the packet and rapidly counted the contents. *'Bon, bon merci'*, she said happily as she pushed the envelope and its contents into the pocket of her apron.

Law turned to Green and Blucher. 'This is your landlady, Madame Claire. She owns the house and does the odd job for me every now and again.' He paused and turned again to Madame Claire. *'Madame c'est Sergent Vert et Blucher Privé'*. He glanced back to Green and Blucher. 'Do either of you speak French?'

'A little,' Green replied. Blucher shook his head.

Law shrugged. 'Ah, pity, but it can't be helped now; I'm sure you'll work things out between the three of you. Well, I must be off. Should you need to speak with me, I can be reached at this number.' He passed a card to Green. 'Other than that, expect me when you see me.' With that Law got back in the car, the driver started the engine, and they departed.

Madame Claire gestured toward the door of the house. *'Viens, viens,'* she encouraged.

'She wants us to go with her,' Green advised Blucher. They picked up their weapons and equipment and followed the woman into the house.

Madame Claire indicated a door at the end of the entrance hall. *'A travers leur est la privy,'* she announced.

'What did she say?' Blucher asked.

'I'm not entirely sure,' Green replied, 'but I think that's where the toilet is. Just nod your head; we can check later.'

They both nodded and Madame Claire beamed at her own

success at communication: '*Tu es fatigue*, no?' she continued.

Blucher again turned to Green for an interpretation.

'She wants to know if we are tired,' Green guessed. 'Nod again, and I reckon she will show us our room.'

Green was correct. Madame Claire led the way up a flight of steep stairs, pausing at a landing and indicating a doorway. '*C'est ma chamber,*' she announced before continuing up the next flight of stairs.

'That's her room,' Green explained as he followed Madame up the stairs. At the top of the stairs, there was another small landing with a door on either side.

Madame Claire pointed at the doors. '*Cette pièce et celle-ci sont à vous,*' she declared.

'These are our rooms,' Green pre-empted Blucher's query. 'Which one do you want?'

'I'll take the one on the right,' Blucher replied, moving toward the door.

Madame Claire made to descend the stairway. '*Vous reposerez maintenant?*' she asked.

Green was not exactly sure what she had said this time, but he figured she planned to let them settle into their rooms, so he nodded politely and entered his room.

Green's room was small but adequate and was clearly an attic built into the roof of the house. At one end of the room, a single window provided a shaft of dull light across the wooden floor. Green walked to the window and looked out. The roof tops of Amiens stretched out before his gaze. Off to the right, he could see the imposing structure of the Cathedral dominating the skyline. His attention returned to the room's double bed on which a large European quilt had been spread. He sat on the edge of the bed and tested the base by gently bouncing up and down. It seemed well sprung. He lay back on the pillows and snuggled down. He was surprised to find he was still tired, given he had slept through the car journey to Amiens, but he reflected, he had had a fairly hectic week. In the next instant, he was sound asleep.

Chapter 17

When Green awoke it was morning, and he was puzzled to find he was naked. Clearly while he slept, his clothing had been removed and he was now under the quilt. He assumed Blucher, or perhaps Madame Claire, had visited the room and seen to his comfort. His rifle and other equipment were neatly stacked against a wall. A large bath robe had been placed on the room's only chair.

He put the robe on and sat on the edge of the bed. He looked at his watch. 'Bugger!' he exclaimed as he noted the watch was no longer working. Padding to the window, he looked out. From the position of the sun, he guessed it was mid-morning. He closed the window and went to the doorway. Stepping out onto the landing, he listened at the door of the room Blucher had chosen. There was no sound. 'Probably still asleep,' Green mumbled. Barefooted, he moved silently down to the second landing and listened at Madame Claire's doorway. The rhythmical creak of bed springs and the muffled sound of Madame Claire and Blucher's voices reached him through the panelled door. He shook his head in wonder. It seemed the landlady's generosity and care knew no bounds.

He reached the ground floor and paused. To his left lay the front door. To his right through an open doorway, he could see the kitchen and he could smell the rich aroma of freshly baked bread. Green found he was famished and eagerly walked toward the kitchen. Disappointingly, there was no one there and in spite of his hunger, he was reluctant to make a search for anything to eat without permission. He continued his exploration.

Through a large window, he could see a clothesline on which his own and Blucher's clothing were pegged and gently swaying in the breeze. He was about to venture further when a polite cough caused him to stop and turn. Madame Claire had come downstairs and now stood behind him. She was flustered, blushing slightly, patting at her hair and straightening her clothing. '*Bonjour monsieur, Ça va ?*'

Green was caught off guard and took several moments to recall his school boy French. '*Ca va bien Madame,*' he replied haltingly, hoping against hope he had responded correctly that he was feeling fine.

Madame Claire beamed happily. '*Tu parle français?*'

'Do you speak French?' Green rapidly translated her question in his mind. 'What the hell was French for "a little"?' Ah yes, that was it. '*Juste un peu,*' he said.

Madame Claire was disappointed, but she quickly recovered and opening the oven door produced a plate of croissants, which she placed on the kitchen table and indicated to Green that he should sit down and eat. Then she poured him a cup of black coffee. 'For you,' she said smiling. 'I too... *juste un peu Anglais*, no?'

She left him alone with his meal and he heard her angrily address someone in another part of the house. From his limited knowledge of French, he understood she was organizing a hot bath. A few minutes later, she returned with a large brown towel and a cake of soap in her arms. She pointed at the door that led to the rear of the house. 'For you,' she said, '*le bain.*'

Green went to the door. A diminutive paved courtyard created by the walls of the neighbouring buildings provided a small back yard to Madame Claire's house. To one side of the area was a clothesline where Blucher's and his uniforms were hanging; on the other, an ancient and gnarled walnut tree strove to reach the sky. The rear partition of the courtyard was provided by a creeper covered wall in which a single window was set high. Backing on to Madame Claire's building was a rather shabby lean-to structure with a smoking chimney. Green assumed this was the laundry, and a few paces from that, a small stand-alone structure that was obviously the toilet. However, his eye was quickly drawn to the middle of the courtyard where a metal bathtub sat in singular splendour. A gentle cloud of steam was slowly rising, from the tub, and another woman, a housemaid Green assumed, was in the process of pouring yet another bucket of hot water into it.

Madame Claire thrust the towel and soap toward Green and gestured toward the bathtub. *'Le bain* for you,' she repeated. *'Vite, vite.* You, how you say... *odeur,'* and she held her nose in pantomime to emphasise her point.

Green took the towel and soap and approached the bath; he had no doubt he smelled—even Law had suggested he needed to bathe. He was so filthy he could actually feel the dirt cracking on his skin when he moved. He dipped a finger into the water; it was luxuriously hot. He looked back toward the house where Madame Claire stood watching, still gesturing for him to get in to the bath. He didn't mind bathing in the open, but he was damned if he was going to take his bath robe off in front of Madame Claire.

He gestured toward her. 'Please Madame, turn around.'

Madame Claire continued to stare.

Green wracked his brain. What on earth was the French for turn around? Ah yes, that was it. *'S'il vous plaît madame, tourner autour.'*

Madame Claire laughed at his modesty, but she turned and went back inside the house, closing the door behind her. The house maid was nowhere to be seen.

Green disrobed and climbed into the tub, gently lowering himself into the water. It was almost too hot to bear, but eventually he sank down until only his head remained above the steaming water. For a few magnificent minutes, he relaxed and allowed the heat to relieve tired and stiffened muscles and to gently soak his skin clean. For a moment, he felt guilty as he thought of the men of the 3 Brigade who were now being withdrawn from the front to rest. He doubted they would be afforded the kind of treatment he and Blucher now enjoyed. He recalled the Bath Units, the military equivalent of a communal bath house that had greeted the ANZACs after their withdrawal from Gallipoli. It had been so undignified, lines of naked men standing on slippery duckboards showering beneath a few minutes of tepid water. He had no doubt that would be the nature of the facilities afforded the Brigade.

'How's it going?' Blucher interrupted Green's reflections.

'Bloody beautiful,' Green replied. 'Have you had one?'

'Earlier.' Blucher replied.

Green sat up. 'Where did you sleep last night, young fellow?' he asked.

Blucher grinned. 'In Madame Claire's room,' he said.

'Really? You're a bloody fast worker, young Blucher. How did you manage that?'

Blucher grinned sheepishly. 'Must be my animal magnetism,' he replied.

'Well, you must keep it well hidden,' sighed Green. 'I'm buggered if I can see what she'd see in you.'

'Well, first in best dressed,' Blucher replied. 'You don't mind, do you? I'm sure you'll find some pretty young mademoiselle soon enough.'

Green laughed. 'Good luck to you mate, and don't worry about me. I'm a big boy—I can look after myself.'

'I'll leave you to it,' said Blucher. 'Don't forget to wash behind your ears.'

Green splashed a handful of water at him. 'Get your girlfriend to check your ear,' he retorted. 'If that wound gets infected, I'll put you on a bloody fizzer!'

Mumbling obscenities against all overzealous NCOs, Blucher returned to the house.

Once again, Green sank back into the water. It amused him to think that three eventful days ago, he considered Blucher to be a useless, ill-mannered prick, and now he counted him as a close friend. Even so as much as he hated to admit it, he was in fact more than a little envious of the additional benefits Madame Claire was providing Blucher. He pondered Blucher's good fortune and his own lack of feminine company:

He had never had much luck with women. Before the war, back home at the parties and dances his parent's organized, he had always been the shy one. He had lacked the confidence to ask a girl to dance, and had spent most of those social occasions sitting watching from the chairs that invariably lined the side of the dance floor. The colour of his skin was another complication and most of the young ladies to whom he had been attracted were warned off by their protective parents who wanted to ensure their daughters did not finish up with a half-caste. It was the same after he'd enlisted; the women he had been brought up to view as the "nice" ones wanted nothing to do with a coloured man.

There had been one exception. He had met that particular lady during his first leave from Broadmeadows camp. She was an unhappily married Melbourne woman who had taken him to her bed to spite her husband. It was a brief affair. After several illicit meetings, the woman had told her husband of the liaison and the husband had informed the police.

Green counted himself lucky that the incident was handled by a more understanding member of the constabulary, for after administering a few well aimed blows with his truncheon to Green's back, so the bruises were not so obvious, the policeman told his fallen victim what would happen to him, if ever he should visit that particular lady again. A quick kick to Green's stomach emphasized this point.

'You've seen 'em geld colts, darkie?' the policeman asked threateningly.

Green had managed a painful groan to signify his assent.

'Good, good boy, and that's just what will happen to you if ever I hear of you playing up again.' The policeman's tone changed as he helped Green to his feet. 'You ought to know better, young fellow,' he concluded soothingly. 'Stick with your own kind. White women are not for the likes of you!'

Green suspected that the police had passed word of his transgression on to the Army, for without the usual benefit of pre-embarkation leave, he suddenly found himself on the list of reinforcements next to sail for the Middle East. He had in fact welcomed the early departure, not because it removed the threat of castration, but because he felt reasonably confident that once overseas the Army would not discharge him on the basis of the colour of his skin. However, it was during that long sea voyage that he decided that women were the very devil and that while he was away, he would avoid all contact with the fairer sex and instead immerse himself in his military training.

He sat up in the bath. Had his self-imposed celibate lifestyle really been worth the trouble? Certainly, he had avoided the pox in Egypt, but after the evacuation, when he had arrived in England, he had thought perhaps he might have met a nice girl and let things develop from there. Somehow it had never happened. Not that he lacked opportunity, for the pubs near the School and London seemed to be full of ladies of easy virtue, but none of these held any interest for him. He just could not see the point to commencing any kind of a relationship, but there were times, like now, as he considered Blucher's luck with Madame Claire, when he wished... 'You're a mug, Green,' he said bitterly to the empty courtyard, 'only good at shooting straight. Women are better off without you.'

A small bird flew down and sat at the end of the bathtub, from where it regarded Green through beady eyes. He flicked some water at it, but the bird turned its back to him and defecated into the bathwater, then it flew away. 'You little bastard,' cried Green angrily. He lunged toward the floating blob of excreta trying to scoop it from the bath and missed. The wave of water created by his sudden movement propelled the mess toward him threatening to attach itself to his chest. Finally, he managed to fling it over the side. Relieved at the narrowness of his escape, he tried once more to relax back into the warmth of the water, but the bird had spoiled the occasion for him and he prepared to climb out of the tub. However, as he stood up, he became aware of the sounds of giggling coming from the direction of the courtyard's end wall. Looking up, he saw that his nakedness was being observed by a bevy of young women who had gathered at the window in the ivy-covered wall. Quickly he covered his manhood with his hands and grinning sheepishly turned his back to their gaze, he stepped out of the bath, scooped up his towel, and fled toward the house. Shrieks of feminine delight and ribald comments followed his retreat, and from his basic understanding of the French language, he knew they were offering a critique of his bare backside and his legs.

He managed to avoid Blucher and Madame Claire and gained the sanctuary of the attic where he found his uniform, now clean and neatly ironed, had been laid out neatly on the bed. He dressed and went downstairs to the kitchen.

Madame Claire was busy at the stove and Blucher was seated at the table eating. 'Some kind of stew,' he said as Green entered the room. 'Do you want some? It's bloody good.'

Green shook his head. 'I'm still full from breakfast,' he said.

'You weren't in the bath long,' Blucher commented. 'I stayed in for almost an hour.'

Green scowled. 'A bloody bird crapped in the water,' he complained.

Blucher laughed. 'There is a lesson in that,' he said, 'but I'm not sure what it is.'

Madame Claire had begun to spoon some of the stew on to a plate, her smile indicating that this serving was for Green. He held up a hand. 'Ah no, Madame,' he said waving the plate away. 'I have had sufficient, er what's the word... *suffisament.*'

Madame Claire looked disappointed, but with a shrug she scrapped the stew back into the pot.

Blucher was impressed. 'I didn't know you spoke Frog, Sarg,' he said.

Green laughed. 'God, Blucher, you don't speak French and she doesn't speak much English. How the hell do you make out in the bedroom?'

Blucher slid an arm around Madame Claire's ample hips. 'She's a good girl, Sarg,' he said. 'She cooks and she...'

'I don't want to know anymore,' Green interrupted. 'Now listen, while we are on leave and living in the same house, you'd better call me Rob, or Bob—I don't care which, but if you want a long life, don't ever call me "Killer."'

Blucher grinned happily. 'Thanks Bob,' he replied, 'I

appreciate that.'

Green grunted an acknowledgement. 'I think I'll go for a walk downtown,' he said, 'and leave you two love birds alone.'

'Are you sure?' Blucher asked anxiously. 'I can come if you like.'

'No mate, you stay here. I'll just walk about a bit. I've got my leave form… make sure you take yours if you go out anywhere.'

Madame Claire understood enough of the conversation to know that she was going to be left alone with Blucher and she was clearly happy at the prospect. She snuggled up to him, sitting on his knee and kissing his neck around his wounded ear. Her behaviour made Green feel uncomfortable and making his excuses he left the table, and pulling his battered slouch onto his head, stepped out into the street.

He began to walk in no particular direction and soon discovered Madam Claire's house was one street back from the river Somme, and not far from the Cathedral of Amiens. The riverbank appeared to be the habitat of well-dressed ladies pushing prams and the occasional couple walking arm in arm. It was not the setting Green desired and so while the cathedral itself held no attraction for him, assuming it must be closer to the town centre, he began to walk in that direction. The streets of Amiens were just as busy as they had been during his first brief visit to the town. The civilian population were going about their daily business. Intermingled with that crowd were British, French, and Australian soldiers taking in the sights, and talking to the local girls. He leaned against a wall and watched the crowded sea of humanity wash backward and forward before him. Then just as he had decided to move on, he was approached by a military policeman.

'Leave pass please, sergeant.'

Green produced his pass. The military policeman checked the pass, found it in order, and with an air of disappointment handed it back before walking away.

Twenty paces further down the street, Green was accosted by another member of the Military Police and then a few minutes later yet another. Their constant attention was beginning to spoil his day, so he decided to find another neighbourhood where the over officious Red Caps were less numerous.

Following a side street, he found his way back to the pleasant boulevard that skirted the river. It was lined on one side with various eateries and on the other with paved stones edging the river. He selected a café that did not appear to be too busy, and sat down at a corner table to watch the world go by. A waiter attended him and not from any need for food or drink, he ordered a glass of wine.

The waiter brought the wine and a small loaf of bread. Green paid him, and thoughtfully sipped his wine. His short time in France had been nothing if not eventful, and he began to give some thought to the real reason for his being there. He had never before carried out what amounted to a political assignation and the idea both excited and appalled him.

'Sergeant Green?'

Green turned toward the sound of the voice, surprised that anyone knew him. A tall and very attractive woman, French by her accent, was walking across the restaurant floor toward him. She was hatless, her dark hair cut in an avant-garde bob ,and she wore a blue crinoline skirt, the kind of style that war shortages had made fashionable. The woman's face was vaguely familiar, but for the life of him, Green could not place where he had seen her before.

She stopped in front of Green's table and stood hands on

hips regarding him mockingly. 'Ah, you do not remember me! How quickly men forget!'

Suddenly, Green recognised her and rose clumsily to his feet. 'Madame Sainson? I'm sorry, I didn't recognise you out of your uniform.'

'May I sit down?'

'Of course,' Green pulled back the spare chair and held it for her.

'I did not expect to see you here,' she said as she sat down.

Green resumed his seat. 'I didn't expect to be here,' he replied.

'And your companion?'

'Blucher, yes, he's here too, but he has stayed at our billet.'

'When did you arrive?'

'Yesterday, in the late afternoon. And you?'

'The day before,' she said. 'I am visiting my aunt and uncle. They are old and the fighting has frightened them, so I have taken leave to care for them.'

'I see,' Green replied. 'We are on leave too. I think we have about fourteen days, and you?'

'The extent of my leave has yet to be determined, but I think I will be here for some weeks.'

'Would you like some wine?'

'No, thank you.'

The conversation died and for several long moments, they sat in silence. Finally, Madame Sainson spoke. 'I heard the battle has been very terrible,' she said. 'Are you all right?'

'Fine, I'm fine, a little tired, but that's all really. Were you close by?'

'Quite close,' her voice became flat and very matter of fact. 'My ambulance was blown up at the Chalk Pit. My driver was killed along with the men we had picked up. All blown to atoms in an instant, I was lucky I was treating another man in a dugout when it occurred.'

'I'm sorry,' said Green.

'It was bound to happen,' she said. 'It was our sixth trip for the day. Everyone's luck runs out in the end.'

'Yes,' Green replied quietly, 'I believe it does.'

Madame Sainson shrugged. 'But so far,' she said, 'you and I we are still lucky, eh?' She rose to leave. 'I must go. I am buying fish for my uncle and aunt's dinner, and if I don't hurry the shop will be closed. It's been lovely to see you again. Be lucky, Sergeant.'

Green stood up and suddenly he was stumbling over his words, blushing furiously, and his heart racing alarmingly. 'Look,' he stammered, 'I'm at a bit of a loose end, I don't know anyone in town and I... I was wondering if you would like to have dinner with me.'

Madame Sainson resumed her seat. 'I'd like that,' she said quietly. 'I'd like that very much.' Suddenly, she clapped her hands with delight. 'I know,' she said, 'we can eat at my uncle's house. You may bring Blucher too if you wish.'

Green grinned. 'I believe Blucher may have other plans, Madame,' he replied.

'Oh, that's a pity, but perhaps it will be better. Oh, and you must call me Stephanie. Madame Sainson sounds so... how do you say... stuffy. Besides, we are old friends, so it's quite proper.'

Green laughed. 'Thank you, my first name is Robert. My mates call me Rob.'

'I like Robert better. Will you mind if I call you Robert?'

Her accent exaggerated the "r" and the "b" of his name; Green liked it. 'Of course not,' he replied.

'Walk with me now, Robert. I will buy the fish and you can

carry it home for me. That way, you will see where I am staying.'

The fish monger was quite close by. Stephanie selected two large carp. 'The war has made food very expensive,' she told Green as she paid for the fish. 'But the River Somme has always plenty of carp, so they are not too dear.'

Green took the parcel of fish and they left the shop. 'I've never seen carp before,' he said. 'We don't have them in Australia. We have lots of other fish though, but not carp.'

'It is a strange fish,' Stephanie explained, 'because it lives in the mud one has to prepare it carefully or it will not taste well. After they are caught, the fish monger keeps them in a bathtub for several days with no food so that they clean themselves out.'

Green was amazed. 'Alive in a bathtub, with no food?' he asked.

'That's right. He would have killed these just before we got to his shop.'

'Poor bloody fish.'

'Ah well, we will respect its great sacrifice by preparing it beautifully for the table.'

They reached a street intersection. 'We turn down here,' Stephanie said. 'My uncle's house is the second on the left; do you see it?'

'Yes.'

'Do you think you can find your way here by say half past six?'

'Of course, but shouldn't you ask your uncle and aunt first?'

'They will be delighted to see you,' Stephanie replied.

Green wondered about that. Even if their niece was in the habit of bringing soldiers home for dinner, he doubted an Aboriginal man had ever graced their table before. However, he kept his thoughts to himself and instead asked, 'Should I bring anything?'

Stephanie smiled. 'Just yourself,' she replied. She stood on tip toe and kissed him lightly on the cheek, then walked briskly away down the street. On reaching the house, she paused briefly at the door to wave, and then she disappeared inside.

Chapter 18

Blucher was highly amused when Green told him of his dinner date with Madame Sainson. 'I knew you were soft on her!' he said gleefully. 'How did you find her?'

'Mate, it was a complete accident, and before you start, there's nothing to it. We met up and she asked me to have dinner at her uncle's house. Besides, she's a married woman.'

'Oh yeah, I forgot she's a Madame. Ah well, mate, so is Claire, but it hasn't slowed her down!'

Green had no desire to indulge Blucher with any further information regarding Stephanie, or to listen to his exposé on Madame Claire's assets. So making the excuse that he had to write a report for Lieutenant Colonel Law, he retired to his room in the attic.

The hours until the time Green was due to meet Stephanie took an age to pass. He had nothing to read and he was unable to sleep. Several times he convinced himself that it would be best if he stood her up and hid in his bedroom. But each time, the pleasure he felt at meeting her again under such unexpected circumstances prevailed, and in the end he determined to keep the date.

He walked the distance back to Stephanie's uncle's house in a state of nervous anxiety. He paused briefly at a flower stall and purchased a small posy of daisies, unsure if he would give them to Stephanie or her aunt. Then right on time, he knocked at the door.

A grey-haired man with a finely trimmed moustache

opened the door. 'Ah,' he said in perfect English with just the hint of a French accent, 'you must be Robert. Come in, come in. I am Henri.'

Henri assured Green through the doorway. 'This is my wife, Micheline,' he said.

'Good evening, Madame,' Green said, and making an instant decision handed Madame Micheline the flowers.

Madame Micheline beamed with pleasure. 'Welcome, Sergeant,' she said. 'Stephanie has already told me so much about you.'

Green blushed. 'I hope it has been complimentary,' he quipped.

Stephanie came out from the kitchen to greet him. 'Should it be?' she said mockingly. 'He did not even remember me this afternoon!'

'Leave the poor man alone,' directed Madame Micheline. 'Come into the parlour, my dear, and leave this brazen woman to prepare our meal.'

The evening was a most enjoyable affair. The meal was excellent. Stephanie had made a carp casserole, which she served with a salad, green peas, potatoes, and a variety of herbs. There followed a desert of rhubarb pie. Conversation was pleasant and studiously avoided any discussion of the war, and at the end of the meal Henri produced a very drinkable port to go with coffee and cake.

After the meal, while Stephanie and Henri cleared the table, Madame Micheline guided Green back into the parlour.

She took a seat beside Green and leaned inquiringly toward him. 'Tell me about yourself, Robert,' she asked directly.

Green found that he was suddenly nervous. 'Well, there is really not much to tell,' he began. 'I'm from a little place in Australia called Penola. My father owns a large sheep and cattle property near there.'

'And you have joined the army and come all this way to fight the enemies of France,' the older woman said with great admiration. 'So many of your young men have come and such a long way.'

Green smiled. 'I stopped off at a couple of other places along the way,' he said.

'And will you go back after the war?' she asked.

Green pondered the question for a moment. 'I suppose so,' he said thoughtfully. 'I don't like to think too far ahead at the moment.'

Madame Micheline nodded sadly. 'I understand,' she said. With an effort, she forced a smile and proposed a new topic of conversation. 'Now, what do you want to know about Stephanie?'

Before Green could answer, Stephanie and Henri entered the room. Stephanie raised her hands to her cheeks in mock horror. 'Aunty!' she scalded, 'don't you dare!'

Madame Micheline regarded her niece smugly. 'Have you anything to hide, my girl?' she asked. Then turning to Green, she added, 'Do you know she is twenty-seven years old?'

Green smiled. 'The same age as myself,' he replied.

Henri stepped in, fearful of any further revelations. 'I think,' he said, 'we should leave these two people, alone my dear.'

Madame Micheline winked at Green. 'Yes, I suppose we should.' She held out a hand to Green. 'Good night, Robert, I hope we will meet you again.'

Green took her hand. 'Thank you for a wonderful evening,' he said. 'You too, sir,' he said to Henri. 'I have thoroughly enjoyed myself.'

When the older couple left the room, Stephanie came and sat beside Green on the sofa. 'That casserole was magnificent,' he said. 'How did you cook it?'

Stephanie shrugged. 'It is a very simple dish,' she replied. 'I cut up perhaps about three cups of the fish, the same amount of potatoes, some onion, butter, herbs, milk, juice of a lemon, two eggs, and let me see, what else? Ah, yes, salt and pepper and then it all went in the oven for a little over thirty, no forty minutes.'

'That does not sound so simple to me,' Green said admiringly. 'I think besides being a skilled nurse, you are a very good cook.'

Stephanie smiled with pleasure. 'Thank you,' she said, 'I'm glad you enjoyed it.'

During the hour that followed, Green and Stephanie talked incessantly, but had they been asked later what they had talked about, both would have struggled to answer. They would, however, have been able to state quite categorically that they held similar views on almost everything, and that by the end of the evening, each had developed an awareness that their friendship was on the verge of becoming something far more intimate. Then Green glanced at his wristwatch. 'Good heavens,' he said, 'It's late,' he announced unnecessarily. 'I should go.'

Stephanie placed a restraining hand on his arm. 'Must you?' she asked. 'I've really enjoyed this night'.

'I have too,' Green replied, 'but yes, I must go... someone needs to check on Blucher and Madame Claire.'

'Really?'

'No, not really, but I should still go.'

'Can I see you again?'

It was a question Green had contemplated asking himself, but hearing it come from Stephanie, the image of his previous affair with the other married woman in Melbourne suddenly appeared before him as a terrifyingly insurmountable barrier. When he replied, his tone was harsher than he intended. 'What about your husband?' he asked.

Stephanie hung her head. 'Oh Robert,' she said quietly, 'I thought you knew. My husband is dead. He was killed earlier this year at Verdun.'

For Green the night seemed to grow suddenly chill. 'I'm sorry,' he said, 'I didn't know.'

Stephanie was weeping. 'I thought perhaps Aunty Micheline had told you.'

'No, no, she didn't.'

'So you see, I am not a bad woman, not unfaithful.'

'I never thought...'

'But you did...'

Green hung his head. 'I'd better go,' he said. 'Thanks for the meal. I enjoyed it. 'He turned and walked away, but he had hardly taken a dozen steps when he heard the sound of running feet and turning was just in time to catch Stephanie in his arms.

'I'm sorry,' she sobbed, 'please be my friend, Robert.'

'Easy, easy,' he whispered into her hair, 'easy now. We are friends; we'll always be friends.'

'There's so little time; you'll go back soon. I may never see you again.'

'I'll see you tomorrow. What time do you get up?'

'I can meet you at ten,' she replied eagerly, 'at the same café?'

Green nodded. 'We can spend the whole day together.'

'And the night?'

'The night too,' he replied, kissing the top of her head, 'but tonight... I'll walk you back to your door.'

They said a brief goodnight and Green walked back along

the streets to Madame Claire's house. He was relieved to find that Blucher and Madame Claire had retired early and were not waiting to quiz him on details of his evening. He tiptoed past Madame Claire's bedroom, smiling at the duet of snoring emitting from behind the door. He reached the attic and was about to open the door, when he heard a soft knocking on the front door. Retracing his footsteps back downstairs, he cautiously opened the door.

It was Stephanie. Quickly and silently, he drew her inside. He held a fore finger to his mouth, signalling her to be silent. Then taking her hand, he led the way upstairs to his room.

As soon as he closed the bedroom door, Stephanie threw her arms around his neck and kissed him. Gently, he pushed her away. 'You're uncle and aunt?' he asked.

Stephanie blushed. 'They sent me to you,' she replied. 'Do you think I'm shameless?'

Green smiled. 'Brazen!' he replied. 'As bold as brass!'

'I don't care,' she pouted.

'Neither do I,' he said, drawing her back into his arms.

They kissed again, this time with greater intensity. Green felt her tongue probing his mouth, her hands pulling him on to her. Almost fearfully he allowed his hands to wander over her body, her back, her hips, her breasts. She emitted little sighs of pleasure at each exploration, but sensing his shyness, she stepped away and quickly unfastened her blouse and skirt, allowing the garments to fall to the floor revealing a delicate cream petticoat. Green was completely mesmerized and stood wordlessly staring at her.

'You have me at a disadvantage,' she said nervously.

Her words broke Green's enchantment and he furiously tore at his own clothing. His tunic and shirt were cast aside and as he bent forward to remove his puttees and boots, Stephanie came up behind him and leaning over his back moulded her body to his. She was naked. Green tried to straighten up, but she held him: 'Boots first,' she whispered into the dark skin of his back.

He flung off the puttees and then carefully, so as not to knot the laces, unfastened each boot. He stood up and turned around. Stephanie was holding her hands in front of her face as Green looked on her naked body. He had never been with a totally naked woman before. The woman in Melbourne had always worn a heavy night gown that was buttoned up to the neck, tied off at each wrist, and only lifted sufficiently once they had been safely under the covers of her bed. Now he looked in wonder at Stephanie's breasts, the tufts of hair that peeped out from her arm pits, her slender waist, and the delicate triangle of hair covering the place where her legs met. She shivered as he reached out and touched her, running his fingers over her skin.

Reaching out, she unfastened his trousers. He stepped out of the garment and gasped as she placed a hand on his manhood where it strained against the fabric of his underwear. 'These must come off,' she announced firmly.

In a moment, he too was completely naked; then she took his hand and gently led him to the bed.

Afterwards, they lay beside each other holding hands and talking quietly.

'How did you know where I was billeted?' asked Green.

'You told me your landlady was Madame Claire. She is a friend of my aunty.'

Green laughed. 'Your uncle and aunt are wicked,' he said. 'Not only do they encourage you, but they knew where I lived. I had no chance, did I?'

Stephanie slapped him playfully on the chest. 'None at all,' she said. Then she grew quiet and serious. 'No chance from the moment I first saw you.'

Rolling toward her, Green took her in his arms. 'Neither did you,' he said, 'but I never thought I'd see you again.'

They made love again. This time in a slower, more deliberate way, until at last their movements terminated in a paroxysm of sensation that left them both breathless.

Stephanie propped herself up on one elbow and idly traced a finger over Green's chest. "You are not very hairy,' she remarked.

'Compared with?' asked Green sleepily.

'Oh, my husband,' she mused, 'and one other man, a long time ago.' Her finger outlined one of his nipples, which hardened in response to her exploration. 'I don't do this kind of thing often, you know!'

Green laughed. 'Believe it or not, neither do I!'

She quickly straddled him, a knee either side of his body, her rump resting on his stomach so that he could feel the wetness of her sex upon his skin. 'Tell me how many women have you pleasured, my lovely Sergeant?' she demanded playfully.

Green was suddenly serious. 'Only one,' he replied, 'back in Melbourne. It meant nothing, well to her at least. Since then, there's been no one.' He laughed and reached to take the weight of her breasts in his hands. "You, my girl, have caused me to break my own rule... no women, only war.'

'Ah hah! And is that a bad thing?' she asked, sliding her rump back toward his wakening manhood. 'Think carefully before you answer, my Sergeant.'

Green shook his head. 'No, Madame, it is certainly not a bad thing.' Then with a deft movement, he was once again within her.

For a time they slept, still entwined from their love making. The squeaking of the attic door hinge woke Green and before he could utter a word, the door opened and Blucher entered the room. He immediately turned away, embarrassed at their nakedness. Green tried to flick the bed sheet over Stephanie's sleeping form.

'Oh shit, mate,' whispered Blucher, 'I'm sorry!' He turned and left the room. 'I'll tell Claire there'll be one extra for breakfast,' he called from the landing.

Green got out of bed and draping a towel around himself, walked to the door. 'Thanks mate, see you down there in five minutes.'

Blucher lingered for a moment. 'Is that the nurse?' he asked incredulously.

'Yes, it is. Now piss off, Blucher.'

'I told you she was soft on you!'

'As a matter of fact, you said I was soft on her.'

'Well, I was right, eh?'

'Piss off Blucher, go get breakfast ready.'

'All right, all right, keep your shirt on. See you in five minutes.'

Green returned to the attic and closed the door. Gently, he leaned over Stephanie and kissed her mouth. She stirred, opened her eyes, and for a moment seemed confused by her surroundings. Then she reached up and taking his face between her hands, pressed her lips hungrily to his mouth.

'You are real,' she said. 'For a moment, I thought it all a dream.'

'It would have been some dream,' laughed Green. He pulled back the covers and playfully slapped her on the rump. 'Do you often have dreams like that?'

'Oh, you beast!' she cried, jumping from the bed and

chasing him around the room.

A knock on the door sent them both scrambling back to bed, pulling the covers up under their chins.

'Come in,' called Green.

Madame Claire entered the room carrying a large tray containing a plate of croissants, a dish of jam, and two cups. A grinning Blucher followed her bearing a steaming pot of coffee.

'Breakfast,' Madame Claire announced grandly. She placed the tray on the side table and then kissed Stephanie on the cheek. She began to weep, rattling off a string of French between her sobs that Green could not understand, and she kissed Stephanie again and again.

'She says,' Stephanie interpreted, 'that she is happy for me. She was very sad when my husband died, and now she says I will be all right and that you are a good man.'

Green inclined his head toward Madame Claire, '*Merci Madame…*' he tried to find the French words to say that he would indeed look after Stephanie, but failed. 'Tell her I'll care for you.'

'There is no need,' replied Stephanie shyly. 'She knows already.'

Blucher poured two cups of coffee. 'There you go, Madame,' he said, 'no milk this morning I'm afraid.'

'Hello Blucher,' said Stephanie. 'It is good to see you again.'

'Likewise, Madame,' Blucher replied. 'I knew we'd catch up again; you two had a certain something about you. It's like you were made for each other.'

Stephanie blushed. 'Thank you, Blucher,' she said. 'That's very kind.'

From the cover of the blanket Green silently fumed.

Madame Claire sensed Blucher had probably said too much and scalding him gently in rapid French she pushed him toward the door. *'Laisse les deux doux coeurs seuls.'*

Stephanie once again translated for Green. 'She said he should leave the two sweethearts alone. Are we sweethearts, Robert?'

Green took her in his arms. 'Yes, love,' he said, 'I reckon we are.'

Stephanie snuggled into his protective embrace. 'I must go and check on Henri and Micheline,' she said. 'Will you come with me?'

'Yes, of course.'

She snuggled into him again. 'What will we do then?'

Green shrugged. 'Rest?' he suggested.

'In bed?'

Green lent forward and kissed the top of her head. 'That,' he said, 'sounds like a plan.'

Chapter 19

Sunlight stole silently through the window and across the bedroom floor, gently caressing the bed with its warming rays, heralding the start of their second day together.

Stephanie woke in Green's arms.

'Did you sleep well?' he murmured into the top of her head.

'She shook her head. 'Too many dreams,' she whispered in reply.

Green kissed her forehead. 'I know,' he said sadly, 'we all have them.'

Stephanie sat up. *'Nous allons seulement avoir des pensées heureuses!'* she said firmly, then translated her words for him. 'We will only have happy thoughts.' She sat up and the blanket fell from her body. Green was transfixed by the sight of her naked breasts and firm white belly. "Ah no, no, no! You naughty boy,' she laughed. 'I know what your happy thoughts are!'

'You were the one who said she wanted to spend the whole of my leave in bed,' he replied.

Stephanie slid from the bed. 'Not this morning,' she said. This morning, I will show you my town!'

'Could it wait for ten minutes?' he asked in a pleading tone.

'Only ten minutes?' she replied mockingly as she climbed back onto the bed.

Sometime later, after they had dressed and taken coffee with Madame Claire and Blucher, Stephanie took Green's hand and together they went to explore the town.

'Now remember,' she reminded Green, '*nous allons seulement avoir des pensées heureuses.*'

Out in the street, the rumble of distant artillery fire was clearly audible and Green immediately tensed.

'It's only thunder,' Stephanie said soothingly.

'It's bloody not, you know!' he replied anxiously.

'It is today, my love,' she pleaded. 'Please Robert, today, just for today, it is thunder.'

With an effort, Green forced himself to relax. 'My, my,' he said with great affectation as they resumed their stroll, 'it looks like rain.'

The sky was cloudless.

Stephanie was not to be deterred; still holding his hand, she skipped ahead. 'Welcome to my town,' she said, waving her free hand in a broad sweep toward the buildings. 'I hope you will enjoy your stay.'

'Seems like a nice enough place,' Green replied. 'What are the women like?'

'Pig,' she chided him sulkily.

He laughed and pulled her back to walk beside him.

'We must go and visit *la Cathedral e de'Amiens,*' Stephanie announced, pointing toward the impressive tower.

'Must we?' Green held a jaundiced opinion of religion.

'Yes we must.' Stephanie's reply had an air of finality. 'I wish to pray for your safety, and for other things.'

'What other things?' Green asked cheekily.

Stephanie blushed. 'Private things,' she replied, 'things for God and me alone.'

Green laughed. 'Well, I'll settle for my safety for now,' he said. 'Lead on.'

It was a five-minute walk to the Cathedral and in spite of himself, Green found he was in awe of the magnificent structure and the beauty of the art it contained. A tinkle of bells indicated that High Mass was being conducted in the main body of the Cathedral. Stephanie covered her head with a scarf. 'Will you wait for me here?' she asked.

'I won't move,' Green promised.

Ten minutes later, she was back. 'I have asked the Saint to protect us both,' she said.

'Good,' said Green, 'but I think so far as I'm concerned, he will have his work cut out for him.'

'*Je ne comprends pas,*' she said anxiously.

'It's nothing love,' he replied quickly, 'just the war. Where to next?'

They walked back to the river. 'I used to visit here in Amiens often as a little girl,' she told him as they strolled along the bank. 'I was an only child,' she said, 'and when I was growing up, my mother was often ill. My father was an engineer and frequently worked away from home, so Uncle Henri and Aunty Micheline looked after me. I even went to school here for a time.'

'It must have been a good time for you,' said Green.

'Not always,' said Stephanie. 'See that orchard over there,' she pointed across the river. 'My friends and I once got into terrible trouble there for stealing fruit.'

'Oh my God,' cried Green in mock alarm, 'I'm consorting with a known criminal!'

'We all received a good beating,' continued Stephanie ruefully, 'but I can honestly say that since that day, I have never stolen anything.'

'Not even a kiss?' laughed Green.

'Oh, I'm not counting those,' she replied cheekily. 'After all, if I share a kiss with someone, that's hardly stealing, is it?'

They kissed and were greeted with a series of whistles and

other encouragement from passing soldiers.

Red faced, but beaming with happiness, hand in hand, they walked on.

Blucher was waiting when they reached the house. His face creased with worry, and he drew Green aside. 'I've just met a bloke down the street,' he began quietly. 'He says he wants to meet you, but he's a nosey sort of a bastard so I told him I didn't know where you were. He seemed to be happy with that, but I left Claire back there to keep an eye on him.'

Green shrugged. 'What's he selling?'

'No he's not a salesman. He's a Digger, name of Bazley. He says he's the batman for that war correspondent bloke Bean.'

'Never heard of him,' replied Green.

'You must have heard of Bean; he was at Gallipoli, sent all kinds of stories back home about the fighting.'

'Oh, I've heard of *him* all right, but not the other bloke.'

Blucher shook his head with exasperation. 'The point is,' he continued, 'I thought that whatever it is we are supposed to be doing here is supposed to be secret. How come this bastard knows you are here, let alone why he should want to talk to you?'

Green was immediately serious. 'You're right, of course. You can bet London to a brick Bean is the one who wants to talk, and the last thing we can afford is to become front-page news.'

'So what do we do?'

'I'll have to think about that, but first let's see if Claire has found out where this fellow is staying.'

'Okay, I'll nip back and find her.'

When Blucher had gone, Stephanie came and put her arms around Green's shoulders. 'Problems?' she asked.

'Hmm... Yes, perhaps.' He glanced up at her anxiously.

'Now there is a fellow downtown somewhere, a war correspondent. Bean's his name, and it seems he might want to interview me. You see, I came to his attention when I was at Gallipoli, and he will be curious as to why I'm here in France, seeing as how the Division I belong to is still in England. Ordinarily, there would be nothing wrong with giving Bean a story, but this fellow has some strange ideas. For instance, he seems to believe the AIF should be an all British force, with races such as the Jews and people like me excluded. Now so far as I am concerned, there is not a lot he can do about me, but my General is a man named Monash, and he is a Jew. Given half a chance, Bean will do all he can to discredit Monash and he would not be above using me to do that.'

'Why don't you just keep away from him?'

'I could, but then he will be even more curious. He might even make something up.'

'How can you stop him?'

'I will arrange to meet him and give him a story he should find believable."

'Will he believe you?'

'I think so, but he will try and find out more. The Army made him an honorary captain, so maybe he will try to use his rank to provoke me in the hope I'll become careless and let something slip.'

'Oh my God!' Stephanie cried in sudden alarm. 'What about Blucher? I like him very much, but he is not as smart as you. What if this man interviews him?'

Green held up a silencing hand. 'Don't worry, Bean won't bother with anyone with a name like Blucher... German, you see, another one that doesn't quite fit his ideal for the Aussie Digger.'

'Can I do anything?'

Green thought for a moment. 'Maybe,' he replied. 'For all his faults, this fellow is a gentleman, a snob, but a gentleman. Perhaps if you were to come along with me, it might put him off his stroke.' He was silent for a moment considering the possibility and then he frowned. 'Yes, I think you coming along would probably work, but it might not be very pleasant. You see, Bean would be shocked that a white woman could lower herself to be stepping out with a half-caste Aboriginal man.'

Stephanie bust into a gale of deep throaty laughter. 'Is that what you call it?' she said when she could at last speak. 'Stepping out... I thought we have been doing rather more than stepping out, my darling!'

Green blushed. 'I don't think we need to provide any greater detail,' he replied defensively.

'Well regardless,' Stephanie continued taking his hands in hers, 'I will come with you and let this Mister Bean do his worst.'

Blucher and Claire returned to announce they had found that Bean was staying at the Grand Hotel. 'What do we do now?' Blucher asked.

'You and Claire stay here and lay low,' Green replied. 'Stephanie and I will visit the Grand Hotel. We'll be back soon and then I'll tell you all about Captain Bean.'

It was a leisurely ten-minute stroll to the Grand Hotel. It was one of the better establishments in the town, but the war had left it showing signs of wear. In spite of this, it remained a popular meeting place and the hotel lobby was crowded with soldiers from a variety of allied nations and of a variety of ranks, making a colourful and noisy crowd.

Green escorted Stephanie to the reception desk. The concierge made a hasty assumption regarding Green's purpose and held up a warning hand. 'I am sorry Sergeant—we have no rooms available.'

'I don't want a room, sport,' Green replied curtly. 'Can you find Captain Bean for me please?'

'Ah Monsieur Bean, but of course, please wait over there,' the concierge pointed at a couch. 'I will have him sent for at once.'

A few minutes later, an Australian private soldier approached the couch where Green and Stephanie were seated. 'Good afternoon, Sergeant,' he said. 'I'm Private Bazley, Captain Bean's batman. I understand you wish to see the Captain?'

Green did not bother to stand. 'Not particularly,' he replied, 'but I understand he wants to see me.'

'And you are Sergeant…?'

'Green.'

Bazley frowned. 'Ah yes, Sergeant Green. I shall just go and tell the Captain you have arrived.'

The Hotel had provided Bean with a large room on the first floor. In deference to his position as a war correspondent and his honorary rank, they did not relet the room while he made his many forays to the front. Bean was extremely grateful for this arrangement and he had Bazley arrange the room with a large desk facing the door with the ample window at his back. He had only just returned from a visit to Pozieres and was writing an article which detailed how accounts given by front line troops, and captured German soldiers, could sometimes be misleading. This he postulated was due to their limited perspective on the battlefield, and also the horrendous effects of shell-shock resulting from the devastating artillery fire which he had now personally experienced. He looked up as Bazley entered the room.

'Sergeant Green is downstairs, sir.'

'Oh good, this should be interesting. I am wondering what one of Monash's Deep Thinkers is doing here while the rest of his division is in England?'

'There is one other thing, sir.'

'Yes?'

'You know the chap has a touch of the tar brush. Will you still want to interview him?'

'But of course, the good Sergeant is better known as "Killer" Green, Monash's pet nigger he kept to do his dirty work at ANZAC. You know I'll bet any sum you care to name that the reason Green is in France is to spy for his master. Monash is after command of the AIF, and that is one thing that must never be allowed.'

'So I understand, sir,' Bazley replied carefully. 'I wonder if we can be sure this fellow is Killer Green? He's rather short; I thought he would be a much bigger man.'

'No, that will be him,' Bean continued. 'He tricked his way into the AIF and then lay low to avoid being sent back where he should be, but he can shoot remarkable straight and somehow he has managed to survive so far. Well, you'd best send him up.'

'There's another thing, sir, he has a woman with him. Will I bring her too?'

'She will be undoubtedly a lady of the night, Bazley. No, just Green. If you feel that way inclined you might find out her tariff, I can keep him busy for half an hour.'

'No thank you, sir. If as you say she is a professional lady, she will probably have every disease known to man and a few that aren't.'

Bean laughed. 'Quite so, Bazley, quite so. Well, go and get our aboriginal caveman. I'm rather looking forward to this.'

Bazley returned to the lobby. Green and Stephanie were

where he had left them.

'Well?' Green asked dangerously.

'Captain Bean will see you now, Sergeant,' Bazley said pompously. 'Miss, if you might wait here, I could get you a coffee?'

'No thank you,' Stephanie replied, 'and it is Madame.'

'Oh,' Bazley was caught off guard, 'I apologise.'

'You can do better than that,' said Green evenly. 'You can tell *Captain* Bean that either Madame comes with me, or there's no interview.'

Bazley scuttled away back to Bean's room and passed on Green's demand.

Bean raised his eyebrows in surprise. 'My first inclination is to send Sergeant Green packing,' he said quietly.

'Quite so, sir,' the loyal Bazley replied.

'However, I am convinced Green is here to advance Monash's ambitions. So see him I must, even if his floosy has to come with him.'

A few minutes later, Bazley ushered Green and Stephanie into Bean's presence. 'Sergeant Green and Madame Sainson,' he announced.

Bean indicated two chairs that faced his desk. 'Madame, Sergeant,' he acknowledged politely. He waited for Green and Stephanie to be seated before resuming his seat behind his desk. He placed his elbows on the desk and regarded Green carefully. 'So you're "Killer Green"?' he said finally.

'It's a name I don't encourage, sir.'

'Oh? Don't you like killing the King's enemies?'

'It's not that, sir; it's just that I feel it is pretentious... something I don't need.'

'The public need heroes though, Sergeant. What do you think of that?'

'I've no doubt they do, sir, but surely they can do without names like that.'

'Hmm,' Bean drummed his pencil on the tabletop and deftly changed the subject. 'I wonder,' he continued, 'how you managed to enlist in the AIF?'

Green smiled grimly. 'I had no difficulty,' he replied evenly.

Bean lips curled into a sardonic smile. 'I'm amazed,' he said, 'I would say that you would certainly fail the AIF's "substantially European background" requirement for enlistment.'

Green laughed. 'The recruiting sergeant wasn't all that fussy,' he said lightly. 'But I'm sure you don't want to talk to me about the AIF's enlistment policies. What is it you really want, Bean?'

Stephanie detected a hint of anger in Green's question and she placed a warning hand on his arm.

Bean stiffened at Green's departure from the normal military courtesy. Green should have called him "sir" and not have addressed him by name. For a second, he considered reprimanding the fellow, but as the words formed in his mind, he decided against it. He could see that Green was not the brainless killing machine he had supposed, but instead the man was an astute judge of the situation. Bean forced himself to smile. 'You're right, of course,' he replied. With another effort he became almost conciliatory. 'You know, of course, I write for the newspapers back home, the *Age* and the *Argus* in particular. Of late I've copped a bit of a bollocking from my editors who claim my writing is too factual, and does not concentrate enough on the Aussie soldier, the Digger. So you can imagine my excitement when I found that a celebrity, Killer Green, no less, was in the same town. Of course, I want to speak to you about your experiences in France, but I wondered first how you come to be here. After all, your Division has yet to deploy.'

Green smiled, matching Bean in his change of mood. 'Well, why didn't you say so, sir?' he said. 'It's really quite simple. My Division is interested in the way snipers are being employed here in France and I have been sent across to study those methods and then to report back. My report will form the basis of training of snipers within the Division.'

'I see,' Bean replied thoughtfully, 'and I suppose General Monash authorised this…' he searched for a word, 'liaison?'

'I've really no idea, sir. Generals are well above my social circle.'

'But that's not true, Sergeant. Surely at Gallipoli you worked directly to General Monash?'

'Ah, those were the days, sir. But no, I've not seen General Monash since the evacuation.'

'So who briefed you prior to your arrival here?'

'Oh, some junior staff officer; I honestly don't recall his name.'

'And you are attached to Brigadier Sinclair-Maclagan's headquarters. So was I, as it happens; in fact, I saw you there in that blasted cellar. As I recall, you did not look at all well.'

'Bit of shell shock. I'm all right now, though,' Green responded casually, but the revelation that Bean had seen him in the 3 Brigade Headquarters dugout shook him. For an instant, he lost the thread of the story he had been creating for Bean and in that instant, he was back in the artillery barrage, cowering at the entrance of the Headquarters dugout. He could taste the rum laced tea that Tollemach handed him, and he could see the disapproving look of the stranger who had accompanied Brigade Major. He realised now that the stranger was Bean. Green shook his head to clear the image from his mind.

'I understand you made yourself very useful while you were with 3 Brigade,' Bean continued. Carrying messages and such, hardly studying snipers, I'd have thought. Are you sure you weren't doing some other job for your General?'

Green had recovered his story line. 'Positive,' Green replied flatly. 'If you know of a better way to study snipers than working at the front, please tell me.'

'Sergeant, sergeant, sergeant,' Bean said beseechingly, 'we both *know* you are lying. The Australian public deserve to know that their men who enlisted to fight the common foe are being well led by professional British soldiers. You have a responsibility to tell me what kind of ridiculous scheme Monash has envisaged for his own benefit, so that I can expose him for what he is!'

Green got to his feet. 'Ordinarily, a man who called me a liar would receive a punch on his nose,' he said calmly. 'However, there is a lady present so I will forgo the pleasure of belting you, Bean. I've told you all you need to know and now the interview is over.'

'It is indeed,' Bean snapped. 'I will certainly be passing on an official complaint regarding your lack of cooperation.' He had not meant to lose his temper, but Green's suggestion that he did not need to know infuriated him.

'Come along, Stephanie,' Green said, offering her his arm, but she remained seated regarding Bean in silence.

Bean returned her gaze and gestured toward the door. 'I believe you are leaving, Madame,' he said curtly.

Stephanie stood up. 'Thank you, Monsieur, for a most enlightening meeting,' she said haughtily, her accent broadened by anger. 'However, I protest your attitude. In the time I have known Sergeant Green, he has *never* lied. He is a man of honour, which is more, I fear, than I can say for you!'

Bean stiffened as though she had struck him. 'And you, Madame,' he retorted nastily, 'what of your honour? Consorting with a man of colour, but perhaps he pays you well!'

'Enough!' Bazley imposed himself between the irate Bean and the furious Stephanie. 'Sir, you will apologize!'

Bean hung his head. 'You are right, old friend,' he admitted regretfully to Bazley. 'Madame, I am profoundly sorry. I can only claim the stress of the past weeks has unhinged me. Please accept my apology.'

Stephanie reached for Green's hand; she was still furious. '*Quel bâtard d' un homme,*' she snapped, glaring at Bazley who scuttled out of her way, and then she turned on Bean. 'I accept your apology, Monsieur, but I find myself wishing never to see you again!'

Bean bowed silently. It was clear he was thoroughly embarrassed by his own behaviour.

Once outside Bean's room, Stephanie looked anxiously at Green. 'Are you all right?' she asked.

Green smiled. 'Sure,' he replied. 'In fact, I rather enjoyed that.'

'The silly man,' Stephanie continued, 'I actually feel sorry for him, but I thought I had to take his mind entirely off your General and whatever really brought you to France.'

'Well, I think you accomplished that,' Green chuckled. 'You had me fooled. I thought you were going to slap him.'

'That was my next move,' Stephanie announced with conviction.

'I think we've done rather well,' Green concluded, 'and I'm sure we deserve a drink. This way, Madame, I know a very nice bar nearby. I doubt he'll even bother to put in a report now. Not that it would bother me if he did. He's a pompous fool.'

Back in Bean's room, Bazley placed an arm around his master's shoulders. 'I'm sorry about that,' he said, 'I should not have spoken to you like that.'

Bean shook his head. 'No, no, my friend, you did what had to be done. I allowed myself to become angry... a failing of mine. I am certain there is more to Green's presence than some damn silly fact-finding mission. He knows more about sniping than most men alive, and if I had not lost my temper, I might have got to the bottom of it. We shall watch Sergeant Green and his fancy lady; there is a story there that may well damn Monash to hell.'

Chapter 20

On Pozieres Heights, the battle continued to rage, with fortune first favouring one side and then the other. However, hostilities were not limited to the front line. At his headquarters in Montreuil, the British Commander in Chief General Haig was on the attack. However, this time his assault was not aimed at the German Army but at the Commander of the 1st ANZAC Corps, General William Birdwood.

The Australian 2nd Division's attack of the night of 29th July on the Pozieres ridgeline had been a costly failure, and the next day a furious Haig had sent for Birdwood, demanding an explanation. Haig was an imposing figure, particularly when he was angry. His moustache seemed to bristle with outrage, his shoulders twitched with indignation, and his steely eyes flashed fury at those unfortunate enough to be summoned before him.

It was particularly unpleasant for Birdwood, for he knew the real reason for his summons. Haig needed a scape goat for the continued British failures and Birdwood had a fair idea he had been selected for that role.

Haig looked up and glared at Birdwood who stood stiffly to attention in front of the Commander in Chief's desk. 'You're not fighting Bashi-Bazouks, now,' he said, his voice dripping with vitriol. 'Your enemy here are real soldiers, the cream of German manhood! You have to be decisive in this theatre; speed is essential! Your colonials were not prepared to adhere to schedule, nor it seems were they capable of maintaining any kind of momentum. They were too concerned with casualties and not prepared to push forward regardless of the Hun.' Haig leaned forward in his chair and even though he remained seated, he seemed to soar above the standing Birdwood like a bird of prey about to swoop. 'Well,' he said loudly, 'do you have anything to say for yourself?'

Birdwood remained silent, staring at a spot on the wall above and behind Haig's head. In truth, there was little he could say. The night attack had not been his idea but General Gough's and Gough's planning, such as it was, had been done in haste and was, as events transpired, inadequate. However, Birdwood knew that Gough was a favoured commander in Haig's suite of generals, so he was sure Haig would not point the finger of blame in that direction. Nor was Birdwood inclined to blame his own staff, men who he had handpicked and who he trusted unreservedly.

'Let me talk specifics,' continued Haig, his voice now low and dangerous. 'The attack was scheduled to commence at 12:15 a. m. Your 7th Brigade failed to reach the start line by that time. Your 5th Brigade made no attempt to move to the start line. Your 6th Brigade was at least on time, but it failed to press on. Lastly, no attempt was made to advise supporting British units of the situation and as a result, they have been exposed to heavy German fire and suffered accordingly.'

Birdwood opened his mouth to speak, but the words would not form. Haig glared at him contemptuously; however, before the Commander in Chief could resume his tirade, a polite cough drew his attention to the third person in the room. Birdwood's Chief of Staff Colonel Brudenell White had accompanied his commander to Haig's headquarters and he now approached Haig's desk.

'With the greatest respect, sir,' White began, 'I wonder if I might correct some of the information you have been provided.' It was a clever ploy, for White was in no way suggesting that the Commander in Chief was wrong, only that his information was faulty.

Haig was caught off guard. 'Eh?' He beckoned for White to come closer. 'What the devil do you mean?'

White took a deep breath and began. He kept his voice calm and even, never allowing the anger he felt at the injustice of Haig's remarks to show. 'Sir, your first point regarding the 7th Brigade overlooks an important factor. To meet the scheduled timing requirements for this attack, the commanders on the ground could not be afforded the opportunity to reconnoitrer the ground they had to cross. As a result, when moving across the unfamiliar terrain in the dark, the Brigade lost its way. In establishing its position, the Germans detected the Brigade and opened fire with numerous machine guns. Unfortunately, the Brigade suffered many casualties, and in extricating themselves from this position, further delay occurred. So yes, they were late to arrive at the start line, but I would argue there are mitigating circumstances.'

'Yes, yes,' Haig blustered, 'you have already made that point.'

'The second point,' White continued calmly, 'is that the 7th Brigade then ran into uncut wire which spread across their entire front. Many more casualties were incurred as they endeavoured to negotiate this obstacle, so many, in fact, that the survivors no longer represented a viable attacking force.'

Haig bristled with indignation. 'I was not told of this!' he said angrily. 'Are you sure?'

Birdwood at last found his voice. 'It is absolutely correct, sir,' he said. 'The 7th Brigade is being withdrawn from the line.

It will need substantial rebuilding before it can return to the front.'

Haig was deflated. 'I see,' he said, then motioned to White to continue.

'The 5th Brigade, sir, did not refuse to join the attack. They were simply mown down as they attempted to leave their trenches to move to the start line. They are still pinned down as we speak.'

Haig grunted.

'The 6th Brigade, sir,' White continued, 'had the least complicated move to the start line and they commenced the attack on time. However, in reaching some of their objectives, they suffered substantial casualties and were prevented from any further advance by extremely accurate machine gun and artillery fire.'

Haig pursed his lips and drummed quietly on his desktop with his fingers.

White had not finished. 'You mentioned communications. Every effort was made by the attacking force to communicate with higher headquarters and with the supporting units. However, the only viable means of communication available to the attacking force was runner. Unfortunately, most of the Brigade runners were killed or wounded and thus failed to deliver their information. The telephone cables provided are brittle and they break. In spite of the continuous effort of our signallers to address this situation, telephone communication during the battle failed. As you are aware, sir, carrier pigeons cannot work at night.'

Haig hung his head in defeat.

'Sir, in the last three days, the 2nd Division has suffered over three and a half thousand casualties. Yes, the Division's attack failed, but it was not due to any lack of endeavour.

Rather, the failure was the result of insufficient planning, the notorious "fog of war," and a lethal response from the enemy.'

Haig looked up at White. 'I daresay you are right, young man,' he said sadly. 'Nevertheless, the attack must be renewed immediately. Once the Pozieres Heights is in our hands, we can concentrate our efforts on the main German position at Thiepval.'

'We are planning a renewed assault as we speak ,sir,' White replied.

Haig smiled. 'Good, good,' he said, then paused reflectively and returned his attention to Birdwood. 'Gough wants General Legge to receive a letter of censure over this last failure. You'll see to that, Birdwood?'

Birdwood almost sighed with relief as he realised he was not to be Haig's sacrificial goat. It was General Legge, the commander of Australian 2nd Division, who was to be censured over the attack's failure. Birdwood had no particular liking for Legge; the two had clashed on several occasions in the past, and instantly he saw this was an opportunity to be rid of Legge for good. However, he still smarted from Haig's earlier unjust criticism of the AIF's efforts, and he felt some shame that he had not defended his command more robustly. He realised if it had not been for White's intervention, Haig would have had his way. Birdwood knew he owed White at least some kind of a show of loyalty to his men and defiance in the face of gross injustice. Legge would keep. He looked directly at Haig. 'I can't do that,' he said firmly. 'A man is entitled to a fair trial before he's hung out to dry. I would seek a formal inquiry into the affair before I'd sign any such letter.'

Haig blanched. An inquiry into the failed attack might well find that his own and Gough's meddling to be the root cause of the attack's failure, and that would never do. 'Good point,' he said quickly. 'Well, I think that's all. Would you both join me for tea and cake?'

———————

A minor skirmish followed this confrontation at the Australian 2nd Division Headquarters. The failure of the attack on the 29th had dinted General James Gordon Legge's usual arrogant self-confidence; he was a worried man. Adding to his concern, Colonel Brudenell White had visited and told him that his planned attack for the night of the 3rd of August must be delayed.

'What do you mean, delayed?' he demanded angrily. 'You people at Corps don't seem to understand the pressure I'm under here. Bloody Gough wanted me to attack three nights ago, Haig is strutting about telling all and sundry I'm no good at my job, and then you turn up upsetting my staff and trying to take over my command!'

White made a soothing motion with his hands. 'Hold on, sir, it's not like that all. We know all about Gough's interference; believe me, we want you to succeed.'

Legge was not convinced. 'Next, you'll be telling me that Birdwood is on my side.'

White could feel his own anger building and he struggled to hide any hint of it in his voice. 'As a matter of fact, sir,' he replied, 'General Birdwood is very much on your side and spoke in your defence to General Haig.'

It was Legge's turn to be surprised. 'I say,' he said, 'is that true?'

'I beg your pardon, sir.' White responded hotly. 'I hope you are not suggesting I am a liar?'

'Oh, for heaven's sake,' responded Legge wearily, 'of course not! I merely find it strange... passing strange that Birdwood would do such a thing.'

White cooled his response. 'Be that as it may,' he said, 'it is true. I was there and heard him. You were to receive a letter of censure regarding the failed attack. The Corps Commander refused to present the letter.' White chose not to mention that it was he, not Birdwood, who had taken Haig to task over his attitude toward the ANZAC 2nd Division. Such a revelation would be counterproductive.

Legge hung his head. 'Well, I must say it was damned decent of him. Please tell General Birdwood I appreciate it.'

White nodded. 'The most important thing at the moment is that this next attack succeeds. General Birdwood fully supports your plan to attack just before dark so that the men will be able to see their objectives and orientate themselves with the ground.'

Legge nodded. 'Yes, they will go in at 9:15 p.m. just before dark; they will be able to see the crest of the ridge and the mound of the windmill and then work things out from there,' he said.

'But,' White continued, 'to avoid mass suicide, the trenches required to position the attacking force must be properly prepared.'

Legge nodded. 'Agreed,' he said. 'The problem is that over the last forty-eight hours, the Hun has shelled the living hell out of every new sap we dig. It's slow work.'

'Therefore', White concluded, 'your men must have more time to dig the trenches and then to position themselves for the assault.'

Legge nodded his agreement. 'Jesus,' he muttered, 'how the hell am I going to tell Gough?'

As White left Legge's headquarters, a feeling of despair

washed over him. What hope did they have when the generals from the Commander in Chief down were bickering like a pack of school children? He knew all too well that in reality, Birdwood did not support Legge and that it was only a matter of time before the two would clash again. It was common knowledge that they had clashed on Gallipoli over Birdwood's plans for the August offensive at ANCZAC Cove and the attack at Lone Pine. Legge had argued that both attacks would prove costly failures, and as events transpired, he was proved correct. Here in France, there had been further disagreement over Birdwood's insistence on manning the front far more heavily than required, a practice Legge saw as a major contributing factor to a high casualty rate. White had been pleasantly surprised when Birdwood had taken the Legge side against Haig, but he knew Birdwood had neither forgotten nor forgiven the 2nd Division's Commander.

In Amiens, another covert battle was about to be joined.

Green thought it prudent to advise Lieutenant Colonel Law of Bean's interest in his presence in France, and to that end he used the telephone number Law had provided to phone through his report.

An unfamiliar voice answered. 'Yes?'

'I want to speak to Lieutenant Colonel Law.'

'He is not available. You may pass your message to me.'

'Tell him Captain Charles Bean is showing an unwelcome interest in Sergeant Green.'

'Very well, is that all?'

'Yes.'

'Call back in two days for further instructions. Goodbye.'

The call ended abruptly.

The next day as Bean was making his way through the crowded hotel lobby, a large man blundered into him. 'Mind how you go,' he warned testily.

The offender turned to apologise but then gave a cry of recognition. 'Good heavens, is that you, Charles? Damn sorry old chap.'

'Lieutenant Colonel Law,' Bean acknowledged, recognising his assailant. 'This place seems to be positively crawling with Deep Thinkers. What brings you to France at this time?'

'Ah, glad you asked; I knew you'd have your finger on the pulse. Well, it's all very hush hush, you know,' Law tapped the side of his nose with a forefinger. 'But as it turns out, you have become inadvertently involved.'

'Oh, how is that?'

'I understand you had a visit from a Sergeant Green the other day.'

Bean was immediately suspicious. 'Now, how would you know that?' he asked.

'Come now, Charles, you know it's my job to keep abreast of things. The fact is my other masters share your concerns about a certain newly promoted General who shall remain nameless. You'll recall there was a report he was actually a German spy?'

Bean nodded. He was all too aware of the story that claimed Monash was actually a German agent. In fact, he had helped spread the rumour to official channels.

'The story was discredited, of course, but we still keep an eye on him. It's one of the reasons I am on his staff. He seemed to be keeping his nose clean until recently when he sent this Green fellow over here, apparently to observe snipers at work. However, our information is the chap's real job is to make contact with a German agent.

'I knew it!' Bean hissed excitedly

'Yes, we soon found out that since he's been here, he's made several trips to the front in the company of a man with a particularly Teutonic sounding name.'

'Blucher!'

'That's the fellow. It makes sense, doesn't it? Monash employs a disaffected Aboriginal as his creature, and another man with obvious links to the other side.'

'Yes, yes it does. What a story, this will finish Monash and we can at last see a true Briton in charge of that Division.'

'Ah, but there's the rub. I can't allow you to speak, print, or even think any further about this affair. We are at a most delicate stage of the investigation, and I hardly need remind you of the consequences should anything go wrong. We need to catch these two in the act and then we can expose their leader.'

'But I represent the free press,' Bean almost wailed as he could see a story scoop slipping from his grasp. 'What of the public's right to know?'

'Stuff and nonsense!' Law snapped. 'I represent the security of the realm and without that, there will be no free press and the public will never know truth.'

'Well, I'm not sure…'

Law leaned forward so that his mouth was close to Bean's ear. 'Let me put it this way, old chap, unless you drop all interest in Sergeant Green and Private Blucher, I shall make it my business to put you away for a very, very long time.'

'Are you threatening me, Law?'

'I certainly am, and you know not take to my threats lightly.'

That night, somewhat reluctantly, Bean burned all of his

notes regarding Green and never mentioned his suspicions again.

Two days later as instructed, Green again telephoned the number Law had provided. 'This is Sergeant Green,' he announced.

'Yes,' a brief pause then the nameless person continued. 'The situation has been resolved. No further action to be taken. Await instructions as originally agreed.'

Again, the call ended abruptly.

A week after White's visit to General Legge's headquarters, a temporary truce between competing Allied Generals had been achieved. Following careful preparatory work, Legge's 2nd Division had captured Pozieres Heights. In the rarefied atmosphere breathed by those of the rank of General and above, the great and powerful could afford to cease their squabbles and acknowledge this success. Great praise was heaped on the Division and its commander, but not everyone involved in the Battle of Pozieres was so impressed.

Their German adversary was not as impressed. General der Infanterie Ferdinand von Quest was not a man given to panic. In his forty years of military service to the Kaiser and the German nation, he had experienced other temporary reversals on the battlefield, but he had always managed to regain the initiative and win through. The loss of Hill 160, the title the German commander afforded the Pozieres Heights, was of concern as it afforded the victorious Australians views of the green countryside leading to the village of Courcelette and the woods around Bapaume. However, the Australian success had not been supported by corresponding advances by supporting

British units. He stroked the wings of his ample moustache and pondered the situation. 'What is the British commander doing?' he asked the young staff officer at his side.

The staff officer pointed to a map board which depicted the battle scene. 'There is little he can do, Herr General. Our forces have halted every British attempt to move forward and match the Australian advance.'

Von Quest now stroked his prominent square chin. 'In other words, the Australians have created...?' he said, leading the younger man to answer.

'A salient, Herr General.' The staff officer looked again at the map where the Australian positions were shown as a stumpy finger protruding into the German line. Unless the British managed to advance a similar distance, the Australians were vulnerable on both flanks as well as their front.

'Exactly!' Von Quest slapped his thigh. 'They will now pay dearly for their victory. Bring every available artillery unit to bear on them.'

'We are already shelling them heavily, Herr General.'

'I know that,' the General snapped. 'Are you deaf? I want the barrage increased.'

'From the front and both flanks?'

'Of course! The barrage should begin at once and continue until the infantry attack, which will take place at first light tomorrow morning. Hill 160 is to be recaptured at all costs!'

The staff officer clicked his heals and walked from the room. 'The old chap certainly has his blood up today,' he told one of his juniors. 'I'm glad I am not an Australian.'

───────────────

The young officer hugged the ground as a veritable hurricane of German artillery fell upon the Australian held salient. It was his first time at the front, but even from his limited experience of war, he could tell this was no ordinary bombardment. Rather, it was an attempt to kill everyone within the beaten zone of German fire, by saturating the area with high explosives. He was finding it difficult to think, but he knew that he had to get on with the task. Hoping that someone else would provide an example, he looked to his left. Through the dust and smoke, he could just make out his friend and fellow junior officer lying in the doubtful shelter of a large clod of earth. His mate seemed to jump at every detonation, but then the young officer realized that the concussion of the explosions was reverberating through the ground and momentarily pushing his mate upwards. He tried to see through the dust, smoke, and flame that had fallen like a curtain about him, but it was becoming increasingly difficult to see anything, for the day seemed to be growing darker.

He looked up. In the sky above him, dark shapes like a swarm of grotesquely huge bees jostled for position above him. With a cry of terror, he realized he was watching the incoming shells and that it was this swarm of ordnance that shielded the sun's rays.

A massive series of explosions erupted in the trench a few yards from where he lay, completely obliterating it and atomising the Australians that sheltered there. A shower of broken body parts and a red mist of blood and tissue swept over his part of the trench. A massive hole some twenty feet deep and five yards across replaced the carefully constructed trench works, providing an instant memorial to the men who died at the moment of its violent genesis. The barrage was now so massive that the ground around the young officer heaved and swayed as though an earthquake were striking at the fields of France. Inevitably, the trench where he lay surrendered to the abuse and collapsed on top of him. In absolute terror, he clawed his way to the surface, and in the time it took to him to disinter himself, his fear vanished and he lost his temper.

He was not angry with the Germans who were trying to kill him, nor was he angry with his men. However, he felt a deep anger at the incompetent fools who had placed him and his comrades in this impossible position. He struggled to his feet and drew his pistol. 'All right, you bastards!' he screamed into the dust cloud. 'Start digging!'

There was no reaction from any of the dim shapes of men who continued to cower in the remains of the trench. For one terrible moment, he thought that he was the only one left alive, so he walked over to one of the prone figures and kicked it in the ribs and received an immediate reaction.

'Piss off, you mad cunt!' the victim of the officer's heavy boot shouted.

The officer kicked the man again. 'Up!' he screamed. 'Get up and start digging, or I shall shoot you where you lie!'

The startled man, seeing that the officer was just crazy enough to carry out his threat, scrambled to his feet and began clearing the trench about him of debris.

The officer left him and strode along the trench, kicking and pushing the frightened men out of cover and forcing them to dig. 'There has to be a trench here in the morning,' he shouted over the shattering noise of the barrage. 'I'll shoot anyone who refuses to dig!'

His friend caught up with him. 'Ease up, old man, you're acting a little strangely. You can't just shoot our fellows!'

The officer turned on his friend. 'I fucking can,' he snarled, 'and I'll fucking shoot you too if you don't help.'

Shocked, his friend began to assist in organising the work parties. Fear of his fellow officer surpassed his fear of the barrage.

The barrage showed no signs of abating. Under the storm of explosion and flying metal, men were blown to pieces, or went barking mad. The wounded were left where they lay; the dead were thrown aside. The living were often buried, exhumed, and buried again. Their uniforms became rotten with the blood and body tissue of their dead and dying comrades. Weapons and equipment were lost and replaced by robbing the dead of theirs. To be wounded and finally attended to by the stretcher bearers was a ticket to salvation. And through it all, the young officer's anger at his far off superiors grew and grew. For if any of them survived this ordeal, he knew the horror would not end. There would be the next day, the next night, the next day, and so on until death finally caught up with all of them.

Jäger Bayerlein had retreated hurriedly further up the Pozieres ridgeline to the second line of German trenches. He had been forced to revise his opinion of the amateur Australian soldiers. They were not only brave, but they were proving to be most resourceful and cunning. On the previous night, a number of them had entered No Man's Land and established a post under the very noses of the defending German infantry, a mere three hundred meters from the German forward trenches. In spite of being cut off from their own lines, the Australians had maintained the new post throughout the day. Bayerlein had managed to kill three of them before the Australian Field Artillery had forced his withdrawal, but he had no doubt the

Australians had used their new post as a jumping off point for the attack from which he had just escaped.

During the renewed attack, he had been surprised when the Australians employed a clever, yet very risky manoeuvre. Their assaulting troops appeared to be moving within their own artillery barrage. When the barrage had commenced, he and his comrades had done what they had always done during previous artillery bombardment; they retired to their deep underground bunkers. Experience had taught them there would be a delay of some minutes between the time the shelling ceased and the enemy infantry arrived on the German parapets. During that period, the attacking enemy would feel the full weight of German machine gun and rifle fire. This time, however, was different. Even as the last of the enemy shells fell, the Australian infantry was upon them. It had been only luck that he had been able to escape. Now he watched in dismay as other survivors from the forward positions streamed back past him. Many were wounded and being carried by their comrades. He saw with some relief, a particular friend, Hans Myer, among the retreating throng and called out to him. 'What news?'

'They are animals,' Myer shouted back and pointed to a blood on his neck. 'I was bitten!' he cried. 'Bitten! And Karl Muller was killed with a spade!'

Bayerlein shook his head in sympathy, but in truth there was nothing unusual in his friend's injury or in Karl Muller's death. In the final stages of an assault, men became animals and fought with whatever they had available, fists, feet, teeth, and even shovels. He himself had preferred a wooden truncheon, the end of which he used to wind rolls of thin wire. But that was before he became a sniper and was not expected to take part in such vulgarity. He lit his pipe and puffed at it thoughtfully. He was certain the setback he and his comrades now suffered would be temporary, and he had every confidence that once regrouped, the German Army would quickly sweep the Australians away.

He finished his pipe and beckoned to his spotter. 'Time to go,' he said. Together the two snipers crept forward to select a fire position overlooking the victorious Australians. It was still early morning, and Bayerlein was determined that at least some them would pay the ultimate price for their victory.

General Gough smiled benignly and passed a plate of scones to the Commander of the 1 ANZAC Corps, General Birdwood. 'These are really excellent, Birdwood. My people have employed a French chap who used to own his own bakery in Pozieres. Of course, the poor chap is out of business now, but it's an ill wind that blows nobody any good, what?'

Birdwood accepted a scone and on taking a bite found that Gough's praise for his new cook was indeed well founded.

'Now, my dear chap,' Gough continued, 'I can't tell you how pleased Haig is that the heights have been taken. Well done, indeed. Legge finally came through. Always knew he would.'

Birdwood almost choked on his scone but managed to control his incredulity. 'Heavy casualties, though,' he pointed out.

'Yes, yes,' Gough soothed. 'Regrettable, I know, but one can't make an omelette without breaking the odd egg.'

'Several thousand eggs, in this case,' Birdwood muttered irritably.

Gough ignored the comment. 'Thing is, now we really

must push on. Haig is most insistent that we take Thiepval, and before we can do that, Mouquet Farm must be secured.'

Birdwood frowned. 'Who do you expect to do that?' he retorted. 'My Divisions have suffered a mauling. I doubt they have the resources to make another push.'

'Nonsense, dear fellow,' Gough replied. 'Why, they have demonstrated skills far beyond anything Haig and I thought possible, and now they have linked up with flanking British units, they are simply best placed to carry out an immediate assault on the farm.'

'And are my men supposed to do this alone?' asked Birdwood, barely able to retain his anger.

Gough waved airily. 'Of course not, my dear fellow.'

Birdwood made one final effort to reason with his commander. 'General, you do realise the scale of the casualties my Corps has suffered. In beating off the counter-attack this morning alone, we suffered over 1,000 casualties.'

'I assure you I am fully aware of all of the costs,' Gough snapped. 'It strikes me that while your troops are capable fighters, the leadership in your Corps lacks an offensive spirit!'

Birdwood got to his feet. 'I will await your further orders, sir,' he responded angrily. Then turning on his heel, he walked from the room.

'The trouble with you, Birdwood,' snarled Gough at his colleague's retreating back, 'you've gone native! We expected you to impose discipline and knowledge to the colonials, but what have you done? You've become one of them!'

———————————

Lieutenant Colonel Law was a most interested spectator at General Birdwood's daily briefing. It seemed inconceivable that so soon after the heavy casualties suffered in taking Pozieres Heights, that the AIF would be required to mount yet another major assault. Law had yet to visit the front, but from the almost mutinous mutterings of some of the officers seated around him, he gathered that the next objective, a place called Mouquet Farm, was asking too much.

An orderly entered the briefing room and on ascertaining where Law was seated, moved unobtrusively around the room and handed him an envelope.

Law murmured his thanks and glanced at the envelope. It was addressed to: "Lieutenant Colonel Law" and carried a stamped security classification in red ink: "MOST SECRET – URGENT – FOR ADDRESSEE'S EYES ONLY."

Law got to his feet and nodding his deference to the briefing officer, he left the room. Once outside he found a quiet spot and opened the envelope. It contained as he suspected a telegram from his masters in London, and with growing excitement, he read the brief text: TARGET HAS MOVED TO COURCELETTE. PROBABLE INTENT TO ASSIST IN INTERROGATION OF AUSTRALIAN POWS CURRENTLY HELD NEAR MOUQUET FARM. BE PREPARED TO MOVE IN NEXT 48 HOURS.

'Well, that is the end of your leave, Sergeant Green,' Law mused. Then he hurried to the Signal Centre where he drafted a message of his own: WILL PICK YOU BOTH UP AT 10 AM TOMORROW. LAW

Chapter 21

Green awoke to find Stephanie already awake. She lay beside him looking at him with the intensity of an artist studying a muse. An empty feeling in the pit of his stomach reminded him this was the last morning of his leave. Law's message had cast a pall over the previous afternoon and the evening had only been rescued when Stephanie's uncle and aunt had visited, bringing with them several bottles of champagne. He was determined not to succumb to the downheartedness that threatened to overwhelm him, and he went to sit up. Stephanie placed a restraining hand on his chest. 'No, please stay,' she said, 'I am etching you onto my memory. You must stay still until I have finished.'

He lay perfectly still while she stared intently at him tracing the outline of his face with a finger. When she had finished, she kissed him lightly on the mouth. 'I love you,' she whispered.

'I love you too,' he replied quietly, and as he did so, he realised it was the first time he had ever said such a thing to anyone other than his mother.

'Nothing must happen to you,' she continued. 'I would not survive your loss.'

'I promise I will come back to you,' he said, knowing he could not possibly guarantee such a thing and knowing she knew it too. There were so many ways fate could conspire to prevent their future happiness. He shuddered, and for a moment he was back in Pozieres listening to the German shells creeping inexorably toward him. He shook his head and the apparition faded.

'I'll come back to you,' he repeated the empty words, and wondered if he was saying it for her, or for himself. He took her in his arms and crushed her naked body to his.

They made love then, and as they ended, she turned away from him and he knew she was crying. He tried to turn her toward him, but she shrugged his hand away. Sorrowfully, he left the bed, dressed, and went downstairs.

Ten a.m. seemed to arrive before any of the occupants of Madame Claire's house had time to think about the hour. It felt as if they had only just finished breakfast when a car's horn sounded in the street and Green knew without checking that Law had arrived and was waiting for them. It was time to go.

'It's been a great leave,' Blucher said as he shouldered his pack. 'Makes me think where I'd be now if you hadn't hitched that ride with me.'

'Or if poor bloody Elliot hadn't cashed in his chips,' Green added.

'Yeah, that too,' Blucher muttered, 'it makes you think.'

Green picked up his own equipment. 'Best not to dwell on it,' he said. 'Anyway, they reckon the war will be over by Christmas; we can come back here then.

Blucher snorted with derision. 'Christmas, I heard that one in 1914!'

Law was leaning nonchalantly upon the car's mudguard and smoking a cigarette which he carelessly tossed into the gutter and stood up as Green, Blucher, and the two ladies walked toward him. 'Good morning,' he called cheerily, 'I'm afraid we are in a bit of a hurry. Place your gear in the trunk, gentlemen; the driver will help.' He turned to Madame Claire. '*Ah Madame Claire, Nousvousdoisplusd'argent*'?

Thinking Law knew of her torrid affair with Blucher, Claire

blushed furiously. 'Non,nonjen 'a étépayéentotalité' she replied.

'And you must be Madame Sainson,' Law said to Stephanie.

Stephanie was confused. 'How do you know my name, Colonel'? she asked bluntly.

Law smiled. 'I'm afraid it is my job to know the names of those people my men spend any time with.'

Green was slightly annoyed. 'Been checking up on me, Colonel'?

Law shrugged. 'Certainly,' he admitted, 'there is a lot riding on our mission; I had to be sure the opposition had not found out about you. I am happy to say Madame Sainson has an impeccable reputation.' He bowed slightly to Stephanie. 'I am sorry for the loss of your husband, Madame,' he said.

Green wondered what would have happened had Stephanie been found to have a less savoury reputation, but he chose not to ask.

Law clapped his hands. 'We must away,' he announced loudly. 'Blucher, front seat with the driver; Sergeant Green, back seat with me.'

There was a brief and awkward silence. Neither couple embraced as they made their farewells. Blucher simply winked at Madame Claire then climbed into the front seat of the car next to the driver.

Green squeezed Stephanie's hand. 'I'll write as soon as I can,' he said as he clambered into the rear of the vehicle to sit alongside Law.

The two women stood together waving as the driver slowly eased the car out into the cobbled street. Just as the car began to accelerate, Stephanie broke away from Madame Claire and ran after the vehicle. 'I love you, Robert,' she shouted through her tears. 'I love you.'

The car picked up speed outpacing the weeping woman,

leaving her standing in the roadway. Green leaned out of the vehicle and waved; then the car rounded the street corner and he saw her no more.

Chapter 22

'Back to Albert, driver,' Law directed. He turned to Green. 'We shall do our final planning there.'

Green nodded and waited for Law to provide more information, but they completed the journey in silence.

On reaching Albert, Law directed the driver to a rubble strewn street near the Cathedral. The car bumped along the damaged cobblestones until they reached the shell of what must have once been a substantial building; now, only the walls remained. 'Stop here,' Law directed the driver. 'Once we've unloaded our stuff, you can return to your unit.'

The driver seemed relieved at his release. 'Sooner you than me, mate,' he said to Blucher as he helped unload the vehicle.

Once the driver had departed, Law seemed to relax. 'This is a supply dump for the 1st Division,' he explained. 'I've secured permission to take whatever we may need for our mission.'

Green glanced inquiringly at the Colonel. 'We...' he inquired. 'Am I to understand, sir, that you are coming with us?'

'I'm coming with you,' Law confirmed, 'but I must stress that the only reason for my accompanying you is the fact that I am the only one of us who can recognise the target. You, Sergeant Green, will be in charge of the mission and I will obey your every direction.'

Green was surprised, but he had to admit the arrangement made sense. 'Fair enough,' he said then he added, 'now would be a good time to fill Private Blucher in as to what we are actually going to be doing.'

'I agree,' Law replied, 'but let's get settled inside first.' He led the way into the building.

In a far corner of the supply dump, a small Bell tent had been erected. 'That's ours,' Law said as he ushered them inside the canvas walls. 'Throw your gear down anywhere and make yourselves comfortable.' He produced a map from the brief case he carried and laid it out on the floor; then he sat down on top of his pack and spoke directly to Blucher. 'Ordinarily,' he began, 'I am a staff officer on General Monash's staff. However, aside from those duties, from time to time I am required to carry out other intelligence work for people further up the chain of command.'

'You mean you're a spy,' Blucher stated bluntly.

'I seem to recall that is exactly what Sergeant Green said when first I met him,' Law replied grimly, 'and so I will provide the same answer... I'm not a spy as such, but my work puts me in contact with people who are. My main work tends to be studying the information provided by spies and then working out what to do with that information. And that is what has happened on this occasion. You've heard of MI6?'

Blucher shook his head.

'No, well MI6 is the British Secret Service organisation responsible for overseas operations. In this case, MI6 have received advice that one of Germany's most senior intelligence officers, Colonel Walter Nicolai, is visiting the town of Courcelette,' he pointed with his swagger stick where the township was marked on the map. 'We are told he is in the area to interrogate some of our lads who are now being held prisoner. We have also learned that he will visit the Mouquet Farm area to carry out this task. This brings me to the reason why we three are gathered here in this tent. Our job is to make sure he never goes home.'

Blucher was startled. 'You mean we are going to knock him off?' he asked incredulously.

'That's it in a nutshell,' Law replied.

'But that Courcelette place,' Blucher blustered, 'that's behind German lines.'

'Yes it is,' Law confirmed.

'Still want to come, Blucher'? Green laughed.

'Of course, I bloody do. It's just a bit of a shock, that's all.'

Law motioned for silence, before he continued his briefing. 'Right, now we all know what we are going to try to do. However, the "how" and the "where" is another matter. You will be aware that a few nights ago we captured Pozieres Heights.'

Green and Blucher nodded. The news of the success had been a major topic of conversation in Amiens and it had even made the Paris newspapers.

'I am told,' Law continued, 'that it is now possible for our forward troops to see into the farmland that lies beyond the Heights, and that they are referring to it as a land of milk and honey. There are, of course, German positions and defences in the area,' he said, vaguely waving his swagger stick over the map. 'Now I understand our target is already at Courcelette, and of course we can't hope to touch him there, but our agent believes that sometime on the 9th of August, he will travel by car along the main Courcelette road,' the swagger stick traced the road on the map, 'to the cross roads here in the "28" grid square. He is to be met there by an escort party who will guide him up to the line at Mouquet Farm.' Law pointed at the place on the map where three roads met, slightly to the north of the halfway point between Courcelette and Mouquet Farm. 'I imagine they'll be feeling pretty safe when they meet, and there will be a lot of handshakes and back slapping, which should give us a good chance of making a clean kill.' He paused, allowing Green and Blucher to digest the information he had provided.

Green studied the map more closely. 'Getting there is going to be a bit of a challenge,' he said. 'It's very open country and the Hun is going to be pretty toey having just been pushed off the Heights. We are going to need some kind of a diversion that will take his attention away from our line of entry to the area.'

'Would a major attack on Mouquet Farm suffice?' Law asked innocently.

Green snorted derisively. 'I know you have influence, sir,' he said, 'but I doubt it extends that far.'

Law smiled. 'Nothing to do with me,' he said calmly, 'but at dusk on the 8th of August, our troops will commence to attack Mouquet Farm in strength. My guess is every German in the vicinity will be concentrating his attention on that farm.'

'I reckon that should do it, Green acknowledged ruefully, 'but we will still have to be bloody careful getting into position, and then of course there's the getting out part after we've done the deed. Our problem at this stage is we only have the picture of the land that the map provides us. Before now, it was impossible to actually view the ground, but now we have the Heights, we have the opportunity to at least scan where we are going with binoculars. I suggest we make for what's left of the Windmill, here,' he pointed to the map, 'carry out our reconnaissance from there, and then plan and rehearse, before we actually cross the start line.'

Law nodded. The Windmill was an infamous landmark of the Pozieres battlefield that the Germans had used to dominate the surrounding land. It had been reduced to rubble by British and Australian artillery, and the ruin was now in the hands of the AIF's 48th Battalion. 'Will we have time to get there by the eighth?' he asked.

Green nodded. 'Take a vehicle forward to Sausage Valley and then walk. We could be there sometime tonight.'

'What about equipment?' Law asked.

'We will need a bit,' Green agreed. He turned to Blucher, 'Want to go shopping?' he asked.

'Whatever you want,' Blucher replied.

'See what you find outside. We will need three strips of hessian, about two yards wide and five in length, the sort of stuff they surround the shitters with in the rear areas.'

Blucher got to his feet.

Green held up a restraining hand. 'While you're at it, find some bully beef, tea, condensed milk, and biscuits, enough for the three of us for two days. Oh, and see if you can get hold of three captured German helmets too.'

Blucher nodded and left the tent. Almost immediately, he could be heard bargaining with someone Green assumed was the owner of souvenir helmets.

'Why do we need the helmets?' Law asked.

Green laughed. 'It won't do us any harm, while we are wandering around Hun territory, if we look like them.'

'Good heavens man—if we are captured, they will shoot us as spies!'

'They will probably shoot us anyway,' Green retorted. 'The Hun is no different to our lads; they don't like snipers.'

Law opened his mouth to make a further comment, but changed his mind. 'I'll go and arrange a vehicle,' he said resignedly.

When Law returned to the tent, he found Green and Blucher busily engaged in a task that was beyond his comprehension. The two men were working on a large strip of hessian. Poking holes through the rough fabric with their bayonets and then inserting ribbons of the same fabric through the rents and tying them in place—the end result was similar to a very rough shagpile carpet.

'That's the last one,' Green said cheerily. He pointed at a small stack of items that included two Mills bombs, a tin of bully beef, a packet of biscuits, a tin of condensed milk, and a roll of the hessian. All this was topped by a German 'coal scuttle' helmet. 'That's your lot, sir,' he said.

Law regarded the pile of items suspiciously then returned his attention to the hessian items. 'Whatever is it?' he asked.

Green stood up and taking one end of the large hessian strip he and Blucher had been working on, shook it out to its full extent. 'These, sir, are what the Pommies call "ghillie suits," man-sized camouflage nets. The Pommie's new sniper unit, the "Lovat Scouts," claim to have developed them, but actually it's an idea that's been around since man first went hunting. In fact, I used something like this a few times on Gallipoli. The topside blends in with the surroundings, while the underside has straps to fix the thing to your arms and legs.' He turned the strip to reveal its underside and Law could see four strips had been tied in place at various positions. 'Here, Blucher, put this one on and show the boss how it works.'

Blucher took one of the suits and slipped his arms and legs through the straps. Law was unimpressed, for the garment seemed grossly too large for Blucher, and he was about to criticise Green's tailoring skills. But when Blucher lay down on the floor of the tent, the suit totally covered him and Law immediately saw how the "shagpile" strips on the upper side of the garment would break up the shape of the wearer's body.

'Rough it up a bit with dirt and throw on a bit of extra

shrubbery from the local area,' Green concluded, 'and it's near as damn is to swearing, makes a bloke invisible. We'll only put them on when we get to the killing ground, so we'll just roll them up and carry them on our packs for now. We've dressed our rifles and the telescope up with hessian too, which brings me to your weapon, sir… are you going to carry a rifle, or will you stick with your pistol?'

'Pistol, I think. I was never much of a shot with the rifle.'

Green nodded. However, Law's response concerned him, for he had no intention of engaging any Germans they might meet, at a range where a pistol with a range of about twenty-five yards would be of the slightest use. He decided against making an issue of it. 'You got a car, sir?' he asked.

Law smiled. 'Same driver as we had to get here. He's not best pleased. I think he thought he'd seen the last of us.'

They packed their individual equipment and then Law led the way to where several vehicles were lined up, ready for tasking.

'It was hardly worth unloading your stuff before, was it?' the driver quipped as he helped stow the equipment in the vehicle boot. He made no comment on the hessian rolls or the German helmets that topped the three packs.

An hour later, after a rough and uncomfortable journey, they reached Sausage Valley.

'Last time you were here, Blucher, a Hun had ear marked you,' Green quipped as he adjusted his pack.

'Yeah, and we won't go into what happened to you,' Blucher retorted. He began to whistle the music hall song "Let Me Call You Sweetheart."

Green laughed. 'Let me tell you,' he said, 'it was well worth it!'

Law was not privy to the joke. He was feeling tired and

nervous. He tried to convince himself this was because the night was much darker than he had anticipated and he was having difficulty gaining a sense of direction, but in truth he knew the real reason was that he was frightened. He had rarely been required to get so close to the front line, but in the next few hours, he would be first at the front, and then beyond it, behind enemy lines. 'Where to from here?' he asked.

'About 3500 yards that way,' Green replied, pointing to the northeast.

The going was somewhat easier than it had been when Green and Blucher had last walked through Pozieres. The German artillery which hitherto had targeted the village itself, now concentrated its venom on the Pozieres Heights and other areas to the north. The eerie glow of star shells pierced the darkness, aiding Green's navigation toward the ridge where the windmill had once stood. No one shot at them, nor did any zealous Military Policemen challenge their progress. Even so, it was dawn by the time the three finally arrived at the headquarters of the AIF's 48th Battalion, and the battalion's Adjutant ushered the trio into the presence of his Commanding Officer, Lieutenant Colonel "Bull" Leane.

Leane regarded Law and his two companions with distaste. He was a man of strong principles and had a reputation for fearlessly expressing his opinions regardless of the consequences. He found no difficulty in addressing any issue he believed to be wrong. He listened silently to Law's explanation as to why he and his two companions were in the location and what they intended to do. 'Why on earth,' he said glaring Law, 'amidst all this ghastly business could it be so important to kill one particular German?'

Law opened his mouth to speak, but Leane cut him off with a gesture. 'In the last forty-eight hours, I've lost the best part of two companies of men to the Hun artillery,' he said. 'Is killing this poor bloody German going to make one jot of difference to them? I mean, even if he were the bloody Kaiser it wouldn't make any difference to my men.'

'Of course not,' Law responded gently, 'but it may save others.'

Leane gave a short laugh. 'You must be using some kind of opiate if you believe that!'

'Nevertheless, if our target turns up, we will kill him,' Law replied.

Leane snorted in derision and turned his glare on Green. 'I'm not surprised that you have employed someone like Sergeant Green to carry out your dirty work. But why he isn't being used in the line to help his mates is totally beyond me!'

Green made a small mocking bow. 'I think you must be missing the adventure of raiding, Bull,' he said. 'I'm sure we could make room for one more should you wish to come with us.'

Thoroughly embarrassed by Green's retort, Law stepped between the two men. 'You will apologise immediately, Sergeant,' he hissed at Green.

Instead of a blast of righteous, angry indignation, Leane laughed uproariously. 'You always were an irreverent son of a bitch, Green,' he said, wiping a tear from his eye. 'It's good to see you haven't changed. Go on, get out of here, the three of you. I still think it's a fool of an idea, but good luck to you.'

Law quickly led the way from Leane's headquarters; he was still shocked by Green's behaviour. 'Whatever did you say that for, Green?' he asked hotly.

'Ah, the Bull is all right, sir,' Green replied. 'If he's got a fault, it's the love he has for his men, and if he's lost as many as he said, he'll be taking it personally.'

'I assume you have met before.'

Green shrugged. 'Once or twice,' he muttered.

'It was the same in Pozieres,' Blucher interjected. 'Wherever we went, someone knew him.'

Green changed the subject. 'We need to rest,' he said. 'Tomorrow we will carry out a reconnaissance, make our final plans, and rehearse.'

There were several disused dugouts in the old German trench line that the 48th Battalion now occupied. They found one that did not seem to have the ordure of death within it, and took possession of it. That night by candlelight, Green penned a letter to Stephanie. It was a long letter and when he had finished writing, he felt a deep sense of sadness and loss.

The next morning dawned warm and sunny. Blucher prepared a billy of tea and they breakfasted on condensed milk poured over their hard ration biscuits. 'By God, I miss Claire's cooking,' Blucher grumbled as he tried to chew the biscuit.

'Too late now,' Green reminded him, 'but you could have stayed there... you're the one who wanted to have a go.'

Law had no appetite for the meal and no interest in the domestic arrangements Blucher had left behind. 'Let's have a look outside,' he suggested.

They climbed on to the roof of the dugout and looked about. Green consulted the map. 'I think that pile of bricks over there,' he said, pointing along the ridgeline, 'must be the remains of the windmill.'

Carefully, they made their way to the pile of rubble. There was nothing to suggest it had once been an impressive windmill; however, it afforded a reasonable view of the land beyond. Green made sure the other two followed his example as he crawled to a high point on the rubble and settled down to watch.

A few hundred yards to their front, they could see the earthworks of the German rear line which was almost as battered and torn as the ground around their observation point. There was no sign of any Germans, but as both sides limited their out of trench activity to the hours of darkness, this was hardly surprising. Beyond the German line were glimpses of green fields, virtually untouched by shellfire, and they could see the rooftops of the village of Courcelette glinting in the afternoon sunshine. Green insisted Law and Blucher were comfortable in relating the vista shown on the map to the land they could actually see.

In the afternoon, having discussed various routes they might take to and from the place where the killing would take place, Green led the way back to the 48th Battalion headquarters where they finalised the plan. They would use the ruins of the windmill as their start point, then following a carefully designed compass march, arrive at a field bounded by the road the German Colonel would take. It was an *agreed* plan, for Green insisted that given the highly hazardous nature of the operation they faced, the three of them had to concur with the strategy. There was no argument, and having agreed on the plan, Green had them rehearse various situations they might possibly encounter on their journey. They practised setting the compass to the various bearings required. They learned the distances of each leg of the route, committing the distances to memory. They practised hand signals, they rehearsed crossing obstacles, and practised dressing themselves in their ghillie suits.

Green was fastidious in his demands. 'When we get into position,' he said, 'put your packs under the edge of your suit where you can get at it for some tucker or a drink, but whenever you have to get to your pack, move really slowly.

Remember, movement is our enemy, and if they see us, we will be for it. Once we lie down, we won't be able to stand up for any reason. If you need a leak, roll to one side and do it where you are; anything else you will just have to keep it with you until we leave. I'll take the middle spot. I like my spotter to work on my right, so Blucher, that's where you'll be, as close as it's comfortable to get. Sir, you need to be close too, but on my left. Blucher and I have to be able to hear your loud whisper when the Hun turns up.'

Law nodded. He was even more nervous now the time for action was drawing near. He took a deep breath and lay down where Green indicated and pulled the overhang of his ghillie suit over his head. For a moment, he felt helplessly encased by the suit and feared it would restrict his vision.

Green knelt by Law's side. 'That's it, sir,' he said encouragingly, 'you can use your pack to hold the edge up, and then you can look out from under the suit.'

As a final preparation, they found a safe spot where Green and Blucher zeroed their rifles and Law test fired his pistol. At last Green was satisfied and by way of rewarding the other two, he volunteered to visit the 48th Battalion's field kitchen to requisition some rations and a billy of tea for the team.

When Green arrived at the kitchen, he found Bull Leane was there enjoying a cup of tea. Leane waved in welcome. 'You cheeky bastard,' he said, extending a hand toward Green. 'Any other officer would have put you on a fizzer!'

Green grinned as he shook Leane's hand. 'I probably deserve it,' he said, 'but I couldn't let you get away with ripping into my boss though, could I?'

'Seems a decent, bloke,' Leane said, 'for one of the Deep Thinker Division. Anyway, what's one of Monash's bum boys doing out here?'

'I'm not so sure he's working for the General at the moment. This little stunt seems to be being run by someone much higher up.'

Leane grimaced. 'Well, I'd sooner you than me, mate,' he said feelingly, 'but then you always did have knack of taking on crazy jobs.' A German artillery shell whirred its way overhead and Leane paused, tensely watching the sky as it passed by. The missile exploded somewhere further down the slope behind them. 'Can't stand much more of their bloody shelling,' he muttered, 'Gallipoli was...'

'Different,' Green said softly.

Leane nodded and with an effort managed to return his full attention to Green. 'What do you want in my kitchen, anyway?' he asked belligerently.

'Why, I thought you might spare this old black man some hot water, and maybe some flour and sugar, boss,' Green replied in a parody of what most white Australians believed was the way Aboriginal people spoke.

Leane smiled. 'Corporal!' he called to a nearby cook. 'Give this Sergeant a billy of tea and enough of that murderous brew you claim as stew for three people.' He turned back to Green. 'I need to know when you are planning to leave on your little jaunt,' he said, 'so I can warn my blokes.'

Green nodded. 'Tonight,' he replied, 'as soon as the attack on Mouquet Farm starts.'

Leane raise an eyebrow and wondered how Green knew of the attack, but he made no comment. Instead he asked, 'And if you come back, are you coming this way?'

'That rather depends on how hard the Hun chases us. It may be we have to try and link up with our blokes somewhere else. But if we can, we will be coming back this way sometime tomorrow.'

'Right, I'll have the forward positions keep watch for you and we will give you what covering fire we can manage.'

'Thanks Colonel, much appreciated.'

'Good luck, Bob,' Leane said, 'keep your head down.' Then he turned and began to walk back to his headquarters.

Green called after him. 'Hang on a moment, Bull.'

Leane turned back.

Green handed him a grubby envelope. 'If anything goes wrong,' he said, 'would you post this to my girl?'

Leane took the envelope. There was a time when he would have tried to impart hope to a soldier making such a request. But he had given up that practice. Death was always close on the Somme. 'I'll see she gets it,' he said.

Green felt awkward. 'Thanks,' he said, 'good luck, Colonel.'

'You too, mate.'

Chapter 23

In spite of Leane's description, the stew proved to be quite edible, particularly when it was washed down with a mug of strong sweet tea. With full bellies, the three men returned to the ruined windmill to wait for darkness.

By way of final preparation, Green made Law and Blucher jump up and down to check their equipment did not clink or rattle; then he had them check him. They blackened their hands and faces with dirt, but when Law went to put his German helmet on, Green stopped him. 'We won't put the Hun helmets on just yet, sir,' he said. 'We don't want to be shot in the back by one of Bull's Diggers.'

Law hastily removed the German helmet and stowed it back in his haversack. 'Sorry,' he murmured, 'I should have thought of that.' He grimaced as a sudden cramp gripped his stomach. 'Blast,' he said, 'I've got to go to the toilet and I've just realised I haven't any paper!'

Wordlessly, Blucher produced a cigarette paper from which he tore a small section. He handed the tiny section of paper to Law.

'What am I meant to do with this?' Law demanded.

'Its' for after you finish,' the straight-faced Blucher replied, 'to clean your finger nails.'

'Leave the Colonel alone, Blucher,' Green interrupted, passing Law a small roll of toilet paper. "There you go, sir. Use that shell hole over there and don't forget to bury your leavings.'

'The attack should go in any minute now,' Blucher suggested as he looked at the lengthening shadows in the valley below.

Green nodded. 'It won't be long,' he agreed.

Law returned. He had finally understood that Blucher had played on his inexperience in the field. 'Clean your fingernails,' he chortled. 'That's very good, Blucher. I must remember that.'

Suddenly, away to the north a veritable storm of the sounds of warfare erupted. 'That's the attack,' Green announced unnecessarily. He stood up and adjusted his pack on his shoulders. 'Ready?' he asked.

Law gulped and nodded.

'Ready as I'll ever be,' Blucher replied.

In single file, Green leading, followed by Law and with Blucher in the rear, they passed through the Australian forward positions and out into No Man's Land. Carefully, they made their way through the wreckage created by recent bombardments and picked their way through the Australian wire. Away to the west, star shells burst high above the Pozieres ridgeline, and a machine gun rattled into deadly life, but neither event posed any risk to the three men as they slowly walked toward German territory.

Green continually checked his compass bearing and Law and Blucher counted every pace they took. The sound of German voices singing wafted across the evening air, indicating they were close to the trench works they had seen during their observations from the ruined windmill. Green held up his hand, signalling a halt. He drew out his German helmet and placed it on his head; Law and Blucher followed suit. 'By the centre, quick march,' Green whispered, and they began to march boldly and quickly through the gloom, as though they really were German soldiers off to perform some task. They passed across the remains of the German wire and through a gap between two badly damaged strong points into the land beyond. All the while, the flash and glare of artillery fire from the attack on Mouquet Farm danced across the night sky like lightning from a massive tempest. The sounds of the distant battle dulled the sounds of their march, and Law was struck by an impression of unreality, as though he and his two companions had entered another realm.

A voice hailed them from nearby. *'Gute Nacht.'*

Green almost froze; had he brought them too close to a German post? With an effort, he kept walking.

'Bleib sicher,' Law called in reply. Moments later, they were through the German front line, swallowed up in the darkness of the night.

Two hours of steady walking passed without incident; then Law whistled softly. The other two gathered around him. 'We have come 1500 paces,' he whispered.

'I make it just under,' Blucher added.

Green looked around trying in vain to make out any recognisable feature of the countryside. 'No sign of a track, but the country feels about right,' he said quietly. 'How about we continue on this bearing for another two hundred paces before we change course?'

The other two nodded in agreement. Silently, they resumed their march. Fifty paces further on, Green signalled another halt beckoned the other two to him. He pointed at the ground at his feet. A well-worn two wheeled track cut across their path.

'This must be the road to Mouquet Farm,' Law whispered. 'Well navigated, Green. The question is, are we to the right or the left of the road junction?'

'Probably,' Green agreed. He knelt down and peered through the gloom at the track's surface. 'It's certainly well used,' he said. 'So if it is the road to the Farm, the junction should be a few hundred yards to our right.' An indistinct noise attracted Blucher's attention. 'Quiet!' he hissed.

They listened. The noise of the nearby battle made it difficult to hear any other sound, but suddenly they could all hear the crunch, crunch, crunch of numerous feet walking along the road toward them. Instinctively, the three men threw themselves into the meagre cover offered by the edge of the road and tried to press their bodies into the earth. Fortunately, the approaching body of Germans seemed to have confined their movement to the road itself. They were moving swiftly, clearly confident that they were safe; one soldier at the rear of the group was even calling the step. They marched straight past the hiding place where Green, Law, and Blucher cowered in the shadows. The German soldiers were soon swallowed up by the night, the sounds of their passing slowly receding into the distance.

Slowly Green got to his knees and waited cautiously, but just as was about to signal the others to resume their march, the glare of an approaching car's headlights pierced the space at the top of the ridgeline. 'Stay down,' he hissed, 'there's a bloody car coming now!'

Law wriggled closer to Green. 'Won't they see us in the lights?' he whispered.

'Only if we move,' Green replied.

Blucher watched with amusement as Law who was hardly satisfied with Green's explanation tried again to press his body into the ground. Blucher felt confident in his own hiding place as he had the good fortune to be close to a small thicket of bushes, and it was from this meagre cover he watched as the vehicle approached.

The car's headlights danced up and down as the vehicle bumped its way down the road. The sound of the engine could now be heard, and above that, the sound of several voices singing happily.'

'Confident bastards,' Green mumbled.

A few yards away from where Green, Law, and Blucher lay, the car slowed to negotiate a particularly rough section of the road. The singing ceased and the singer shouted jovial abuse at the driver as the clung desperately to their seats. The rough section negotiated the driver began to increase speed again, when an authoritative shout from the rear of the vehicle interrupted this endeavour.

'*Einhalt!*'

The driver brought the vehicle to a halt directly above the Australian's hiding place, and for one terrifying moment, Green thought they had been discovered. Careful to avoid any sudden movement that might be seen by the group of Germans, he slowly began to take a Mills bomb from his basic pouch. Law gently restrained his hand, indicating that Green should wait. Almost imperceptibly, Green nodded, acknowledging the Germans were showing no sign of alarm. Then the same voice declared happily: '*Pisse zu stoppen!*'

The driver seemed less than impressed. '*Sei schnell,*' he said grumpily.

Green slowly moved his head in the direction of the now stationary German vehicle. It was so close he could almost reach out and touch it. Three people were climbing down from the rear of the car; they seemed to be in high spirits, for there was considerable laughter and back slapping between them. From his position on the ground, the three Germans appeared to be unnaturally tall, and as he watched they lined the edge of the road, unfastened their trousers, and began to urinate into the darkness. Then they climbed back into the vehicle, the driver gunned the motor and clumsily engaged the gears, scoring a tirade of jovial abuse from his passengers; then, the car proceeded on its way into the night.

'Close,' Law observed as they listened to the receding sound of the vehicle.

'Too fucking close,' Blucher grumbled. 'The bastards pissed on me!' He turned his back toward his two companions to reveal his discomfort.

It was too dark for Green or Law to see Blucher's sodden tunic. 'Bloody well done, Blucher,' Green said enthusiastically. 'I'm not sure I could have stayed still if it had happened to me!'

'Nor me,' Law agreed, 'but what's to be done about it?'

'I'll dry out as soon as we get moving,' Blucher replied; then he added jokingly: 'It's too far to go back for a change of clothes.'

'I wonder what that lot were doing here,' Green remarked thoughtfully. 'I'd have thought with the attack going on, they would be sending reinforcements up this road, not taking people away.'

'Maybe it was the leave draft,' Blucher offered. 'The Other Rank's marching, and the officers in the car...'

Green nodded. 'Maybe, but even then, with that lot going on,' he jerked his head toward the sounds and flashes of the attack, 'you'd think they would have cancelled all leave. No, I think it might be a sign our attack isn't going too well. The bastards are confident'.

'Does it matter?' Law asked.

Green shrugged. 'In the short term, probably not. If we have to withdraw that way though, it might be a bit tricky. One thing I think our visitors have shown us though, this track is almost certainly the right one, and if we follow it downhill, we'll find the crossroads.'

'Agreed,' Law said.

'Are you ready to move, Blucher?'

'Sooner we walk, the sooner I'll dry off,' Blucher replied resignedly.

Quietly they moved forward, and twenty minutes later, they were standing at their objective. 'Closer than I thought,' Green muttered. 'I thought we were further up the hill. Well, let's not stand here; we have to find somewhere to shoot from.'

The initial search was fruitless. There was a single tree and a broken down animal shelter near the crossroads, but Green dismissed these as being too close to the crossroads and too obvious.

Law lifted his German helmet and scratched his head. 'It seems to me that leaves us with open paddock,' he said, casting a worried glance at the darkened field in which they stood.

Green shook his head. 'It's not such a problem,' he said. 'It might even be better in a way. We've got our ghillie suits and just enough darkness left to set up a decent hide.'

Even Blucher, who trusted Green implicitly, doubted his Sergeant's choice. 'But it's open paddock,' he said quietly.

'Don't worry, mate,' Green replied, 'when I've finished, we will be hard to see at five yards, let alone two hundred.'

The paddock contained the remnants of a crop of sugar beet. Clumps of the leafy plants remained pocking up above the furrowed soil, while discarded tops of the harvested roots lay all around. 'This is good,' Green muttered.

Law was unconvinced. 'How can this be suitable?' he asked hotly. 'There is absolutely no cover here.'

Green poked at a stub of beet with his foot. 'Maybe not

cover from fire,' he countered, 'but with our ghillie suits on, a man could walk on top of us in this stuff and still not see us.' To prove his point, Green took his suit from his pack and rolled it out on the ground. It was indeed remarkably difficult to see the garment. 'Pull a bit of this stuff over it,' Green continued, raking some of the beet leaves over the suit, 'and it's invisible. Don't forget, we don't want to be involved in an exchange of shots here. One shot and that's it.'

Law was still a worried man. 'How far is it to the crossroads?' he demanded huffily. 'Are you sure you can hit him from here?'

Green glanced in the direction of the crossroads. 'Still too dark to be certain of the range,' he replied, glancing toward the sky and the thin ribbon of moon that drifted far above them, 'but in daylight, anything inside eight hundred yards is an easy enough shot, and at a guess, I'd say the road is no more than six hundred yards away. No, we are well within range.'

Law's shoulders sagged in resignation. 'Well, you're the expert,' he muttered. 'What do we do now?'

'First thing is make ourselves comfortable,' Green replied. 'Give us a hand, Blucher. We'll make a bit of a scrape to lie in. Sir, will you keep watch and let us know if anyone is moving about?'

Using their hands and feet, Green and Blucher smoothed out an area that would accommodate three men lying here side by side. 'Make sure you get any of the beet roots,' Green warned. 'Once we lie down here, we can't be moving about, no matter how uncomfortable it gets.' After about five minutes' work, Green was satisfied the scrape was ready for occupation. He stood up and gestured to the other two to come close. 'We'll put on our ghillie suits now,' he said. 'Have you dried off, Blucher?'

'Dry enough, let's get on with it.'

Just as they had practised during their rehearsals, the three men slipped their arms and legs through the straps that held the suits to their bodies. They made a macabre sight, like caped creatures from the underworld performing some ghostly rites under the night sky.

'Now I want everyone to take a piss,' Green announced. 'Blucher, you go over there a few yards, sir, you go that way, and I'll do the front and rear. Spray it around a bit.'

'Is this some kind of weird Abo thing?' Blucher asked.

'Maybe,' Green replied, 'but it might stop a fox or some other kind of wild creature walking on our hide and giving us away.'

Law nodded in appreciation. 'Clever,' he said, 'very clever. The smell of our urine will warn them off.'

'That's the way, sir. It's an old bushman's trick.'

'I'd have thought there was already enough piss on me to keep most creatures away,' Blucher quipped. Nevertheless, he joined the other two as they marked their territory before returning to the hide.

'Everyone comfortable?' Green asked, and received a duet of nods in response. 'Well, good luck, one and all,' he concluded.

Chapter 23

Law and Blucher positioned themselves either side of where Green would lie. Law uncased his binoculars and Blucher placed his pack to allow him to poke the telescope out from under the folds of his suit. Green made some last-minute adjustments to both men's suits and scattered handfuls of beet leaves over their suits. 'Looks good,' he whispered encouragingly. He lay down between the two of them and gently pushed his rifle forward. 'Snuggle in,' he murmured, 'nice and close now; don't be shy.'

They had previously arranged a three-hour sentry roster. Two men would keep watch while the third slept. However, opportunities for rest proved to be fleeting. An hour after they had occupied the hide, a heavy artillery bombardment fell on the German line to their north west. The noise and flash of exploding shells, although safely distant, made sleep difficult. Then at around two in the morning, the sounds of marching feet and singing voices caused another alarm. They waited tensely as the martial sounds seemed to grow closer and then receded in the direction of Mouquet Farm.

Soon after, another column of marching troops passed invisibly by, followed by another and then another. 'They must be reinforcing the Farm after the attack,' Green murmured. 'Just as well we got here when we did.'

'My oath,' Blucher replied with feeling. 'There seems to be a hell of a lot of them.'

'Well, at least they are not looking for us,' Law observed.

'So far so good, eh?'

At around four o'clock, the first hint of dawn etched itself across the eastern sky. The hedges and fences dividing the various fields became faintly visible. Green and Blucher were on watch while Law rested. Blucher allowed his head to lull forward, easing the stiffness in his neck and shoulders. 'Couldn't half do with a fag,' he muttered.

'Quiet!' Green hissed, 'I thought I heard something!'

The sound of a horse's whinny and a man's voice drifted across the field from the direction of Courcelette. 'There!' Green said.

Blucher turned his head toward the sound. 'I heard it,' he whispered. 'Can you see anything?'

'Nothing, keep quiet; it might be cavalry!'

The horse whinnied again and then they heard a dull scraping sound.

'It can't be cavalry,' Blucher muttered, 'not making a noise like that. What the hell is it?'

Green listened for a moment; then he chuckled. 'It's a bloody farmer,' he said, then added in amazement, 'He's going to plough this bloody field.'

'Shit,' Blucher hissed in reply. 'I didn't join up to be ploughed into the ground by some bloody French farmer!'

'Keep your shirt on,' Green replied. 'It couldn't be better. It will take him all day to reach this spot with his plough. So long as he doesn't spot us, he'll make the perfect decoy for any Hun travelling along that road.'

Law stirred sleepily. 'What's going on?' he asked. Green gave a rapid explanation.

'Let's hope he doesn't see us and give the game away,' Law mused.

'Not a chance,' Green said confidently. 'We may as well eat

something while it's quiet. I'm for a nice tasty biscuit.'

'Mind you, don't break a tooth,' Blucher grumbled.

When the sun's rays allowed, they could see their hide was in the middle of a field of approximately six acres in area. A man and a team of two horses pulling a plough appeared like wraiths in the half light, slowly and methodically working their way back and forth across the northern end of the field. The man was clearly unaware of the hide that had been covertly established in his paddock.

Blucher watched the man with some envy. 'You wouldn't think there's a war on,' he muttered. 'I mean look at him, not a care in the world and here we are hell bent on doing some poor bastard in.'

'That's the way of it,' Green agreed, 'but I don't like his chances of seeing a crop out of this ground.'

'Me neither,' Blucher said, 'if he waits a week or two, the artillery will plough it all up for him, and later it will get a good dose of blood and bone all over it too.'

'That sounds a bit pessimistic,' Law said. 'The war can't last much longer surely.' But if he expected to promote a discussion he was disappointed, for he received no response.

With the daylight, they continued the same sentry routine they had observed during the darkness. The morning hours dragged slowly by, occasionally German supply wagons clattered along the road, and several times small patrols of three or four German soldiers walked along the edge of the field, but none of these passers-by paid any attention to the middle of the field and the morning passed uneventfully.

At midday, the farmer rested his horses in the shade of the single tree and ate his lunch. 'Beef and pickled onion by the look of it,' Law commented as he trained his binoculars on the man's lunch.

'Nice,' Blucher replied, 'I wonder if he'd swap a couple of these army biscuits for a pickled onion?'

'Not if he has any sense,' Law muttered.

The afternoon sun blazed down and it became uncomfortably hot beneath the hessian ghillie suits. Perspiration began to ooze from their bodies. It stung their eyes and attracted swarms of flies and other insects that crawled annoyingly over them, entering their eyes, nostrils, and ears. 'I don't know how much more of this I can stand,' Law muttered as he attempted to dislodge a particularly persistent insect from a nostril.

'Keep still,' Green hissed, 'they won't eat much.'

'They won't be around much longer anyway,' Blucher offered. 'I reckon it's going to rain.'

'How do you work that out?' Green asked.

'It's me bunion,' Blucher replied. 'It always aches when rain's on the way.'

Green looked up at the cloudless sky. 'Don't give up your day job, mate.'

Blucher took his turn to rest and promptly dozed off. Moments later, he began to snore, only to receive a sharp elbow in the ribs from Green for his trouble. 'Snoring?' Blucher asked.

'How did you guess?'

'Sorry.'

The farmer had returned to the shade of the tree to rest his team and one of the horses seemed to have heard Blucher's snore, or perhaps it sensed the presence of something hidden in the middle of the field, for it pricked its ears and turned toward the hide. For a moment, the three men hiding beneath the hessian and sugar beet camouflage held their collective breaths in case the farmer noticed his horse's interest. But with a quick flick of the reins, the farmer called his team to attention and returned to the ploughing.

'There is something funny going on there,' Blucher whispered as he lay back to rest again.

Green focused the telescope on the farmer. 'How do you mean?' he asked.

'Well, it seems to me he's going backwards and forwards over the same bit of dirt. I reckon he should be halfway out to us by now, but he's still on the same first couple of rows.'

Law swung his binoculars toward the farmer. 'You're right,' he said. 'I wonder why he's doing that?'

Green grunted. 'Must be harder ground over there,' he suggested, 'or perhaps the new crop needs a really fine seed bed.'

'Probably,' Law replied, and he turned away to study a supply wagon that bumped its way dustily along the road. Blucher had already gone back to sleep.

The farmer remained their only companion, continuing to plough the northern end of the field. Green and his two companions had become used to the man's presence and no longer concerned themselves with his agricultural pursuit.

The afternoon dragged on, their target was late, and Law was beginning to be concerned that the German colonel would not appear. 'I'm sorry, chaps,' he whispered, 'I think we should call it a day and head back.'

Green grunted. 'Not yet,' he replied, 'if he doesn't show, we will go back in the dark.'

The sun was hovering on the very rim of the horizon, and lengthening shadows stretched their fingers across the land toward the hide, when Law saw the car. 'Look to the left,' he said. 'I think something is about to happen.'

A German staff car drove slowly along the road from the

direction of Mouquet Farm. Law focused his binocular onto the vehicle. 'Three Huns,' he announced quietly, 'a Colonel, a Major, and their driver. By the look of it this could be our man's welcoming committee. Are there any cars coming from the other direction?'

Slowly, Blucher carefully swung the telescope to watch the road from Courcelette. 'Nothing,' he replied quietly.

The staff car came to a halt at the road junction. The two German officers remained in the vehicle. 'Good opportunity to check the range,' Green said. 'Blucher, how far do you reckon it is from here to the car?'

Blucher thought for a moment. 'Four hundred and twenty yards,' he replied.

Green turned to Law. 'Sir?'

'A bit less.... three hundred... say, three eighty yards.'

Green nodded. 'Averaged out, that makes the distance four hundred yards. I'll set my sights at that. Any wind?'

'Left to right but very slight,' Blucher replied.

'Hardly an issue then,' Green muttered as he adjusted the sights on his rifle.

Law watched with interest. 'I thought you'd use a telescopic sight,' he said as Green took aim at the driver of the car.

'I don't like the Army issue scopes,' Green replied. 'Bloody things are off set for some reason. Anyway, I get pretty good results without. Mind you, this rifle has a few modifications that make it a bit more accurate.'

'Oh?'

Green gently slid his hands over the weapon in an almost loving caress. 'The barrel's "floated" and I've made some adjustments to the trigger.'

'Watch right,' Blucher hissed, interrupting Green's

explanation. 'There's a car coming from Courcelette!'

At the head of a dust cloud of its own making, a second German staff car sped along the road toward the junction. Blucher watched them through the telescope. 'Four, no six of them in the car,' he said.

Green nudged him gently. 'Forget them,' he said. 'Concentrate on the two at the crossing. Let's do a quick practice.'

Blucher refocused the instrument on the first car. 'Reference the car's steering wheel,' he intoned quietly, 'half a point left, a German major.'

'Good,' Green breathed as he took aim, 'very good.'

Law interrupted. 'The second man, the Colonel, is getting out of the car and walking to the front of the vehicle.

'Blucher?' Green asked.

'Reference the steering wheel, one point right, loan man standing at the road's edge.'

'That will do nicely,' Green murmured as he readjusted his aim. 'Good teamwork.' He opened the breech of his rifle and worked a round into the chamber. 'Now all we have to do is wait.'

The second car was travelling at speed, and for a moment it appeared as though it was going to drive straight past the stationary vehicle, but at the last moment it came to a sliding halt. Law was watching the occupants of the car intently. 'Damn dust,' he muttered. 'I can't get a clear look at them. Wait, yes, it's him. Blucher, the little bloke in the Colonel's uniform. The one shaking hands with the other Colonel. I think that's him.'

Green watched... the German group were clearly introducing one another. 'You have to admire the German race for their manners,' he muttered, 'I'm surprised they haven't kissed!'

The German officers continued, shaking hands and saluting. Blucher concentrated the telescope on the short Colonel. 'Can't get a clear look at him yet,' he whispered. 'I'll use the same reference point.'

'Hang on,' Green said in sudden alarm, 'what's going on here?' The farmer was now ploughing across the field and rapidly placing himself between Green and his target. 'Get out of the way!' Green muttered angrily. The farmer was now about twenty yards from the Germans, completely blocking Green's line of fire.

'I don't like this,' Law muttered, 'something's wrong here.'

Blucher was studying the farmer through the telescope. 'Bloody hell,' he hissed, 'he's no bloody farmer, he's got a grenade in his hand.'

Green watched in horror as the farmer pulled the pin from the grenade and lobbed it toward the crowding group of German officers, their shouts of alarm drowned in the ugly crump of the exploding bomb. The sudden and horrific noise caused the farmer's horses to bolt, the single furrow plough bouncing crazily behind them. The farmer turned and ran directly toward the snipers hide.

'Shit, shit, shit!' Law snarled, 'and look... the silly prick missed the lot!'

Law was wrong; the farmer had not missed everything. The grenade had exploded beneath the first staff car and that vehicle was now burning fiercely. Two of the German officers were down, one lay still, while the other clearly in agony from his injuries was flopping about on the ground like a freshly landed fish. The driver of the burning car remained behind the wheel of his vehicle, dead and enveloped in flame. However, the man Law had identified as Colonel Nicolai seemed to be unharmed, and one of the other officers had pushed Nicolai into the remaining car and climbed into the driver's seat where he was desperately trying to start the vehicles. The other two officers had drawn their pistols and were firing at the retreating farmer, the bullets inadvertently flying dangerously close to the snipers hide.

Completely oblivious to the danger posed by the pistol firing Germans, Law was in a state of intense excitement. 'Get Nicolai!' he shouted at Green. 'Shoot the bastard!'

Green calmly regarded the scene of carnage to his front. Dense black smoke from the burning vehicle billowed across the second car, obscuring his view. 'Speak to me, Blucher!' he said quietly.

'Reference the dead German on the ground,' Blucher began, 'half a point to the right, target in the passenger seat.'

Green was proud of Blucher. Even in the excitement and surprise of the moment, he was still thinking clearly. Robbed of the car's steering wheel reference point that they had previously practised, he had calmly selected another. Green had worked with other spotters who under similar circumstances would have panicked. 'Seen,' he said, 'the bloody smoke is making it difficult... damn, this bloody farmer keeps running in front of me.' For a millisecond the smoke cleared, and the farmer's running figure swayed out of the line of fire. Green squeezed the trigger, but just as he did the German officer in the driver's seat of the remaining car succeeded in starting the vehicle and it jerked forward.

'A hit,' Blucher commented as he steadied the scope on the erratically moving car. 'Right shoulder, you'll need another shot to finish him.'

Green worked his rifle bolt, easing another round into its chamber. The effect of his first shot was amazing. The German officer driving the car tried to execute a three-point turn to gain the cover the burning vehicle, all the while screaming at the two officers in pursuit of the fleeing farmer to return to the car. The farmer had felt the wind created by Green's bullet on his right cheek and the shock caused him to stumble and fall. In the same instant, the two pursuing Germans caught a glimpse of the hide and began to fire their pistols at the ghillie suited men inside it. Green knew he had no choice. He quickly changed his point of aim and shot the closest German officer through the head. Blucher shot the other through the body. When Green returned his attention to the car, it was already too late. The driver had managed to complete the turn and made good his escape, the car bouncing crazily as it sped along the road back toward Courcelette.

Law watched the retreating vehicle intensely through his binocular. 'Well done, Green; you too, Blucher. Not your fault of course, but what a bloody stuff up!' he growled. 'If it hadn't been for that bloody peasant, we would have had Nicolai on a plate.'

Green showed no interest in either Law's praise or the retreating Germans. He stood up and threw his pack on to his back. 'Let's get the hell out of here,' he said. 'In less than five minutes, there is going to be a big mob of Huns crawling all over this place.'

Green's words galvanized Law and Blucher into action, and they stood up, the stalks of beet plant falling from their ghillie suits. The farmer, who still lay where he had fallen, managed to struggle to his knees and stared in amazement at the three figures that suddenly appeared before him. It seemed to him that three devils had erupted from the earth. With a startled shriek, he jumped to his feet began to run across the field in the direction of Courcelette.

Green led the way at a brisk jog, across the field, upwards toward the Pozieres ridgeline. They were not a moment too soon; the hand grenade's explosion and the bevy of small arms fire had attracted the attention of the nearest German outpost. A guttural shout caused Blucher took a glance over his left shoulder. 'That's nasty,' he said hastily as he ran onward. 'There's a platoon's worth of Huns trotting in our direction.'

Law glanced fearfully toward Green. 'What do we do now?' he asked.

'Save your breath and keep running,' Green replied sharply.

'But we can't go this way,' Law panted. 'We are going to finish up at Mouquet Farm!'

'Can't go back down there either,' Green replied grimly. He looked desperately ahead at the ridgeline. It seemed to be further away than ever.

Chapter 24

Jäger Bayerlein had been out of the line, resting in a safe area near the village of Courcelette, when the crumping bang of the exploding grenade reached his ears. Moments later, a staff car had careered into the position and a slightly wounded Colonel Nicolai shouted the news of an assassination attempt. Within moments, the officer in command of the position had mustered and deployed a forty strong rapid response force. Bayerlein and his spotter were included in the response force and now the force was trotting determinedly toward the crossroads where the attack had taken place. However, there was something about the whole event that puzzled the German sniper, and as he hurried forward, he considered the facts as he knew them.

A peasant believed to have been responsible for throwing the bomb at Colonel Nicolai's party had blundered into the response force and had been summarily executed. No attempt had been made to question the peasant; the fact that he was running away from the area where the attack had taken place and the brief description provided by Colonel Nicolai had been sufficient proof of his guilt, and the officer in charge simply drew out his pistol and shot the fellow. Bayerlein thoroughly agreed with the execution. Any interrogation of the peasant would only have given his accomplices time to escape, but the very fact there were accomplices puzzled Bayerlein. According to Colonel Nicolai, three snipers had acted in support of the bomb thrower. That puzzled Bayerlein. He could understand the bomb thrower being support for a sniper, in case the shooter missed his target, or lost his nerve, but why have the bomb thrower as the primary method of attack? It did not make sense. No, Bayerlein decided, there was the smell of a botched attack associated with this event; someone on the enemy's side had blundered.

An excited shout from somewhere to the front of the response force formation interrupted his thoughts. 'Half right... three men running up the ridge!'

Bayerlein glanced toward the direction indicated. A thousand yards away, he could see the tiny figures of three men who seemed to be running ever so slowly toward the top of the ridge

Someone, possibly the man who had shouted, began to fire his rifle at the retreating figures.

'Fool!' Bayerlein snapped at the shooter. 'They are out of your range; cease fire!' He gave the man a vicious shove, sending him sprawling on to the roadway. For a moment, there was confusion among the pursuing force as men swerved away to avoid the fallen man, and bumping into others pushing them out of the formation. With a few curt orders, the officer in charge regained control and swung the formation to the left so that it faced the ridge. 'Forward,' the officer shouted, theatrically waving his pistol. 'Fire at will!'

———————————

A bullet cracked past Blucher's head and he turned toward the dull thump that followed its passage. 'They've definitely seen us,' he called to Green.

Green risked a brief glance at the following German troops. They were about nine hundred yards away and moving steadily. 'Bugger!' he growled. 'There's at least another ten minutes before it gets properly dark. You two keep running up toward the ridge top. I'll slow them down a bit.' Without waiting for a reply, he sat down where he was, the skirts of the ghillie suit flicked carelessly about him, and quickly set the sight on his rifle to nine hundred yards. A young German officer was enthusiastically urging his fellows on after their prey was his first target. He took a deep breath to steady himself, then exhaled slowly. When about half of that breath had gone, he squeezed the trigger home. The bullet caught the young officer in the chest, slamming him backward to the ground. Green ignored the dead man and quickly changed his aim to two other German soldiers who had stood stock still, staring at their fallen comrade in horror. Seconds later, they too were dead. The others went to ground and were desperately trying to present as small a target as possible to the killer who was further up the ridgeline. Green killed three more of them before jumping to his feet and running after Law and Blucher.

He caught up to them in a low depression, about two feet deep at its lowest point, but sufficient to shield them from the pursuing Germans fire. Blucher was aiming his rifle back down the slope ready to support Green had it proved necessary. Law was clearly spent. 'My God,' he gasped, 'I'd forgotten how hard soldiering can be, but I'm glad you're on our side, Green. I don't think I've ever seen such shooting.'

Green ignored him and hastily checked his own weapon and equipment. 'What are they doing now, Blucher?' he asked.

Blucher stole a glance over the lip of the depression. The German troops were still in cover. 'They 'haven't moved yet,' he announced, then he ducked back as several rifle bullets cracked over his head.

'We're safe enough here for the moment,' Green said. 'I wonder why they aren't following up...' He turned and looked further up the ridge. 'Shit!' he said, 'they aren't as green as they are cabbage looking!' He pointed up the slope. A line of around twenty grey clad soldiers were moving cautiously down the slope toward the depression. Clearly, the troops that had been pursuing them were aware of their comrades' advance, and were now waiting as a blocking force to prevent the Australians' escape.

'Can we hold them off till dark?' Law asked.

'It's our only hope,' Green said, knowing this was a lie and there was really no hope at all. 'If we can... we'll make a break for it off to the left, and make our way back to our blokes. Sir, would you mind watching those pricks down the hill? Let me know if they move.'

Law nodded, and wriggled into position.

'Blucher,' Green continued, 'when I give the word, you and I will see how many of these bastards on the uphill side we can kill in five minutes.'

Green made himself comfortable on the uphill side of the depression and aimed his weapon at the advancing line of German infantry. 'Right, Blucher,' he said quietly. 'I'm going to take that bastard that's waving his arms about; choose any of the rest for yourself... fire when ready.'

Green squeezed the trigger and was rewarded when the man he had targeted was flung viciously to the ground.

Blucher had selected the man on the extreme length of the German formation. 'Christ,' he muttered, doubting his ability to hit a target at that range, 'they're a fair way up the ridge.' He too fired, and a German soldier spun away holding his right thigh.

By the time Blucher fired, Green had already killed another

man and was zeroing in on a third; nevertheless, he shouted his encouragement to Blucher. 'That's the way!' he shouted. 'Good shot, mate!'

The Germans began to employ their battle drills, one group taking cover from where they fired at Green and Blucher forcing them to shelter, while the other group dashed forward. Even so, Green killed two more of their number and Blucher another, but it was never going to be enough. The nearest Germans were now little more than eighty yards away. Green could see their long bayonets glinting in the last of the sun's rays. In another twenty paces or so, he knew they would break into a run and then he and Blucher could never knock them all down in time. He, Blucher, and Law would die on this slope, and there was nothing he could do about it. His thoughts momentarily turned to Stephanie and felt a deep sadness that he would never see her again.

———————————

The initial pride Bayerlein had felt in the swiftness of the German response was beginning to wane. The young officer's enthusiasm for the chase had placed all of the response force in danger, and so he felt it was simple justice that the young fool had been the first to die. However, the manner of the officer's death interested Bayerlein. A nine hundred-yard shot to hit the officer squarely in the chest was a demonstration of the enemy rifleman's skill, a skill he confirmed by shooting another five of the pursuing response force. Bayerlein glanced toward his spotter. 'Binoculars!' he demanded harshly, then added urgently, 'stay down, you young fool! Just pass them across.'

The new spotter, the man who had taken the long dead young Himmler's place, cautiously passed the binoculars across to where his master lay in the doubtful cover of a ploughed furrow.

Bayerlein focused the glasses on the place where the sniper had taken cover. Occasionally, a head would appear above the top of the cover, those appearances attracting a bevy of ineffectual shots from the response force. Then he saw German troops advancing down the ridge toward the snipers' cover. Clearly, the snipers were now doomed; all the response force had to do was wait. He passed the glasses back to the spotter.

'Watch,' he said curtly. Let me know when it's over.'
The spotter refocused the glasses. He watched as two of the enemy desperately engaged the German troops moving down the slope. One of the enemy was clearly a superior marksman, and as the spotter watched, he noticed something else about that man... he had dark skin. Almost casually, he advised his master of the fact.

'What?' Bayerlein was instantly interested. A dark-skinned marksman? Surely, he thought, there could not be many such men in the British forces. He wriggled into a fire position and focused his telescopic sight on the enemy position. He made a silent prayer: 'Please God, give me the chance to avenge young Himmler before those oafs with their bayonets rip the sniper and his comrades to pieces.' Then as if in answer to his supplication, British artillery provided a response.

For the three Australians, the sudden flurry of sound that ended in a climatic reverberating crash was a welcome miracle. The artillery shells fell squarely among the advancing uphill Germans, and in a matter of seconds their well-ordered advance was reduced to ruin. Two brave men, the Germans closest to Green and Blucher, began to charge toward the depression that hid the Australians, screaming challenges as they ran. Green shot them both.

'How did that happen?' Blucher shouted, pointing toward the still exploding shell fire.

'God alone knows,' Green shouted in reply, 'but I hope they keep it up!'

The artillery barrage began to creep slowly down the slope toward them and Green waved for Blucher to join him.

'This is great,' Blucher grumbled as he slid to ground beside Green, 'we miss out on being bayoneted to death by the Huns, only to be blown to hell by our own side!' Almost as Blucher spoke, the barrage checked in its advance down the slope, to fall with even greater vigour onto the German positions further up the slope. Then quite suddenly, the rain of shells ceased altogether.

———————

The casualties and the artillery shoot seemed to take all the fight out of the Sergeant who had assumed command of the response force. 'Fall back!' he shouted. 'Fall back!'

The artillery fire ceased almost as suddenly as it began, but this did not seem to reawaken any desire within the new commander to resume the fight against the enemy sniper. In ones and twos, the men of his new command began to run back down the slope toward the crossroads. However, Bayerlein did not move. He knew with complete certainty that the next few seconds would be decisive.

'Come on,' his spotter urged.

'Quiet!' Bayerlein snapped. 'Concentrate on the enemy position!'

Reluctantly, the spotter resumed his position. He glared angrily at his master; he had been told Bayerlein was a mad bastard, and now he was beginning to think his informant was right.

Bayerlein was not interested in his spotter's concerns. He was concentrating all his attention on the enemy position. Something told him that if he did not take the dark-skinned sniper now, he would never have another opportunity. Once again, he peered through his telescopic sight. It was already late in the day, the light was fading, and the range a little over eight hundred meters. Every ounce of his experience screamed at him that this was an impossible shot. He tensed. The enemy snipers had noticed the response force's withdrawal; their heads were above the cover of their hide. Through the telescopic sight, he could not quite make out the enemy soldiers' features, but he could see enough to see that one of them had dark skin. He aimed at the dark-skinned face, regulated his breathing and gently squeezed the trigger.

'The Huns are leaving,' Law called from his position watching the first German group. Green crawled to Law's position, crouching so that his head was just above the lip of the depression; in the very last of the sunlight, he could see the grey figures moving back the way they had come. They had done it! All that remained now was to safely navigate their way back to the 48th Battalion's position near the windmill. He rose to his knees to get a better view of the retreating Germans, and suddenly his world was filled with a searing flash of light and he knew no more.

'A good hit,' Bayerlein's spotter announced in surprise. 'Do you want to try for another?'

Bayerlein ejected the spent round from the chamber of his rifle and swiftly reloaded. 'No,' he said quietly, 'that's enough... let's go.'

Chapter 25

'Blucher!'

The urgency in Law's shout of alarm frightened Blucher more than the artillery barrage. He turned toward the Colonel and saw Green was lying, unmoving, on his back and Law was desperately trying to staunch the blood that was flowing from the right side of Green's head.

'More bandages, man. For God's sake, hurry!'

Blucher tore open his pack and seized two field dressings from within. 'Here,' he gasped, handing the dressings to Law.

Law applied the first dressing. 'Push on this pad,' he directed Blucher.

Blood flooded over Blucher's hands as he pressed the dressing Law had applied. 'It's not stopping!' he cried.

Law tightly bound the second dressing in place and then followed with a third. 'Pressure,' he said, more to reassure himself than to explain what he was doing to Blucher, 'that will stop the blood.'

'Is he still alive?'

Law felt the pulse on Green's neck. 'Yes, but for how long I don't know. The whole side of his head... I don't think his skull is broken, but his face... We have to get him to a doctor.'

'Jesus,' Blucher muttered, 'how the hell are we going to do that?'

Law smiled ruefully. 'I was rather hoping you might have some ideas,' he said.

'Me? Mate, a month ago I was a bloody driver! If Rob Green

hadn't found me, I'd still be there or more likely in prison for belting some bastard.'

'You are a good soldier, Blucher. Green would never have brought you along if he did not believe in your ability. Now between us, we have to help him.'

Law's simple statement stilled the rising panic that threatened to engulf Blucher. 'Sorry, boss,' he said contritely. He thought for a moment. 'Well, we shall have to wait until it's properly dark,' he said finally. 'Some bastard will knock us off if we step out now.'

'Agreed.'

'And we will have to take turns carrying him.'

'I'll take the first turn,' Law said emphatically. 'You will have to carry the rifles and find the way.'

Blucher looked worried at the prospect. 'Shouldn't be too hard,' he muttered. 'Keep the ridge on our right and don't go any further downhill.'

'What about Hun patrols?'

'Nothing we can do about them. So long as we see them before they see us, we should be okay.'

Darkness eventually fell.

'Best be off,' Blucher muttered. He picked up Green's rifle and slung it over his shoulder; then holding his own rifle across his body, he climbed out of the depression.

Law bent down and carefully picked Green up, adjusting his load to that of a fireman's lift. The deeply unconscious Green hung limply across his shoulders.

'Right?' Blucher whispered.

'Let's go,' Law grunted in reply.

Blucher sniffed the night air. 'I still think it's going to rain,' he muttered, and then he led the way along the ridge.

Blucher was carrying Green when rain began to fall.

'Just a shower,' Law suggested hopefully.

'Nope,' Blucher panted in reply, 'it's going to piss down.' He lowered Green gently to the ground. 'We'll have to cover him up.'

'How is he?'

'I'm not sure. I thought I heard him groan before.'

Law checked the bandages around Green's head. The bleeding seemed to have stopped and his breathing was regular; however, he was still unconscious. 'No change really,' he sighed.

'Probably a good thing,' Blucher observed. 'I don't know how he'd take this if he were awake.'

Law took his own ground sheet and arranged it over Green's body. 'Do you want me to take over?' he asked.

'He's right. Just drape the sheet over him when I lift him up.'

The rain was now falling in torrents making it impossible to see more than a few yards and making the ground slippery and treacherous to walk across. Law and Blucher were soaked to the skin and Green's bandage had washed clean, the coagulated blood leaving a gory trail down Blucher's back.

Two hours later, they were both exhausted, but Law, unused to the physical nature of frontline soldiering, was utterly spent. He set Green down in the shelter of a shell hole and looked appealing at Blucher. 'I don't think I can go on,' he admitted unhappily.

Blucher nodded. He could see that the situation was irrevocably turning against them. If Law were to collapse, he would have two casualties to deal with and they could all die.

'I'll go for help,' he said. 'We can't be far from the 48th now.'
He handed Law Green's rifle. 'Don't move from here; I want
to be able to find you when I come back with a stretcher
party.'

'We'll be here.'

Blucher took a long drink from his water bottle then
handed the bottle to Law. 'If I'm not back by morning, you'll
know I'm done for and you'll have to make your own
arrangements.' Then he turned and walked away into the rain
and the terrors of the night.

An hour or so after Blucher had left for help, Law heard
footsteps moving toward the shell hole in which he and Green
lay hidden. Convinced they were saved, he was about to call
out when he heard a voice speaking in German. For a brief
moment, he wondered if he should not in fact surrender to
enable Green to receive medical attention. However, against
this course of action was the possibility that the Germans
would soon deduct that Green and he were part of the group
who had tried to assassinate Colonel Nicolai. Once that
connection was made, he doubted either of them would
receive good treatment.

Law quickly pushed the unconscious Green into the water
that the rain had deposited in the bottom of the shell hole.
'Sorry, old chap,' he murmured, 'there are Huns about. I'm
going to play dead and if they think you're dead too, they
might leave us alone.' He placed his pack under Green's head
to prevent his drowning, and then draped himself across the
side of the shell hole in a pose he hoped would convince the
casual observer he was dead.

The footsteps of the German patrol receded into the night, but a few minutes later Law heard them return. They passed the very edge of the shell hole, but if any of them looked down into the hole, Law could not tell. Again the footsteps drifted away, and this time they did not return.

In the first glow of dawn, the artillery fire returned with renewed fury. Law had no idea if it was British or German shells that pounded the ridge above him. He had removed Green from the water and tried to warm him with the ghillie suits and ground sheets, but Green was shivering, and Law could see they were running out of time if he was to be saved.

As the light grew stronger, Law lost hope of Blucher's return and he began to plan how he could carry Green to safety on his own.

'Colonel Law! Colonel Law!'

Law almost cried with relief. 'Blucher! We're here, over here!'

Moments later, two stretcher bearers slid into the shell hole beside him.

'Where's Blucher?' Law demanded.

'Wounded,' one of the stretcher bearers replied curtly. 'You're dead lucky, sir; we were just about to go back, the light you know. We had best be off.'

'What about the shell fire?' Law asked fearfully.

'We'll have to risk it. At least it will keep the snipers' heads down.'

As gently as possible, the two stretcher bearers lifted Green on to the litter. One of the bearers gave Law a thin stick with a small Red Cross flag attached to one end. 'Hold this up as we go along, sir; it might make the Huns think twice before they take a pot at us.'

Law took the flag. The rules of war that he had studied at

Staff College seemed to be just so much technical theory in this place, and instead of guaranteeing safe passage, he wondered if he was simply telling the enemy where they were.

With a groan of effort, the stretcher bearers took up their burden and with Law waving his little flag, they began their perilous journey across No Man's Land to the Australian trenches.

Chapter 26

Luck is a fickle providence, but on that particular day it was with Law, Green, and the stretcher bearers. They reached the relative safety of the 48th Battalion's trenches where the unconscious Green was delivered to the Aid Post. It was there Law learned that Blucher's luck had run out.

'The pity of it was he had reached our forward positions,' the Battalion's doctor explained, 'when the Hun had fired a single artillery shell, probably a ranging shot, and the shrapnel hit your man. Someone carried him into me, but he was a hopeless case. Nothing I could do for him, and I told the lads to set him aside to die. Then a damnable thing happened! I mean, the fellow's throat was laid open... I didn't think he was conscious, let alone able told speak! Somehow, he managed to tell one of the stretcher bearers where he had left you.'

Law shook his head in disbelief. 'It's so bloody unfair,' he said fiercely.

The doctor had seen too much of death and suffering to be greatly moved by the fate of one man, no matter how unfair the circumstances might seem. 'A brave man no doubt,' he sniffed as he pushed tobacco into the bowl of his pipe. 'His last act to try and save his comrades... commendable, I'm sure.'

'Can I see the body?' Law asked sadly.

The doctor held a flame to his pipe and sucked in a mouthful of smoke, then blew it out of the dugout door. 'Probably not,' he said shortly. 'It has almost certainly been buried... we don't like to let the bodies pile up; it's bad for morale.'

Law hung his head in disappointment and listened half-heartedly as the doctor completed the explanation as to how he and Green had been rescued. It seemed Bull Leane himself had ordered the stretcher party out to look for them. 'Rather lucky, really,' the doctor observed casually as he drew in another lung full of smoke. 'It seems Bull has a lot of respect for your Sergeant; I'm not sure he would have risked men to find anyone else.'

Law ignored the inference that had he been injured, Leane would not have bothered to rescue him. 'How is Sergeant Green?' he asked.

'Difficult to say, really. I don't have the facilities or the time to delve too deeply into the wounded. His head wound is nasty, but there's no sign of it turning septic. Not yet, anyway. We will evacuate him, of course. If he survives that, they will almost certainly send him back to Blighty to recuperate. But if the wound festers...' he shrugged.

Law's next call was to Bull Leane. 'Bad business all round,' Leane concluded once he had heard Law's account of the mission. 'Pity about young Blucher, to be struck down just as he reached safety; it seems so bloody unfair. Green too, of course, but believe me, he was lucky to have lived this long. That man has taken too many risks, and in the end, everyone's luck runs out. He was a bit of an enigma really. I mean considering the way he and his people have been treated, I'm fucked if I know why he bothered to help us.'

Law nodded sadly.

'What will you do now?'

'I'll return to London and report to my masters, although I've no doubt they will have already had news of the failure.'

'Oh?'

'I am of the opinion it was they who sent the farmer with the grenade in the belief that we would never get near the target. Either that or they believed we would provide a decoy to enable the bomb thrower to get close.'

Leane sniffed derisively. 'I'm not surprised,' he said. 'As each day passes, I become more and more convinced that those who are responsible for the conduct of this war should be certified and committed to the nearest mental asylum.'

Law made to leave and extended his hand. 'Good luck, Colonel. I shall try and look in on Green and I'll let you know how he is.'

Leane shook Law's hand. 'I would appreciate that. Take care.'

It was only after Law had left for his lonely walk to the rear that Leane remembered Green's letter. 'What do you think I should do with this?' he asked his Adjutant.

The Adjutant glanced at the unopened letter. 'Well, the fellow is still alive so far as we know. I'd keep it until we hear one way or the other. No use upsetting the lass whoever she is.'

The doctors at the Field Hospital did not expect Green to live. The obvious aspects of his wound were quite shocking, but not necessarily fatal. The bullet had hit his skull just above his right eyebrow. The fact that Green had been leaning forward to speak with Law when he had been shot had saved him, for had he remained upright, the bullet would have entered his brain with deadly effect. Somehow, the bullet missed the eye, and travelling downward it had laid open his cheek, finally exiting through the bottom of his jaw.

This trauma had left the right side of his face a mangled mess, but like the 48th Battalion's doctor and the doctors at the field hospital believed, so long as infection could be avoided, he could recover from these physical injuries. However, the same doctors assessed that the more critical damage Green had suffered was concussion. The impact of the bullet striking his head had they believed, bruised his brain. Still deeply unconscious and with no prospect of recovery, Green was placed in a tent with other hopeless cases to wait for the end.

Some days later, the hospital received an important visitor.

'General Monash,' the senior doctor blustered, 'we were not advised you would visit us.'

'This is not an official visit,' Monash reply hurriedly. 'I understand you have a Sergeant Green here as a patient.'

'Yes sir, we do. Unfortunately, he is gravely ill. Quite frankly, I don't believe there is much reason to hope.'

Monash's shoulders slumped. 'I see,' he said heavily.

'How well do you know Sergeant Green?' the senior doctor asked.

'Quite well,' Monash replied. 'We were at the ANZAC Cove together. Look, I am in rather a hurry. Can I see him?'

'Certainly,' the doctor led the way toward the hopeless case ward. 'It's rather strange, sir,' the doctor commented as they walked, 'but we can't establish anything about the fellow through official channels, almost as if he is in France illegally. Do you know if there is anyone we might contact on his behalf?'

Monash was in no position to explain Green's presence in France. Indeed, MI6 in London had strongly suggested to Monash that he made no attempt to see Green. Law had failed to inform him of Madame Sainson and Madame Claire and so, as he was unaware of their existence, he could not provide the doctor with any information regarding the two women. 'No,' he sighed resignedly, 'I don't know of anyone.'

'Well, here he is,' the doctor said, indicating the bed containing Green. 'He's quite unaware you are here; he can't hear or speak. I'm afraid in many ways it would have been kinder if he had died. His face, well, at least one side of it, has been almost destroyed... massive tissue loss and bone damage. Of course, they can do wonderful things now, the specialists in England you know, but we rather fear in Green's case there will be brain injury as well...'

Monash wasn't listening to the medical prattle. Not for the first time in his life, he felt deep regret at his part in ordering men into battle. He placed a hand on Green's unresponsive shoulder. 'In thy face,' he murmured sadly to the unconscious man, 'I see the map of honour.' Then he turned and walked out of the tent.

Historical Note

Robert Green is a figment of my imagination. However, the commitment, tenacity, bravery, and skill he exhibits were characteristics displayed by some 1,000 Aboriginal men who fought in the First World War. Those men enlisted in spite of the nation's best attempts to prevent their service. At over 100 years' distance, it is impossible to say what motivated these men to enlist, although in spite of their treatment at the hands of the wider Australian society at the time, loyalty and patriotism certainly seems to have played a part. However, the fact that they received the same pay and conditions as their white comrades must also have been a factor. For many it would have been the first time in their lives they had experienced equal treatment with white people. No doubt some of them hoped that on their return to civilian life that equality would continue, but this hope proved to be a vain one.

Like Green, numerous Aboriginal soldiers were promoted during the war, although none achieved commissioned rank. The first commissioning of an Aboriginal would not take place until the Second World War when Reg Saunders was promoted to the rank of lieutenant. So Green had to be content to reach the rank of sergeant.

The AIF had a strong presence in England where it maintained a number of training establishments, some of which were located on the Salisbury Plains. However, the First Australian Imperial Force School of Musketry was not one of these. Most of the AIF Divisions conducted their own musketry training. For ease of introducing Green and providing a reason for him being in England, I have introduced a central school to the AIF order of battle.

The mission to assassinate Colonel Walter Nicolai, the head of the German Secret Service, is another product of my imagination. However, Nicolai did exist and was, if not the head of the German Secret Service, was certainly an important member of the organization.

The Battle of Pozieres, into which I imposed Green and Blucher, was all too real. The battle was fought in and around the small French village of the same name in July 1916. The village was initially captured by the AIF's 1st Division but at great cost. The Division suffered 5,285 casualties. The 1st Division was relieved by the AIF's 2nd Division, which after some initial failures, seized the German positions beyond the village but at the cost of a further 6,848 casualties. The AIF's 4th Division then entered the line and consolidated the initial Australian gains. At the end of the battle, the War Correspondent Charles Bean stated that Pozieres Ridge "is more densely sown with Australian sacrifice than any other place on earth."

I took yet another liberty by writing Green and Blucher into the tragic issue of the dead runner at Pozieres. The actual incident was recorded by Sir Neville Smyth of the AIF's 2nd Infantry Battalion:

"One of the two runners fell on his way to the road. The second one, who belonged to the 2nd Battalion, seeing the great peril which he must face, and realising that if he fell the fact of his being a runner bearing a message might be overlooked by those who passed him among so many fallen soldiers, he must have deliberately taken the message from his breast pocket and as he was struck dead he held it up in the air so that a small party of men making their way forward

with ammunition within about 20 minutes saw that he held a paper in his hand and taking it from his fingers carried it on to the officer it was addressed to, thus enabling the further advance to be successfully carried out. The man was fair and muscular, wore the Second Battalion badges on sleeve and a red band to denote that he was a runner. The bands were made very raggedly by the men themselves of red calico bought in the villages. Sleeves were rolled up above the elbow (as a recognition mark in the night and afterwards). The man's name and number is not known."

With the exception of Green, Blucher, Law, Stephanie, Madame Claire, and Major Cook, who are all fictional characters, the other main characters in the story actually existed and took part in the Battle of Pozieres.

It is also true that Charles Bean, aided by Keith Murdoch, endeavoured to discredit Monash and have him removed from command. Bean was also well known for his opinions regarding the need for racial purity in the AIF. He had issues with Monash being a Jew, and would certainly have had issues with Green's Aboriginality. Indeed, the media tended to ignore the presence of Aboriginal soldiers in the AIF to an extent that it was many years before their presence at Gallipoli was acknowledged.

Would Monash have formed an association such as the one I have attributed between him and Green? Monash was a very ambitious man, and he would not have risen to the heights he achieved by being "nice." However, during the war and in the peace that followed, he recognised the debt he owed the men who had served him and was always concerned for their welfare. I like to think that if he and Green had really met, their shared experiences of discrimination and war might have led Monash to act toward Green in the manner I have described.

Other incidents that Green and his comrades are involved in are based on fact. The incident where Major Cook was struck down by a can of tinned peaches may actually have a basis in truth, but not, of course, involving any of the characters involved in this story. The unconfirmed story follows much the same situation as I have presented, with the exception that the officer who was assaulted was repatriated to Australia after he recovered.

The accounts regarding Green and Blucher's activities in and around Pozieres are based on a report provided by a French liaison officer Paul Maze DCM MM Croix de Grurre. Maze was sent forward by General Gough to ascertain the true dispositions of British and Australian troops. I saw no reason why Green and Blucher should not undertake a similar mission. The incident where Green becomes stuck in the culvert pipe escaping German machine gun fire, I have borrowed from a similar episode that occurred during the 1917 Battle at Gavrelle. During that battle, Able Seaman Downe of the Royal Naval Division crawled to safety through a culvert, became stuck, and fortunately, like Green, was able to free himself. Both the Paul Maze report and Able Seaman Downe's account are contained in a very old book I was bequeathed titled *The Great War, I was There,* Volume Two, edited by Sir John Hammerton (London Amalgamated Press Ltd.).